M000032869

A Talent
FOR MURDER

—〰—

A Polly Pepper Mystery

R. T. JORDAN

AMALFI
BOOKS

A Talent for Murder
Published by Amalfi Books. www.Amalfibooks.com

Copyright © 2019 by Amalfi Books and R.T. Jordan

All rights reserved. No part of this book may be reproduced in
any form or by any means without the prior written consent
of the Publisher and/or author, excepting brief quotes used in
reviews.

All Amalfi Books titles, imprints, and distributed lines are available as e-books and print on demand. For details, contact Amalfi
Books at www.Amalfibooks.com.

Cover Illustration and Design provided by
Virtually Possible Designs
Interior Design & Typesetting by Ampersand Book Interiors

ISBN-13: 978-1-7337937-0-4

Amalfi Books logo Reg. U.S. Pat. & TM Off.

Printed in the United States of America

BOOKS BY R.T. JORDAN

—❧—

Remains To Be Scene
Final Curtain
A Talent For Murder
Set Sail For Murder
"Naughty Or Nice"

PUBLISHED BY AMALFI BOOKS.
WWW.AMALFIBOOKS.COM

"Hollywood is a place where they place you under contract, instead of under observation."

— *Walter Winchell*

CHAPTER 1

"Lush Hour, at last!" Polly Pepper exclaimed as she stepped out of her Manolo Blahnik heels and joined her son, Tim, on the sofa in the great room of Pepper Plantation, her fabled Bel Air mansion. Polly rested her bare feet on his lap, anticipating Tim's large, strong hands to knead away her aching arches. "I plan my life around this time of day!"

"For the massage? Or the bubbly?"

"Both make me tingle, dear," Polly said, wiggling her toes.

At the wet bar, Placenta popped the cork from the chilled bottle of Veuve Clicquot.

"Pavarotti's high C never sounded as intoxicating!" Polly called out as she watched her maid fill three Waterford crystal champagne flutes and sighed as her son gripped her instep. "This is heaven. We can all sit back, take a few dainty sips of God's golden cure-all, and wash the world away," Polly said.

"Temporary amnesia is all I expect," Placenta said as she handed chilled glasses to Polly and Tim.

Polly raised her flute and clinked it against Tim's and Placenta's. "I'm the luckiest star in the universe," she trilled. She drained her flute in one long swallow. With a satisfied "Ahhhh," she withdrew her feet from Tim's lap and leaned forward to reach a slice of Placenta's famous salmon tortilla appetizer from the glass-top coffee table. At the same time, Placenta refilled her employer's vessel up to its lipstick-smudged rim.

"Yum!" Polly said, acknowledging both the refill and the salmon tortilla. Then she groaned. "Guess which of the crazies in my life called today?"

"Who is ... Alex Trebek?" Tim played along.

"J.J. Ol' reptile-eyelids himself."

Tim groaned at his mother's reference to her unctuous agent, J. J. Norton. "I suppose he wants a character reference for one of the gads of employee harassment lawsuits pending against him."

"Believe it or not, he actually has a job for me," Polly said.

"A healing purple pill commercial?" Tim mocked.

"I should be so lucky! Old stars hawking pharmaceuticals is all the rage. Dorothy Hamill made a killing—literally— shilling for Vioxx! Kathleen Turner, Lauren Bacall, Delta Burke, Peggy Fleming, who hasn't made a few million shekels pushing drugs? Don't get me started about Bob Dole's erectile dysfunction pill!" Polly, Tim, and Placenta simultaneously shuddered. "As a matter of fact, I'm up for a *reality* series," Polly said. "I'd be perfect."

Tim coughed in mid-sip. "Perfect for what? 'The Biggest Boozer'?"

—❧—

Polly winced. "I'd never diminish my dignity by appearing as a *contestant,* for crying out loud! No, there's a spot open for the 'nice' judge on a summer replacement talent show. Think darling Carrie Ann Inaba, but tons more famous. FYI"—she glared at Tim—"I'm totally aware of the ten warning signs of alcoholism. I only have..." She made a mental tabulation, stuck her tongue out at her son, then took a defiant swallow from her glass.

Placenta cackled. "The 'nice' judge, eh? Don't get me wrong, take away dear dead Cyd Charisse, and you and Carol Burnett and Betty White are in a three-way tie for everybody's idea of the nicest living showbiz legend. But when it comes to faking praise about others' lack of talent, you're more like Kelly Ripa feigning devotion to some flash in the pan's latest CD. You're both transparent."

Polly looked concerned.

"Actually, this could be an ideal job," Placenta continued, "if you don't mind lying to poor young wannabes, telling them that they have the potential to achieve fame and fortune, when in fact they stink."

"Just as modem maids don't have to know anything about cleaning moldy bath mats, one doesn't require talent to succeed in show business," Polly sniffed. "Just look at Charlie Sheen."

"Just look at your bath mats!" Placenta snapped.

"So what's the show about?" Tim asked. "Dating?"

"Home makeovers?" Placenta added.

"Extreme retribution in the workplace?"

"Celebrity colon irrigation?"

Polly thought for a moment. She shrugged. "They sing. They dance. They swallow scorpions. Who knows? Who cares? Just cheap thrills for a viewing audience weary from news of wars, dummy presidents, the sucky economy, melting ice caps, and Naomi Campbell's latest assault and battery charges against her domestics. But it pays well, and it's only for the summer. It's called, um, *I'll Do Anything to Become Famous.*"

Placenta rolled her eyes. "Accent on the word *anything*, I suppose. I swear I don't know who on earth would want to expose their lack of talent to millions of television viewers. Frankly, I'm embarrassed for them. They're too stupid to realize they're practically wearing 'Kick Me' signs!"

Tim nodded in agreement. "At least you'll have a summer job that doesn't include steaming July nights at an amphitheater in St. Louis! Fans may miss seeing you in perspiration-soaked Victorian gowns and wigs playing *The King and I*, but we'll all be safe and sound in an air-conditioned television studio."

"God knows, it's easy money," Polly said. "I mean, how much work can it be to sit around and watch telegenic amateurs, and telling 'em how delightful they are?"

At the thought of being around attractive contestants, Tim became animated. "I'm very compassionate toward losers. I may have to help comfort more than a few cute dancers or singers or sword swallowers. I'll be indispensable in helping to restore their self-worth!"

"Just don't turn Pepper Plantation into a haven for Hollywood's ne'er-do-wells," Polly said. "Actually, I have a rather good feeling about this job. That is, if I accept it. I still haven't decided. There are always negotiations to hammer out. Billing. Per Diem. Expense account. You know J.J. and his penchant for getting me involved in crummy projects. Lately they've been murder. Literally!"

"A primetime program could give your career another leg up," Placenta advised. "That *Dancing with Pseudo Stars* sure helped bring Marie Osmond back—for a minute. And the previously unknown judges on that show are now household names."

"Very well, I'll do it!" Polly announced. "These programs are the closest we'll ever get to good old-fashioned variety shows. But if I'm the 'nice' judge, I'm a little concerned about who I'll be sparring against. You know how much I loathe confrontation. I couldn't handle a Simon Cowell clone."

Tim and Placenta both sniggered. "When you have an opinion, you don't let go until everybody agrees with you!" Tim sassed. "You're still insisting that the last *Indiana Jones* flick was a masterpiece! And that's only because you think Harrison Ford is still hot. Which he is."

Placenta added, "Your pigheadedness is why Jamie Lee Curtis won't play Scrabble with you anymore. There's no such word as *glurg!*"

The great room was quiet for a long moment. Polly, Tim, and Placenta thought about the phenomenon known as "reality shows." With the airing of every new program, Z-list celebrities were instantly created. They achieved quickly fleeting fame for doing things as brainless as dating a dweeb or having Tyra Banks judge how well they performed bikini waxes.

Will my conscience allow me to encourage vain acts of hedonism such as fashion and grooming? Polly thought.

Polly Pepper sparring with cranky judges is likely to make the show a water-cooler hit! Placenta considered.

I'd better take ballroom dance lessons in case I run into one of the studs from Dancing with the Stars, Tim daydreamed.

Their reverie was shattered by the sound of the telephone ringing. "Oh, let the machine pick up," Polly moaned. "I'm not in the mood to negotiate with J.J." The trio listened. "Honeybabycookiesweetie! It's Phil. Just heard about your new job offer! Listen. I'm awaiting a new trial. I suppose you've heard about that dead wannabe actress playing with my shotgun. Nobody believes that she was cleaning it … with her tongue. I'm a rotten judge of women, but I still have a damn good sixth sense about talent. So if you decide not to do the show, please put in a word for me. *Ciao, bella!*"

"Oh Lord," Polly snorted. "Next we'll be hearing from Bobby Blake!"

Again, the telephone rang.

As the elevator doors opened onto the foyer of J. J. Norton and Associates, Polly Pepper threw out her arms and sang in her powerful imitation of Ethel Merman, "There's no business like show business…!" With Tim and Placenta in tow, she confidently walked across the blond hardwood floor to the reception desk. "You're new." She smiled at a young man wearing tortoiseshell eyeglasses, a white oxford cloth button-down dress shirt, and a conservative striped tie.

He was startled by Polly's sudden appearance.

"This place is like Oz," Polly said. "People come and go so quickly here."

"My agency offered me combat pay if I could last until Friday," the receptionist admitted.

Polly reached out and caressed the young man's smooth cheek with her hand. "Poor baby," she cooed. "J.J. can be a beast. The only way for a boy of your angelic beauty to survive is to … Well, never mind. You're safe as long as you sneeze a lot."

"And make a point of scratching as if you itch all over," Placenta added.

Polly turned to Tim. "Don't you think so too, dear? Isn't he adorable?"

"Absolutely," Tim said, appraising their host.

"What's your name, dear?" Polly asked, holding out her hand to shake.

"I'm not supposed to give out my name or become friendly with clients," the young man said, looking around to make sure that he wasn't being observed interacting with guests. "Mr. Norton is very strict. I had to sign a confidentiality agreement and swear that when I leave each day I'll forget all the celebrities who may have come to the office."

Polly rolled her eyes. "One can never forget *moi,* dear," she said. "As you know, I'm—"

"Polly Pepper!" the receptionist said.

"He's smart, too!" Polly said, looking at Tim. "This pet you can take home and keep."

"You're younger than Mr. Norton described you," the receptionist said.

Polly blanched.

"Take a deep breath," Placenta coaxed, as she patted Polly on the back. "Reel yourself in, honey. Don't succumb to J.J.-bashing in public."

Polly found the breath to speak. "Where is dear Mr. Congeniality, anyway? We have a luncheon appointment."

"He had an emergency meeting with a potential new client," the receptionist said.

"Potential?" Placenta tsk-tsked.

"The Best Western down the street again?" Tim sniggered.

"His usual room?" Polly suggested.

"Mr. Norton wanted me to personally hand this envelope to you," the receptionist said.

"J.J. didn't have the decency to call before I had to battle midday traffic to get here," Polly said, trying not to sound too perturbed. "What's in the package?" Everybody watched as Polly opened the large manila envelope and withdrew what appeared to be a script. *"I'll Do Anything to Become Famous,"* she read from the cover page. "I thought these programs weren't scripted." Polly flipped through the pages and discovered that it was a breakdown of the show, complete with bios of the contestants and judges. There were suggested words and body language to use when evaluating a particularly pitiful performance. Polly looked aghast. "I can't say such things to those poor sweet and probably embarrassed innocents."

The receptionist looked around the foyer again for eavesdroppers. "I could get fired on the spot for this. But since I

Googled you this morning and remembered you're the star my grandparents used to love, I'll take a chance."

"Grandparents?" Polly raised an eyebrow. "How old are you?"

She and Tim and Placenta leaned in closer as the receptionist whispered, "If it's any indication of what you're in for, the FBI used the casting call as a sting operation to round up a horde of fugitives. They got a whole lot of criminals who responded to the *Craigslist* ad that called for contestants who would be willing to do anything, and it stressed *anything,* to become famous. Also, the six who were selected had to go through a mental evaluation to make sure they aren't dangerous to the judges."

Polly swallowed hard. She then straightened her posture, squared her shoulders, and pasted a smile on her face. "Sweetums, the moment that Mr. Norton returns from his emergency *mating,* would you please tell him to ring me? Contract or not, there are still a few things to hammer out. It was lovely meeting you. Good luck with your combat pay."

As Polly turned to leave, the receptionist called out, "Please don't tell Mr. Norton that I spoke to you!"

"My lips are sealed. And tell your *grandparents* that Polly Pepper sends kisses."

"They're dead."

"That happens a lot."

When the elevator car arrived, the trio stepped in and Tim pushed the button for subterranean parking. As they dropped through the shaft, Polly clutched the show material to her chest and silently stared at the digital readout as they passed each floor. It was only when Tim was driving his mother's Park Ward Rolls-Royce down Sunset Boulevard toward Beverly Hills, with Polly and Placenta buckled into their seats behind him, that Polly emerged from her silence. She retrieved the synopsis of the show and began to read aloud:

"'A fusion of *American Idol, Celebrity Detox,* and *The Miss America Pageant, I'll Do Anything to Become Famous* is a high-octane laser light show of a talent competition program with one major difference from others in this genre glut. While contestants are encouraged to give the best artistic performance, they also have to convince the judges and the voting television viewing audience that they understand that talent isn't enough. To be a success in Hollywood, one must be as nefarious as Glenn Close on *Damages.* They'll have to literally do as the title of the show suggests—*anything*—in order to become the next Dina Lohan, Denise Richards, or the Geiko gecko.

"'When each week's remaining wannabes reach the interview segment of the program, the judges pose *Truth or Dare*-like questions about celebrity ethics and morality. The answers and the lengths to which each contender says he/she would go to become a star will help decide the ultimate winner.'

"My stars!" Polly sighed. "This is *America's Got Talent* for the Menendez brothers!"

Tim looked back at his mother through the rearview mirror. She was lost in a fog of thought. Then he looked at Placenta, who was beaming. "Why the smile?" Tim asked.

"'Cause this show is going to be a hit!" Placenta said. "Who wants to see boring singers and dancers with nothing more on their mind other than emulating whoever is on top at the moment? This show'll give the public a look at how mean and cunning some people are. I hope it gets nasty. Every looky-loo loves a train wreck!"

"It'll be a lot harder to be the 'nice' judge if the contestants are undisciplined thugs," Polly countered. "I don't want to jeopardize my public's opinion of me! I can't let happen to me what happened to Bing Crosby's widow. One appearance on Johnny Carson and poof, she was instantly recognized as not so grieving."

"Who are the contestants?" Tim asked.

Polly riffled through the papers for the bios. "These are more like personality evaluations. Yikes! Listen to this: 'Toe Nail: A surly self-absorbed rapper thug. Short on vocal agility but long on intimidation. Observed during auditions bullying others and sharing body-piercing horror stories. A+ among the three thousand applicants.'"

Placenta cackled. "Would one call him 'Toe' or 'Mr. Nail'? I'll never understand the crazy names these so-called artists make up for themselves! '50 Cent, Pitbull, Bow Wow,' indeed!"

"'Amy Stout'," Polly continued. "'A Miley Cyrus clone. Southern drawl that comes and goes like the color of a mood ring. Has at least two faces: Ellen De- Generes fun, and Lily Tomlin caught in an *I Heart Huckabees* soundstage snit, when she doesn't get her way. Disingenuous, but has a lovely voice.'

"Another A+ score," Polly noted. "And how rude of them to bring up my darling Lily's little diatribe on that movie set. She wouldn't have been so nasty if she'd known that some meany was videotaping her tantrum for an axe-grinding broadcast. Poor baby!"

Tim smiled. "She's always been nice to me. But I still have fun watching her meltdown! Pretty scary stuff. Like watching a Bill O'Reilly tantrum!"

"Who are the other Antichrists on the show?" Placenta asked.

"Um, let's see. Oh, here's one. Miranda Washington. 'Strong and cultivated voice, reminiscent of Broadway legends.' Finally, someone with talent!" Polly read on. "'Contestant is more likely to become a maximum-security penitentiary guard than a recording star. Audition interview responses often peppered with colorful expletives. Be prepared to bleep during broadcasts. A+.'"

Tim drove past the UCLA campus and approached the Bel Air gates. "This show is *Jerry Springer* meets *Sweeney Todd*. Who are the other judges?"

Polly shuffled through a few more pages. She stopped and smiled brightly. "Me!" she said. "My standard bio. Nice to see it's been updated to include my Ovation Award nomination for last year's production of *Mame.*"

"The other judges?" Tim prodded.

"Nobodies," Polly said, skimming the pages. "Or at least not somebodies. A Brian Smith. It says he was once a *Pip*, dancing behind my eternal love, Gladys Knight. The other is someone named Cornwall. Thane Cornwall."

"Thane Cornwall?" Tim and Placenta simultaneously barked.

"Not 'The Royal Pain of England'!" Placenta said. "'The Terror From the Thames'!"

"'The Nut Job of Nottingham'?" Tim added.

Polly was incredulous. "Terror? Nut job? Who is this creep?"

Tim sighed. "You do too know Thane Cornwall!"

"Not even if you put a gun to my head."

Placenta prompted, "Made Barbara Walters cry on her network interview special."

"Where was I that night?"

"He's considered almost as venomous as that rabid rodent Ann Coulter. Famous for his put-down phrase, 'From which medical research lab did you escape, monkey moron?'" Tim said.

Polly bit her lower lip. "I do seem to remember reading something in the *National Peeper*. "He's that actor who—"

"Yep!" Tim said, anticipating his mother's recall.

"—put his fist through his dressing room wall in a London theater just because the air-conditioning wasn't cold enough," Polly said.

"No! Well, yes, but that's not what he's most noted for," Tim countered. "Don't you remember? Before Thane Cornwall became famous, he was living off a very rich wife. He was often seen insulting her in public. And the tabloids said that he neglected her privately."

"Didn't two of his wife's lovers go missing?" Polly asked.

"According to the *Peeper*, Scotland Yard couldn't prove foul play," Placenta added, "but those two guys have never been heard from again."

"Could be that they just moved on to other people," Polly said.

"Sure," Tim conceded. "But I've heard that Thane left England because the whole country thinks that each time he found out that his wife was playing around, he got rid of the Lotharios to ensure that he didn't lose his meal ticket."

"The irony," Placenta said, "is that as soon as Thane became rich and famous himself, he traded in the starter wife for a supermodel he'd been boinking for years. Then she dumped *him*."

Polly exhaled loudly and shook her head. "I'll have no problem being the 'nice' judge compared to a guy who needs anger management classes, and probably a healing purple pill!"

CHAPTER 2

—⁓—

When Polly, Tim, and Placenta arrived for the first *I'll Do Anything to Become Famous* production meeting, the conference room in the Writers Building on the Sterling Studio's lot was already crowded with network executives and the show's judging panel.

Standing in the doorway and posing as if she were on a red carpet entertaining paparazzi, Polly made her entrance. With her hands on her hips, her head tilted up at a forty-five-degree angle, and her camera-ready smile beaming toward Jupiter, Polly sang out, "I'm hee-eer!" All eyes instantly focused on the lady in the red Armani pantsuit.

Polly was effulgent. However, when she spied an impossibly handsome twenty-something young man occupying the chair at the head of the conference table, she suddenly felt like an ugly stepsister sentenced to the plus-size dress department at Neiman's. Polly swallowed hard, as the poster boy for human genetic engineering stood and offered a wide and enthusiastic smile. "You're the famous Polly Pepper. I'd recognize you anywhere."

"Please don't tell me that you have grandparents who watched my show," Polly teased, only half joking.

He reached out to shake Polly's hand and introduced himself as Richard Dartmouth, president of unscripted programming for the Sterling Network. "It's so cool that you're on our team," he said.

"Yes. Cool. And you're ... *muy caliente!*"

"Mother!" Tim whispered harshly as he poked Polly's ribs with his elbow.

"I meant 'tall,'" Polly backtracked. "I'm learning Spanish. I get confused," she said.

Richard Dartmouth smiled and shrugged. "Gotta blame my otherwise perfect parents for something," he said. "Let's get this boring bit of business out of the way so you can do something more meaningful with your magical life."

Still blushing, Polly smiled broadly and finger-waved to everyone seated around the table. She took the one empty leather chair, while her entourage found seating in the back of the room.

"I'll keep this short." Richard Dartmouth began his meeting. "I just wanted you to get to know each other before the first show on Friday. I'll start by saying that I have complete trust that *I'll Do Anything to Become Famous* is going to be a ratings winner. I expect that we'll be picked up for a full season after we end our summer run in September. Of course we have to be a hit from the get-go, but with the media blitz, plus our amazing contestants, and of course the luminous Polly Pepper"— he nodded to the star—"as well as the charming Brian Smith"—he acknowledged the second judge—"Thane Cornwall, and our host, Steven

Benjamin"—he smiled at both men—"we're going to be a Friday night fave."

Polly tried not to stare at Dartmouth. That, however, was impossible. Not only was he articulate and bright, but he presented an air of absolute confidence. He also wore a neatly trimmed shadow of a beard, and an amazing mane of dark, feather-soft hair, which he frequently tossed with an unconscious whip of his head. Without looking over her shoulder, Polly knew that Tim and Placenta were equally rapt.

Polly surreptitiously looked at the ring finger of Richard Dartmouth's left hand. It was bare. *No one that good looking is single,* Polly thought to herself as she looked at his green eyes. Then she heard her name and realized that she hadn't been paying attention to what was being discussed. Polly intuited that introductions were being made, so she reanimated her smile and modestly thanked Richard and the others for the opportunity to join their show.

Dartmouth continued the introductions, giving brief comments about each person at the table. "You all remember Brian Smith from his work with Gladys Knight."

"No one remembers that," Brian said. He was modest—and right.

"What they also might not know is that for the past decade you've been running the Actors' Workout Fitness Center," Dartmouth continued. "So he's eminently qualified to judge a talent competition. He's also the best darned cook in Hollywood." Dartmouth pointed to a paper plate on which rested a pyramid of chocolate brownies. "Brian made treats for us."

"Double fudge," Brian boasted.

"Our other judge is, of course, the famous—or, as some would say, *infamous*—Thane Cornwall." Richard chuckled good-naturedly as all heads turned to look at the smug man with his arms folded across his T-shirted chest. Thane's body language suggested boredom and arrogance. However, he forced a tight smile and shrugged. "Infamy. Yeah, that works for more than a couple of people in this room." He nodded to Polly and the others.

"You're British?" Polly asked Thane innocently. "I haven't seen your Queenie in decades. Did she ever replace those ancient bathtubs for stall showers at Buckingham Palace? Do you think the evil Prince Phillip did you-know-what? Wink, wink."

Thane sniggered. "Fascinating observation about my accent. You're certainly a bright bulb. As for Elizabeth, I quite like her. And Phillip is … Well, princess killer or not, he's done well for a short man. Wink, wink, yourself."

Polly camouflaged her annoyance by smiling even more broadly. "I'm not exactly a royalist. I know what those inbreeds are capable of doing. As Anglophiles, you and I are bound to have a ton o' fun on this show. I'll be Anne Boleyn to your King Henry!"

"You wouldn't be the first to lose your head over me," Thane said.

Everyone laughed. "I know that we'll *all* get along *very* well," Richard interrupted. "Speaking of losing a head, I have a bit of bad news. We've lost one of our contestants."

"Lost, as in misplaced, departed, or … deceased?" Brian Smith asked.

"Yes, and no. Jewell Jones was picked up by the FBI this morning for the murder of her grandmother in Georgia," he said. "Someone saw her on one of our television promos and snitched. When they cuffed her she kept screaming that she should win our competition anyway because when Granny wouldn't lend her the money to come to California, she did what she had to do to get it, which, she said, proves that she'll do *anything* to become famous."

"Very resourceful," Thane Cornwall agreed. "She's set the bar high as far as I'm concerned."

Polly gave Thane a look of disbelief. "Do you have a granny? Would you do something sinister to her in a bid to make your own showbiz dreams come true?"

Thane stared at Polly. "Save the Dr. Laura judgments for the contestants' Q & A, Miss *Used to Be*."

Polly gave Thane an equally icy stare that chilled the entire room. "I don't know you, and yet I'm getting a very disturbing vibration."

"Old motors make odd noises." Thane smirked. "When was the last time you had your engine tuned up?" Polly looked at Thane with contempt. "As a matter of fact, I get serviced regularly."

"Okeydoke," Richard declared uncomfortably. "Let's call it a day. Be sure to review the rules of the show and your individual responsibilities before coming to rehearsal on Friday. And it's important that you *not* become friendly with the contestants. We don't want a Paula Abdul situation on this show. At least, not until we need tabloid publicity."

With that, the meeting was adjourned, and Polly reached for one of Brian Smith's double fudge brownies. "I need something to take away the slimy taste of that annoying Thane person," she said with her mouth full. "May I have three?" she asked Brian. "My herd over there"—she pointed to Tim and Placenta—"will do to me what Jewell Jones did to her poor granny if I don't put something sweet in their feeding troughs."

"They're all yours," Brian said. "Nobody else touched 'em."

Polly stopped mid-bite. "No E. coli? Ebola? Tetanus?"

"FDA approved," Brian said. "Unless you're allergic to Duncan Hines."

"In the spirit of reciprocity, you'll come to dinner at the plantation before the next lunar eclipse," Polly said as she pushed the plate toward Placenta. "And bring another Pip or two, or three or four. How many are you, anyway?"

As Tim and Placenta joined Polly and began to follow the others out of the conference room, Steven Benjamin, the dimpled-for-days and boyishly sexy soap stud-turned-reality show-host, wheeled his way into the group. "Miss Pepper," he called.

Although Tim was the big fan, Polly knew that Steven was someone of note from the world of pop music radio and daytime drama. She smiled and gave Steve a warm hug, then intimately pushed a bit of Brian Smith's brownie into his mouth. "Isn't this exciting?" she said.

"Double Dutch chocolate, or judges who hate each other?" Steve said, swallowing the morsel of brownie.

"All of the above. But if Mr. Cornwall thinks he can intimidate me, he's way off base," Polly said. "I survived Trish Saddleback when I was a guest on the dumb-ass

24

daytime coffee klatch show *The Shrews*. Still, this Jewell Jones tragedy is upsetting and Thane's lack of respect for the dead is just plain weird. Isn't it amazing what one will do to court the limelight?" Polly said as she unconsciously played with an ostentatious diamond dragonfly brooch on her jacket. "What do you make of that dreadful refugee from the U.K.?"

"Danger," Steven said with a roll of his eyes. "Just ignore him. He hates everybody, including me. And I'm totally lovable!"

"You are indeed," Placenta said. "I adored you on the radio, even when your picture on the back of that bus caused me to crash my car. And I have the DVD of that movie you made with Jessica Alba!"

Steven Benjamin gave Placenta an even wider smile that showed off his beautiful white teeth and twin dimples. "That bus poster ad campaign wasn't a very good idea. You're just one of hundreds of hit-and-runs. I have a face made for radio, not marketing," he said, pretending that he didn't know he was considered one of the sexiest men on the planet.

Steven looked at Polly. "You're going to be a terrific judge. Also, I've met the kids and they're pretty awesome ... if a bit creepy." He shuddered. "Oh, forget what I just said. I don't want to be accused of influencing a judge!" he chuckled. "Chin up. Don't let the creatures, er, contestants, bite. And don't lose any sleep over Thane Cornwall, of all people! Although, judging by your response to someone else in the room this morning, I imagine that any sleep you get will be filled with dreams of a tall, too-handsome-to-be-real stud with a smile as insincere as an undertaker's."

Steven Benjamin made a hasty retreat into the crowd and sidled up to Richard Dartmouth. Polly and her troupe watched as the two walked away, giggling like sorority sisters.

Polly sighed. "Why must they be so young and attractive? And what the hell was that Thane altercation about? I was only trying to be the friendly star that everybody expects me to be."

"You just touched a sensitive nerve," Tim said.

"Nerve is all he's made of," Polly said. "And what'd Steve mean when he said the contestants are creepy? How does he know? We're not supposed to interact with them."

"Everyone we've met here is creepy, including your heart-throb Richard D., who looks like he was manufactured rather than born," Placenta said.

"He doesn't do a thing for me," Polly lied. "Anyway, I have my own sweet beau. Detective Randal Archer is the only man I have any interest in. At the moment."

"Then don't pay any attention to Thane 'Stupid Name' Cornwall," Placenta suggested. "Some folks just love to start trouble. But perhaps you'd better make it clear that you're dating a cop."

Lying on the chaise beside Polly's Puddle, the name she gave to her elegant Olympic-size swimming pool at Pepper Plantation, Polly reread the *I'll Do Anything to Become Famous* contestant bios. "A live television show is just too exciting for words," she said to Tim, who was also soaking up the UVs, but paying more attention to the perspiring landscaping crew than to his mother. "This is going to be like stealing money!" Polly said. "I get paid fairly well just for critiquing a few kids who are trying to sing, then asking them nosy questions that are supposed to reveal how nutsy-cuckoo they are. Why didn't someone invent this concept for throwing cash at celebrities sooner?"

Tim divided his attention between his mother and his favorite gardener, Fernando. "I read the outline of what's expected of you," he said. "It seems as though we'll be on the go most of the week. You're required to give interviews and to tape promos for the show. I saw something in there about personal appearances at malls and stores and clubs where the demographic audience hangs out. And Friday's sound grueling. They can keep you at the studio from ten a.m. until midnight. Remember how tough shooting days were for your own show?"

"But this is a live broadcast, dear, so the program can't last more than two hours," Polly said.

There was indeed more work to do to prep for the debut of *I'll Do Anything to Become Famous* than Polly had antic-ipated. The rest of the week was punishing.

Along with the other judges and the host Steve Benjamin, Polly spent three days taping a series of national television commercial spots, and being interviewed for *TV Guide, Parade, Redbook, People, O,* and the *National Peeper.* She appeared on the talk show circuit and visited Stephen, Conan, and James. When Polly finally got to Ellen, she brought a gift beautifully wrapped in wedding paper. "For you and Portia. A little late, but then I wasn't invited to the nuptials." The studio audience laughed when they saw the gift was a copy of Polly's old record album, *Priceless Polly.*

The low point in the week came when she was ushered by limo to the Snake Pit, for a live local news interview at 11:00 p.m. The Snake Pit was a trendy bar on Sunset Boulevard, made famous by a string of drug-related deaths among young up-and-coming actors and models. The establishment was indeed a pit. It stank of alcohol and mildew, and other odors that Polly identified with her trip to Calcutta in the dead of summer. The so-called music was heavy on bass, and light on understandable lyrics. It was so loud that Polly had to communicate with Tim and Placenta by writing on cocktail napkins.

"When I was their age, we had real music," Polly cheerfully yelled out to the Channel 7 reporter who was covering her club visit for the *Eyewitness News* broadcast.

"Um, Mother, you're insulting the very demographic audience the show wants to reach," Tim loudly whispered into her ear.

Embarrassment played across Polly's face and she immediately laughed and said, "There I go, sounding like Methuselah—or Diana Ross. Personally, I love all the new music and stars! I keep Big Bow Wow's CDs on a leash! Usher, and that pretty what's-her-name—Mary O'Blige, too."

When the reporter turned the broadcast back to the studio anchor, the too-perky-for-television newsgirl said, "Polly Pepper. She's certainly history."

By the time Thursday night finally arrived, Tim and Placenta returned Polly to Pepper Plantation and had to help
her ascend the Scarlett O'Hara Memorial Staircase. At last in
the sanctuary of her luxurious bathroom, she immersed her
tired body in the hot, scented, sudsy, and curative waters of
her Jacuzzi jet tub. There, with a glass of champagne resting
on her bath caddy, she listened to Whitney Houston piped
throughout the house sound system. "Didn't I say that J.J.
is a lying beast? He promised easy money. What a crock! I
haven't even had time for a date with Randy this week!"

Tim reminded his mother that it was actually she who
had expected a big payoff for nearly zero effort. "As for
Randy," he said, "you haven't even mentioned him since
melting over pretty boy Richard Dartmouth."

Polly waved Tim away. "Can I help it if I have excellent
taste in God's own works of human art? Anyway, Randy's a
keeper. I wouldn't jeopardize our relationship for anything.
At least not at this early stage in the game. And don't tell me
that you didn't have the exact same response to Mr. Sterling
Studios' executive boy wonder as you did to James McAvoy!"

Tim blushed. "He's just okay. At least he took your mind
off Thane Cornwall."

Polly took another therapeutic sip from her champagne
flute. "I'm more than a little concerned about blowing my
image if Mr. Cornwall attacks me while we're on the air. I'm
not one to easily step away from an altercation, especially
if I'm in the right."

"Which is always," Placenta said. "After tomorrow's show,
things will calm down."

"We'll get into a comfortable routine, and life will once again be sunshine and lollipops," Tim added.

"Then we'll invite Richard D. over for a little tea and sympathy," Polly said. "Now, please refill Mummy's glass and allow her to die in private."

CHAPTER 3

—⌣—

Although the morning sun had been shining over Pepper Plantation for hours, the mistress of the manor and her son were still tucked into their respective beds, each of them dreaming—of Ryan Seacrest.

When Placenta knocked on Polly's bedroom door, pulled down the bed sheets, and swatted her boss's behind to wake her up, Polly complained, "Nightmares come true. You're still in the house!"

"Su casa mi casa!" Placenta said. "Rise 'n shine, Golden Oldie! Breakfast is on the bed stand: two Advil and a Bloody Mary."

Polly groaned in protest, but managed to lean over and retrieve her drink and pills. Within an hour she was showered, dressed, coiffed, and seated behind Tim in her Rolls-Royce. Placenta, too, was enjoying the ride, and completing the *New York Times* crossword. The trio arrived at Studio B on the Sterling Studios lot just as the gloved hands on Polly's Mickey Mouse edition Cartier wristwatch pointed to the inlaid diamonds that indicated it was time to put on her meet 'n greet face.

With the exception of her appearances on talk shows, it had been years since Polly had set foot on a television studio soundstage. Now memories of practically living on the set of her own show, *The Polly Pepper Playhouse,* flooded back to her. She consciously inhaled the scents wafting through the cavernous stage. She absorbed the hullabaloo of the tech crews running microphone and lighting checks and testing the strength of the staircase from which the contestants would descend when introduced by host Steven Benjamin.

Polly blinked as if she were a camera lens shutter, capturing all the visual information for replay. It was an exhilarating moment for her. And for Tim and Placenta, too. They knew what this opportunity meant to Polly. She was where she belonged.

However, that peace lasted only a fraction of a moment. Before Polly had an opportunity to say how very Norma Desmond she felt, Thane Cornwall flounced onto the soundstage, shouting at a skinny young man with large glasses, a freckled nose, and a losing battle to keep up with Thane's pace. Tears were trickling down the young man's cheeks as he tried to take notes on a pad.

"You're incompetent!" Thane roared. "When Richard Dartmouth calls, I'm *not* available. Why wouldn't you know that?"

"Because he's the boss."

"I am *never* to be summoned like a common mutt! I may as damn well say it, you're as thick as a brick!"

Polly and her troupe watched in horror. "I'm trying to do the best I can!" the young man begged.

Thane stopped, turned around, and looked down at the young man. "*Trying* is not *doing*!" Thane bellowed. "And stop your girly crying! I can't be the first with the guts to tell you the truth, that you're a hopeless twit! Your parents? A high school teacher? Someone *must* have held a mirror up to you! Just go away and bring me coffee! And, Michael, don't ask me again how I like it! I hate repeating myself. But if it isn't right … so help me!"

As the young man scurried away, Thane noticed Polly and her entourage staring at him. "What?" Thane roared. "He's an idiot. I don't have time for fools! This amateur show assigned a dimwit to be my assistant. A worthless piece of…" He paused and took a deep breath. "Okay. I lost my temper. But it's his fault. When he comes back, if he comes back, send him to my dressing room." Thane Cornwall stormed away, yelling, "If he brings me anything latte, I'll kill him."

Polly, Tim, and Placenta watched dumbfounded as Thane left the stage. "I've worked with more than a few bombastic jerks in my time, but he definitely tops my Paul Lynde vicious list!" Polly said.

At that moment, a cheerful older man with a walkie-talkie and a clipboard appeared at Polly's side. "Miss Pepper? I'm Curtis Lawson. Your director," he said. "We weren't properly introduced at Monday's meeting."

Polly's smile grew wide as she held out her hand to greet Curtis. "That was entirely my fault," she cooed. "You're an extremely busy man. I should have pursued *you*. In fact, I wanted to tell you how much I adored your last feature film ... that Disney thing ... with the talking tarantulas .... So cute! So big! So hairy! So John Travolta." Tim had Googled Curtis Lawson and tried to get his mother to memorize his credits.

Curtis's pleasure was obvious. "And I'm a huge fan of yours, from way, way back," he gushed.

"That far, eh?" Polly deadpanned. "The Natural History Museum is exhibiting my bones next month. I can get you a VIP pass." She forced a laugh. "Speaking of bones, I have one to pick with that Mr. Thane Cornwall. Did you see the fuss he made a moment ago?" Curtis lost his smile. "I've had just about enough of Mr. Ego Cornwall, and those misfits they call contestants," he said. "If I get one more demand for rose petals to be floating in the ladies' dressing room toilets, or minibars to be stocked with something stronger than Mountain Dew, I swear I'll jump off the Sterling Studio's water tower!"

"Hold off until you need a ratings boost," Placenta suggested.

"I haven't got the cojones anyway," Curtis admitted. "I'm not really complaining. Jobs are few and far between these days. But the lack of respect from these kids, and the crass Thane Cornwall—even Richard Dar—" Curtis abruptly stopped. "Never mind. I'm just exhausted. It's been the week from hell, but we're finally to show number one. If we're a hit, then all the chaos and ghoulish experiences will have been worth it."

"What's on the agenda?" Polly asked. "Any more interviews today?"

"Channel Seven may want you after the broadcast. For now, you can relax. I'll show you to your dressing room," Curtis said. He cocked his head toward the backstage area and cautiously escorted Polly and her troupe across the studio set, and over a floor that was booby-trapped with thick black electrical cables snaking everywhere. He looked at his watch. "If all goes well, the audience will be let in at three o'clock. Then we'll do the blocking and camera queues and have the run-through by four o'clock. Then we go live at six and judge the demons."

"What about the questions and answers segment?" Polly said. "I haven't received my script."

Curtis gave Polly a blank look. "That was covered in the material that production sent to you," he said. "They're supposed to be extemporaneous."

"You mean I have to make up my own?" Polly said as they stopped in front of a door labeled with her name on a gold star. "There should be writers for this sort of thing!"

"Can you say, 'cheap-o network'?" Placenta said.

"What should I ask? I'm not prepared," Polly panicked.

Curtis suddenly looked as nervous as his star judge. "Um, er, you can ask them anything you want. Just make the questions as provocative as possible. Encourage the contestants to tell a ton of lies about the lengths to which they'll go to get the most votes and thus win the grand prize."

Tim asked, "What exactly is the big payoff? A million dollars? A new Lamborghini? A shopping spree with The Fab Five?"

Curtis smiled. "At the end of the summer, the contestant with the most votes from the judges, combined with the television audience's votes, will get a totally legal *Get Out of Jail Free* card. It's redeemable at their first misdemeanor court appearance in Hollywood."

"Exactly what every star needs these days," Placenta said.

"God knows how many off-their-pedestal celebrities would have killed for such a card! Jan Michael Vincent could have had a career. At least for another moment," Polly added.

"That's a pretty nifty prize, especially since, from what I've heard, this group of contestants is one step below schizophrenic," Tim said. "But isn't there something more fun, like a ticket to one of Britney and Jamie Lynn Spears's Family Values seminars? Or a date in the Los Angeles County Prison's laundry facilities with Shia LeBeouf?"

"The winner also gets an appearance on *Good Morning, America,*" Curtis said with pride. "To be interviewed by Gail King."

"Oh dear, what questions will I ask these kids? I need darling Bruce Vilanch to write my material!" Polly fretted. She thought for a moment, then turned to Tim. "To become famous, would you be willing to auction off your kidneys on eBay?"

He played along. "Duh! Ever hear of dialysis?" Polly turned to Placenta. "Would you kidnap a studio executive and ransom him for a role on *Grey's Anatomy*"?

"As fast as you can say, 'B-bye, Isaiah Washington'," Placenta harrumphed.

Again Polly looked at Tim. "Costar in a film with Rob Schneider?"

"Um, that's going too far even for the most desperate wannabe," he said.

36

"That's it!" Curtis said. "Just ask insane questions like those and you'll be home free! Now, I've got to get over to Cell Block D, otherwise known as the contestants' dressing rooms. I'll send a PA to escort you to the set when we're ready." He shook his head and his face turned white. "God, give me strength." Then he left the room.

When the door had closed behind Curtis, Polly plopped herself down on the love seat. "Tiny bubbles," she began to sing, which was Placenta's cue to pop the cork from one of the champagne bottles she always carried in her temperature-controlled backpack. Polly picked up a copy of *Architectural Digest* that was lying on the coffee table. She unconsciously flipped through the glossy pages depicting homes that were inferior to her own. She thought about the live, unscripted, flying-by-the-seat-of-her-pants television program with which she had found herself involved. *I'll just say nice things to each performer and be as encouraging as Sally Field pitching an osteoporosis pill,* she said to herself. "You're my personal savior," she said as Placenta handed her a plastic cup filled with her effervescing amber cure-all.

A knock on the dressing room door brought Polly out of her reverie. "Makeup!" a voice called from the corridor. Tim opened the door and cast his beaming smile on a petite young woman with a mop of unruly red hair. He couldn't help thinking that she was Bernadette Peters—in a Bozo the Clown fright wig.

"I'm Katie," she said, holding out her hand and staring longingly at Tim. "You're Tim Pepper. You're even better looking than the pictures on your mother's official Web site."

As Tim's smile increased, so did the depth of his dimples.

"You've obviously got good genes. And I don't mean your Wranglers," Katie joked, her Brooklyn accent becoming more pronounced. After a long pause during which she looked adoringly at Tim, she turned and looked to Placenta and Polly. "Look at the star lady!" Katie enthused as she moved toward Polly. She smiled at Placenta, who looked Katie up and down. "Ach! You don't need me!" Katie said to Polly, and nudged Placenta for her to agree as she scrutinized the star's face. "Perhaps a little rouge here, a bit of mascara there. You're very well preserved!"

Polly smiled. "Every night after I brush my teeth and slather my face with a tube of imported monkey semen, then my darling maid, Placenta, pumps my veins with formaldehyde. After that she and Tim tuck me into my satin-lined Red Cross-approved blood bank refrigerator. By morning I'm as fresh as Doris Day."

Katie's jaw dropped. "That's some awesome beauty regimen! Certainly does the trick! You big stars know all the secrets. Someone should pass that one on to Cybill Shepherd. At least the formaldehyde part. She's already got the icy temperature thing down pat."

Polly, Tim, and Placenta all exchanged looks of amusement.

Katie stopped examining Polly's pores and wrinkles. With her arms crossed, she said, "Before we get started, I need to make myself clear about something. I don't play games."

"We weren't mocking you, dear!" Polly said. "We simply thought your summation of Miss Shepherd to be right on the money. She's a dear *old* friend of mine. We all know her well. Her icicles, too."

Katie rolled her eyes. "Puleez! I'm not talking about your silly private jokes at the expense of my self-value. You can laugh behind my back all you want. I'm a pro. I've plastered the puss of practically every putz in the biz. Nothing bothers me. Except…" Katie paused. "Let's just go back to my rule about no games. And I don't mean 'Hangman' or 'Pin the Tail on Queen Latifah's Weight Watchers hiney.' You must be civil toward me. Not necessarily nice, but at least treat me as a member of the human family."

"Egalitarian is my middle name!" Polly protested.

"That's not how the contestants of this soon-to-be-canceled show, or the despicable Mr. Cornwall, are treating me. I can't work with them!"

"Then I'm the last star standing. I'll have you all to myself!" Polly smiled.

"Practically," Katie said. "I'll make up the darling Brian Smith. And I suppose our cutie host. But the Neanderthals they have caged up in the contestants' wing of the studio are a different animal!"

Polly stood up and put a hand on Katie's shoulder. "What did those nasty trolls do to you?"

"Let's just say there's a malevolent vibration that permeates all their dressing rooms," Katie said. "I feel as though I've taken a wrong turn and ended up in a Wes Craven horror flick: *The Walls Have Eyes.* Oh, and before you hear any rumors, that Miranda chick deserved my cuticle stick up her nose!"

"Ouch!" Placenta said, holding her own nose.

"It didn't go very deep. But if she bleeds while descending that ridiculously high staircase, you'll know it's not the altitude. And Mr. Toe Nail needs to know that some people don't want to see that every body part has the potential to be pierced."

"I'm with Placenta," Tim said. "Ouch, indeed! No piercing stories, please!"

Katie waved at Tim. "I only looked for a nanosecond. Yawn. Not terribly exciting. I need this job, so I'll probably have to return to that den of insanity after all." She turned to Polly and smiled. "Let's get started. As I said, you're stunning! I have just the thing for that gnarly mustache."

The afternoon moved swiftly. Soon, Polly was escorted to the set and her seat at the judges' desk, while Tim and Placenta were ushered to their reserved front row seats in the audience. Polly could feel the excitement coming from everywhere in the studio. The set reminded her of what she imagined the main deck on an alien spaceship would look like: a vast, open, oval, raked stage with an enormous and steep stairway leading down from a height just below the ceiling. Billows of smoke and fog issued from the top of the stairs.

Laser lights sliced through the air, scanning the audience, and splitting into green cones and blue tunnels and magenta fans. Eerie metallic music that sounded like anvils being struck by hammers echoed through the studio's sound system.

As Polly took her seat, she nodded to Brian Smith and Thane Cornwall, who seemed to be enjoying the chaos. "The noise level is insane!" she shouted into Brian's ear.

She studied the audience. Collectively, they looked like they'd all been bused in from the Snake Pit. The age spread appeared to be a slender sixteen to twenty- one. Polly suddenly realized that she wouldn't be critiquing Julie Andrews or Johnny Mathis wannabes.

Instead, she would probably be witnessing some primordial toxic material that had evolved from the death of pop music in the 1970s. "Dear John Denver! Where are you when the world needs you?" Polly yelled, but her voice was drowned out by the cacophony.

At exactly 5:55, a spotlight hit the stage, the music was muted, and the audience roared and pounded their feet on the floor. Steven Benjamin stood under the bright lights as a half-dozen steadicam operators maneuvered around the stage and covered the audience. Overhead, three large cranes with cameras mounted on them glided through the air ready to capture every aspect of the event for the television-viewing audience.

At precisely six o'clock, the cheering from the audience became explosive, and Steven Benjamin lapped it up. His wide smile offered brilliant white teeth, and his hand seductively rubbed his two-day growth of beard. He welcomed the audience.

Not wanting to lose a moment of *I'll Do Anything to Become Famous* airtime, he plunged into his rehearsed introductions.

Within five minutes, Steven Benjamin had explained the rules of the game, introduced the judges, and individually called to the stage the five contestants—who, one after another, cautiously descended the staircase. The crowd was eager for the entertainment to begin. And Steven was equally excited as he introduced Miranda Washington.

Miranda, a beautiful, young, African-American woman swathed in a chiffon dress of deep rose, with a ruffled neckline that exhibited her ample bust, walked down the stairway and smiled for the audience. She sang *Road Kill.* Although Polly had never heard the song, it was obvious from the ovation that not only was the audience familiar with the music, but it seemed to be an anthem for the newly incarcerated.

Miranda's voice was sensational. Polly was as impressed as the first time she heard Linda Ronstadt. By the end of her song, which suffered only from the repetition of the lyrics—"Road Kill! Road Kill! Tires down your front and rear. Road Kill! Road Kill! I wish I hadn't run you down, my dear"—Polly was again reminded of why she had never given contemporary music a fighting chance.

When the applause died down, Miranda took her bow and was escorted by Steven Benjamin to face the judges. "We'll start with the legendary Polly Pepper." He beamed as Polly wildly applauded Miranda and put her hands to her heart.

Polly smiled warmly. "Such a big voice and such a pretty young woman. I loved every moment of your charming performance. If I still had my old variety show, I'd have you on as a special guest star! That's how much I enjoyed your work, dear. I think you're going to be very big! I'll drink a toast to you after the show. I award you a hundred points!"

Miranda's smile grew wider and she wiped away a tear. The audience completely agreed with Polly's assessment.

Steven Benjamin turned to Brian Smith.

"Oh yeah, what a voice!" Smith said. "Everything about your performance was exceptional. Love the outfit! The glitter in your hair is divine! And it's good to hear the old songs given a new interpretation!"

Old songs! Polly thought. *I have the entire Rogers and Hart catalogue, Noel and Cole, too. "Road Kill" isn't on any record I own.*

"A hundred points from me, too!"

Again the audience roared with approval of Brian Smith's comments and whooped it up in the stands. Steven Benjamin then brought Miranda to stand before Thane Cornwall.

Thane was poker faced. He sat with his arms folded across his chest and offered a loud sigh. "You're very clever," he said.

Miranda smiled with relief.

"Did you deliberately select a song for your debut that perfectly describes where your career is headed?" Thane asked.

Miranda cocked her head and knitted her eyebrows.

"I mean, your voice sounds like a seriously injured little forest creature that wandered onto the motorway only to be pulverized by an eighteen-wheeler," Thane said.

Miranda rolled her eyes, set her jaw, and put her hands on her hips. "Anything else, Mr. Think-You're- Such-a-Hotshot-With-A-Phony-English-Accent?"

"As for your lack of stage presence, you're not even as interesting as the carpet under your feet. Zero points. Dismissed."

The crowd booed Thane, while Miranda stared at him like a cobra at a mongoose. Steven Benjamin uncomfortably announced that the show would return after a series of commercials. As Miranda was escorted offstage and back to her dressing room, Polly and Brian looked at each other. Thane picked up his cell phone and began to scroll through his messages and tweets.

In a matter of minutes, Steven Benjamin was back before the cameras and welcoming the next performer. "He's a hip-hop and rap master with as much star quality as you'll find anywhere on the planet. Please welcome Toe Nail!"

The audience was enthusiastic as a swarthy, barely out of his teens young man came out from the wings. Toe Nail wore long black sideburns, a soul patch, fly fishing bait dangling from his earlobes, and a leather vest under which was nothing but muscles, more piercings, and a large tattoo of a *no parking* sign over his ripped stomach. As his music began, Toe Nail started to move with the rhythm, and strutted around the stage.

The audience felt the rhythm and could not help moving to the beat. Although Polly couldn't understand the lyrics, she was enamored of the way he seemed to own the crowd. He was in command and one couldn't take their eyes away from him. Sexy? Yes. Talented? Polly was a good judge of those who had something special, and although she wasn't sure what Toe Nail's talent was, she was very much impressed with what she saw.

At the conclusion of Toe Nail's performance, Polly and Brian joined the audience in wild applause, while Thane sat with his arms crossed and his legs stretched out under the judge's table. When the cameras were fixed on her, Polly exhibited genuine excitement, "You were absolutely marvelous, dear!" she exclaimed. "Your dancing reminds me of the brilliant Ken Berry's or even Michael Jackson's. And your confidence tells me that you're a very secure young man. I suppose anyone with a body like yours would be confident, but I think you have something extra special. Even if you weren't so sexy I'd give you high marks! One hundred points!"

Toe Nail didn't smile, but he nodded to Polly as if in agreement with her praise and the appropriateness of his score.

"Absolutely sexy!" Brian Smith echoed Polly's observation. "Not only did you deliver a first-rate performance, but your No Parking sign tattoo should be your trademark. Bravo! Well done! One hundred points!"

Toe Nail nodded and moved on to Thane Cornwall. For a long moment, Thane seemed to be examining his fingernails.

"What's your problem, dude?" Toe Nail said, which brought a wave of applause from the audience. That anyone would blithely take on the notorious Thane Cornwall, especially when it could make or break his career, was exciting.

Finally, Thane shrugged. "Now that you've finished your so-called performance, I haven't got a problem. However, if, God forbid, you return for next week's show, I'll have a huge problem because you're what we call a triple threat: can't sing, can't dance, can't act. Even if you had just one of those attributes, you probably wouldn't find work in this town. I don't think you could even serve me in a restaurant. Pretty boys are a dime a dozen here. But I'll give you ten points. The No Parking tattoo makes a perfect statement: that you'll be towed away if you don't soon move on to another career. Dismissed."

As the evening continued, Polly and the world were introduced to three more contestants. Amy Stout was a Miley Cyrus clone. Danny Castillo was a third-rate Zac Efron, and Socorro Sanchez was Ugly Betty, without the braces. Polly Pepper and Brian Smith continued to give each contestant one hundred points, while Thane Cornwall gave the others withering looks, scores of zero, and the deafening pronouncement, "Dismissed!"

With only twenty minutes remaining in the debut broadcast of *I'll Do Anything to Become Famous,* the five contenders for the most votes reassembled onstage for the interview phase of the program.

As the music became less intrusive, and the laser light show augmented the vibrations in the studio, Steven Benjamin explained the process of this portion of the contest. Each of the three judges would be assigned contestants to whom they would pose a question about the lengths one might hypothetically go to make it in Hollywood. The novelty of the answers would be rated not by the judges themselves, but by the television-viewing audience.

Steven Benjamin looked at Polly Pepper. "Ladies first." He then opened a sealed envelope and read the name Amy Stout. "Polly. Please pose a question to lovely Amy."

Although Polly was a nervous wreck, she'd had much practice emceeing charity auctions and benefits, which required her to quickly come up with funny lines when things went awry.

Now Polly called forth all of her talents for ad-libbing. She smiled at Amy. "Honey," she said, "I know that stardom is the most important thing in the world. If I could wave a magic fairy wand and tell you that you could make your dream come true, but that you only had until midnight to accomplish your goal, what would you do?"

The laser lights scanned the crowd, as the background music started to sound like the film score from *The Omen*. Amy put a hand on her hips, shifted her weight to one leg, and tossed her long blond hair over her shoulder. With a voice that sounded as serious as a hooker making a deal with a U.S. senator, she said, "Lady, wave that wand and get me into the Golden Globes dinner. I'd spike every actor's salad with a dressing laced with cyanide. I'd be the only one left for producers to cast in their movies."

Polly was appalled, but the audience cheered. She wanted to scold Amy for thinking such perverse thoughts, but was cut off when Steven Benjamin drew another envelope.

"This one is for Danny Castillo. Go for it, Brian." Brian smiled and nodded to the young man whose, singing talent wasn't actually worth a hundred points score, but Brian hadn't wanted to hurt his feelings. "Okay, you've just arrived in Hollywood. You're broke. You wanna be a star. What will you do?"

Danny gave Brian a sly smile. "So, it's like this. I get a job with a producer. I hear they're all jerks who brutalize their assistants with a lot of yelling and screaming over stupid things like salt not being salty enough. So I take the abuse for a while. But as I'm being held responsible for his French fries not being French enough, or his toilet paper not soft enough, I'm secretly taping his phone calls and keeping track of all the personal stuff he or she is charging to whatever production they're working on. When the time is right, I show him the evidence and demand to star in his next flick. He agrees because he doesn't want the world to know that the guy who makes fuzzy family films is subhuman scum." Steven Benjamin nodded in agreement. "Ah yes! Nothing says Hollywood like blackmail and extortion!" He then opened a third envelope. "Thane, you get to see how far Miranda will go!"

Thane smiled evilly. "Hypothetically, you've been hanging around Hollywood for years. You've never achieved anything because you haven't got an ounce of talent, and you have a reputation for a nasty disposition. Finally you're packing your bags and heading back to Nowhere, U.S.A. But a friend tells you that an old director, some hideously ancient man who used to be important, will try to open doors for you in exchange for sleeping with him three times a week for a year. Would you trade sex for fame?"

"The barter system is as much a part of Hollywood as power lunches at The Ivy," she snapped. "You should know that better than most. When a girl's got these"— she put her hands on her breasts—"she can get a lot of old men to do nice things for her. There's only one old man in town who I wouldn't sleep with. His name is Thane Cornwall. I hear he's a snore in bed."

The audience roared with approval.

Steven Benjamin smiled. "Polly! It's your turn again." He opened another envelope and withdrew a card. "Socorro!"

Polly looked at the young Latina. "Complete this sentence. 'I'll Do Anything to Become Famous because—'"

"I'll do anything to become famous because ... fame equals money, and money *can* buy happiness," Socorro

48

quickly said. "When I win this competition, I'll be able to buy my mama a big house." Polly's heart melted. "I'm sure that your mama's already very proud of you. And you're right, money does buy happiness. I have a lot of both."

With one contestant left to interview, Steven Benjamin called on Thane to pose a question to Toe Nail.

Thane folded his arms across his chest and tilted his head from side to side, as if inspecting Toe Nail. "This show is about doing some ultimate act in order to become famous. Since we, the judges, probably hold your fate in our hands, which of us would you kill to win the competition?"

A collective roar from the audience erupted. They exhibited the same lust for blood that made jousting tournaments popular during medieval times, or attracted huge crowds to gladiator fights in ancient Rome, and created a media frenzy over movie stars on trial for killing their spouses.

"Go on," Thane baited Toe Nail. "You can do it. And I think everybody here is confident about who you'd pick. And guess what, it *would* indeed make you famous." Toe Nail stood facing Thane Cornwall, his upper lip twitching, his fists clenched at his side.

The judges, as well as the studio audience, held a collective breath. Finally, Toe Nail spoke: "Polly Pepper."

CHAPTER 4

— ❧ —

When Polly's Rolls-Royce drove up to her PP-monogrammed iron gates at Pepper Plantation, Detective Randy Archer was already in the cobblestone car park
waiting for her. Rolling down to the front portico, Tim
eased the car to a stop by the front steps. Randy opened the
rear passenger door of her car and offered his hand, first to
Polly, then to Placenta. "That hip-hop dweeb threatened to
kill you!" he said as Polly stepped out of the car.

"Isn't live television exciting?" Polly said as she gave Randy
a quick kiss on the lips. "Glad you're using the remote I gave
you. And you're a dear for tuning in. Ach! I've had threats
before. Nell Carter said the same thing when I deservedly
won the Emmy the year that our musical variety specials
were both nominated. Nell, bless her departed soul, couldn't
face the fact that the Academy unanimously selected my
superior *PP with Elton John,* over her mediocre *Heaven
and Nell.*"

Placenta said, "The important thing is that Polly was the
top story on news radio all the way home!"

As Polly and her entourage entered the mansion, they automatically headed straight for the great room. "Bubbles and Brie please," Polly called out as her maid raced ahead to pop a cork.

As they entered their main play area of the house, Polly continued. "Forget Toe Nail. I'm much more miffed with Brian Smith. Who does that brownie-baking ex-Pip think he is, copying me! I signed on to be the *nice* judge! I gave each contestant the full one hundred points and cooed lovely lies about their half-assed performances. He copied me exactly."

"Being nice got you insults and a death threat from a lunatic gangsta with so many body piercings, he'd never make it through any airport security," Randy said as he settled himself comfortably on the sofa.

"Toe Nail is just a young blowhard and braggart. Of course, with a body like his…" Polly stopped and looked at Tim. "Did you get any vibes, dear?"

"Um, no," Tim said, helping himself to a glass of champagne, and trying to evade the ongoing issue of his mother always being on the lookout for someone who might take him away from her.

Polly cleared her throat. "As I started to say, with a body like his, and all the work that goes into crafting such a sculpture of flesh, he's won bragging rights." Desperate to change the direction of the conversation, Tim picked up the television remote and turned on the wide-screen television. "Let's see how Channel Four spins the story," he said.

Everybody focused on the honey-blond female reporter who was holding a microphone to Toe Nail's face.

Polly said, "That little twerp is stealing my limelight! Channel Four didn't ask *me* to do an interview!"

"You didn't threaten to be the next star-turned-killer," Placenta reminded her.

The reporter said, "Tonight, probably a bajillion viewers watched as you said a few mean things on *I'll Do Anything to Become…*" She stopped to look at her notes. "*Famous.* In fact, you threatened to murder one of the judges." She stopped and spoke to the anchor in the newsroom. "Roll the tape, please." A replay of Toe Nail telling the world that he'd be famous if he killed Polly Pepper filled the screen.

The camera returned to the overly serious reporter. "Do you have any comment?"

Toe Nail looked at the woman as if she had green teeth. "Aren't there a couple of wars in the Middle East that you should be covering? Or a drive-by shooting on the freeway? Or a sex scandal starring a Disneyland costume character?"

The reporter looked taken aback. "We're also told that the police are taking your threat seriously and have placed Polly"—again, she looked at her notes—"Pepper, under round-the-clock protection."

Polly smiled and leaned against Randy. "Are you my big and strong security detail?" she purred.

"If Bambi LeVitz, the Wonder Reporter who doesn't seem to know you, says so, it must be true," Randy said.

As Toe Nail tried to move away from the camera, the reporter grabbed him by the arm. "One last question. How, when, and where will you kill Polly … Pepper?"

"I'm not killing anyone or anything!" Toe Nail roared. "Except maybe my competition! Dang! That old judge should consider my remark a huge compliment. I hear she used to be a star. Thane Cornwall is nobody. The headlines would be bigger if I took *her* down. D'ya think?"

"Old? Used to be?" Polly fumed. "From now on, he'll never get more than fifty points from me! Refill, please," she called to Placenta, wiggling her glass above her head.

Unless the household was preparing for one of Polly's legendary soirees, Saturday morning at Pepper Plantation was never any different from every other day of the week. Placenta was up by six, but the mistress of the manse crawled out of bed only when the mood hit her. This morning it was nearly ten when Polly and Detective Archer wandered in their bathrobes and bare feet to the poolside patio breakfast table. "Does the sun always rise this early?" Polly said to Placenta as she slipped on her sunglasses, then walked straight toward her Bloody Mary, which had been set on the table.

Placenta poured coffee for Randy Archer and placed a glass of fresh-squeezed grapefruit juice at his setting. "Muffins." She pointed to a basket covered with a linen napkin. "Breakfast will be out in a jiff."

"You're a gem, Placenta." Randy smiled.

"I'm on my best behavior to keep you around." Placenta nudged him with her elbow.

Polly, too, smiled and sighed with contentment. She placed a hand on Randy's and gave it a quick pat. "You were a dear to protect me from unimaginable *Twilight Zone* evils last night," she said, looking into his dark brown eyes. "You have a way of making me feel—sweet sixteen."

Randy's smile radiated brighter than the light reflecting off the water in the swimming pool. "And you have a way of making me feel—like the guy in the Cialis commercial who's always ready."

Polly sighed again. "Nothing can spoil this splendid day."

At that moment, the telephone rang. "Naturally!" Polly said, and gritted her teeth. She called out to Placenta, "If it's J.J., tell him I'm hiding from killer fans!" Then she took another sip from her BM.

In a moment, Placenta appeared with a breakfast cart on which rested plates of berry-topped heart-shaped waffles, caramelized bacon, sausage links, poached peaches, and fruit compote. From her apron pocket she withdrew the cordless phone. "It's your producer, Richard Dartmouth," Placenta said, holding the handset out for Polly, who grimaced.

"I'm in Bolivia." Polly pushed the phone away. "I'll be damned if I'll do another promo spot. Especially not today!"

Placenta grumbled as she pushed the On button. "Miss Pepper's keeper says her cage is empty. When the bounty hunters drag her AWOL butt back I'll ask her to call you." She listened a moment longer, then added, "That's the only section of the newspaper that she ever reads anyway."

As Polly and Randy were playing footsy under the table and enjoying bites of their breakfast, Placenta said, "He's summoning everyone for a meeting tomorrow at ten."

"On a Sunday?" Polly protested. "What if I want to go to church?"

"And give the pope a stroke? Mr. Dartmouth said to tell you to read the Calendar section of the *L.A. Times* before you call him back."

Polly looked across the table and picked up the morning newspaper, which was face-up with a large picture of an entire town in the Midwest submerged under floodwaters. Polly tsked in sadness for the victims. "If they lived here on Stone Canyon Road, such things wouldn't happen." Polly pulled out the Calendar section and started to skim the contents. "What am I looking for?" she asked. Then Polly's jaw dropped and her eyes bugged out.

"What's the scoop?" Randy asked as he watched Polly's lips move as she read the words on the page.

"*I'll Do Anything to Become Famous.* It's a dud!" she whined.

Tim finally wandered to the table, his hair disheveled, and still wearing his bedclothes: a diaphanous threadbare T-shirt and a pair of gym shorts. Until his first infusion of caffeine for the day, it was impossible for Tim to be fully conscious. He automatically wrapped his hands around a mug of organic Mayan blend coffee that Placenta had set before him. Tim took a long swallow. Then, looking at his mother's face, which showed a combination of anger and resentment, he managed to ask, "'Nother dead body drop by?"

"We're all dead! Everyone associated with this stupid summer show. Apparently the ratings for last night's debut stank!" Polly snapped. "I'm sunk."

"You always float to the surface," Tim grumbled, his mind beginning to limber up.

Randy took the paper out of Polly's hands. He found the article and began to read aloud. "Headline," he said, "'Famous Flops.'" He looked up at Polly, and then continued reading. *"I'll Do Anything to Become Famous* made its big, splashy network debut last night. However, someone forgot to tell the Sterling Studio executives that their target audience of tweens dash out of their cribs on Friday nights. Thus, the ratings were lower than the calories in a Diet Coke.

"An *American Idol* wannabe, *I'll Do Anything to Become Famous* is scraping the bottom of the dirty clothes hamper reality genre. It rates somewhere between *America's Most Moronic Medical Mistakes* and *Britain's Worst Teeth.*"

Randy looked at Polly, then continued. "Although it's scheduled to run for five weeks, we'd rather be dodging stray bullets in South Central than wasting time watching this drivel. To quote one of the judges (Thane Cornwall), after passing judgment on an assembly line of pathetic non-talent, we'd like to say to this show: 'Dismissed!'"

Polly looked morose. "They didn't even mention my name."

Placenta handed Polly another fortifying Bloody Mary.

Polly had lost her appetite. She nibbled on a slice of caramelized bacon, then set her utensils on her plate and patted her lips with her napkin. "I suppose I'd better call Dartmouth. They'll be pulling the life support plug on the show, but I'd rather hear the death rattle from his lips."

Placenta handed Polly the telephone and called out the numbers that she'd written down. In a moment, Polly was connected to the president of unscripted programming. The conversation was brief, and when Polly disconnected the call she had a slight smile on her face. "He and Sterling are willing to let the show try to find its audience. I'm not out of work after all. At least not yet. The meeting tomorrow is to talk about strategy and promotion. I suppose I'll have to make the rounds of all the talk shows again. I need a vacation."

Polly didn't have to travel far to attend the Sunday morning meeting in Richard Dartmouth's home. He lived in the posh Benedict Canyon area of Beverly Hills, which was close to Polly's own estate. Tim drove his mother and Placenta up the steep incline of Tower Drive and found the address that Richard had e-mailed to Polly. They parked on the street, then rang the front gate doorbell at which a plaque on the iron bars read

BIENVENUE A MON MAISON HUMBLE.

"Humble, my foot!" Polly said, looking up at the grand house. "A house should speak for itself. You don't see a sign on Pepper Plantation announcing *Ma maison est plus grande que votre maison!*"

"Always on time!" Richard said when he opened the door. He looked at Tim and Placenta, and back to Polly. "Does your posse always travel with you?"

"Can't shake my shadows," Polly trilled as she eased her way past Dartmouth and into the house. She oohed and aahed, pretending to admire Richard's designer home. "The view is almost as breathtaking as my own!" she exclaimed, looking from the foyer through the vast open space to the floor-to-ceiling windows in the distance. There was a view of the Pacific Ocean.

"The others are in the study," Richard said. "May I get you something to drink before we start? Some juice? A Pellegrino?"

"Don't bother about me, dear," Polly said absently as she examined the spacious, modern decor of the open floor plan and doted on several bizarre *objets d'art* that looked like large paper clips bent into contorted shapes resting on display pedestals. "Mother and Child," she read from a brass plate in front of one piece. "The way they're tangled together, I suppose child is suckling. If you're making mimosas, I'd kill for one."

Richard hesitated before looking at his wristwatch. "Um, gee. Mimosa. Yeah, okay. Let me look into that. It's Sunday. Maid's day off. Er ... In the meantime, my study is down that corridor." He pointed in the vast distance. "Join the others and make yourselves comfortable."

Polly and company made their way down the long sandstone-tiled hallway that took them past a gallery of what Polly called "the weirdest collection of paintings I've seen since that horrible Orbinthall exhibit of Ted Bundy's, Richard Speck's, and John Wayne Gacy's thumbprints on canvas."

When they arrived at the study, Polly, Tim, and Placenta walked in to find director Curtis Lawson, Steven Benjamin, Brian Smith, and three unfamiliar people, two of whom quickly identified themselves as executives at Sterling Studios, and the third as Richard's secretary, Lisa Marrs.

Polly introduced her son and maid before shooing them to the other side of the room and promising the group that her family would be invisible.

While waiting for Richard to arrive, Lisa sidled up to Polly. "Oh! My! God!" she said, the color draining from her face. "I swear, I never do this—slobber all over movie stars, I mean. But you're you! I mean, you're Polly Pepper! Duh! Of course you know that. Everybody does. Well, not everybody, but most people are pathetic. I'm rambling. When I was a little girl I watched you all the time. I wanted to be you when I grew up! My family thought I was a freak."

"You look perfectly normal," Polly said, not sure if she should encourage further conversation.

"It's just that I made them nuts with all the loud laughing that came from my room," Lisa said.

Polly embraced Lisa's effusiveness and beamed her most sincere smile. "You look way too young to remember *The Polly Pepper Playhouse.*"

"Oh, hell, your show was canceled long before I was born."

Placenta inadvertently cackled from her seat in the comer.

"But I found a set of videos of your show at a garage sale," Lisa continued. "Of course, now I have the boxed special collector's edition of DVDs with commentary from the entire cast, as well as Carol Burnett and Sandy Duncan. When I first came to Hollywood, I took a bus tour of the stars' homes. Of course Pepper Plantation was the highlight. I've always dreamed of going to one of your famous parties. Maybe someday—"

Lisa was interrupted when Richard arrived with a tray of three mimosas. "One for each of you," he said, looking at Tim and Placenta.

"They're driving," Polly said. "Just set the drinkies here." She pointed to the place directly in front of her on the coffee table.

As Lisa moved back to her seat on the sofa, Richard looked at his watch again. "We'll wait a few more minutes for Thane. I'll say one positive thing about him, he's almost always on time."

"The more opportunity with which to be nasty," Steven Benjamin cracked.

To fill the next few minutes, Richard discussed the previous night's show. "The studio audiences loved the program!"

"Too bad the rest of the planet wasn't home," Polly sniffed.

"Regardless, you all did an amazing job," Dartmouth added, looking at Polly, Brian, Steven, and Curtis. "I'm proud of your work, and you should be happy too."

"Forget about career-destroying reviews, eh?" Polly added. "This is the only time during my illustrious internationally acclaimed career that I'm thrilled to have *not* been mentioned in the paper!"

"The *Times* critic should be strangled," Curtis added.

Placenta called out from the other side of the room, "You could do the deed and blame it on that Toe Nail person." She ignored Polly's withering look. "I'm just saying that since that boy has already made death threats, someone might get away with doing in a critic or two, then blame it on Toe," Placenta added.

61

Richard Dartmouth looked at his wristwatch again, then at his assistant. "Lisa, call Thane's cell *and* his BlackBerry. He loves to make an entrance, but this is ridiculous."

Another fifteen minutes passed. "Lisa," Richard said, "run over to Thane's house and tell him to get his faux British butt over here, pronto. The man has no consideration for others!"

During the next hour, Richard Dartmouth laid out his marketing plans for capturing his coveted Friday night television viewing audience and saving his expensive summer replacement show, as well as his own reputation as a young Turk in Hollywood. As Polly suspected, she was to be a key instrument in getting the word out that what *Fear Factor* was to the phobic, *I'll Do Anything to Become Famous* was to the creatively challenged but sadistically exceptional.

Eventually, Polly stood in the front foyer of Dartmouth's mansion saying good-bye to her television family. "Repackaging the program's publicity to present the show as proof that for one to become famous, all one has to be is mediocre is brilliant strategy," she said as Brian Smith and Steven Benjamin anxiously played with their car keys. "Hell, it worked for Pammy Anderson. And whatever happened to that Neanderthal, Steven Seagal?"

When Polly was finally out the door, air-kissing her colleagues good-bye, the sound of helicopters hovering in the sky made everybody stop and look up. "The paparazzi must have discovered that I'm in the neighborhood." Polly waved. "Will a telephoto lens make me look fat?"

"I think they're police helicopters," Tim said.

"Leave it to snooty Beverly Hills to have a neighborhood watch that includes surveillance by air," Polly said. "Although

one would think they would muffle the noise from their blades." She then bade, "Ta!" to her friends and climbed onto the backseat of the Rolls.

As Tim maneuvered the car down Tower Drive and prepared to turn left onto busy Benedict Canyon, Polly said, "I'm in the mood for a little Veuve and Carly Simon, please."

As Tim simultaneously tried to keep an eye on traffic and find his mother's favorite CD, Placenta opened the bar refrigerator.

"Careful not to upset the champers, dear," Polly called out to Placenta as Tim found a break in the line of cars and stepped on the accelerator.

When Tim was safely driving down Benedict toward Sunset Boulevard, he pushed the button to the stereo system. Before he had an opportunity to insert the CD into the slot, a news announcer said, "... dead at his home in Benedict Canyon. Cornwall was thirty-seven."

CHAPTER 5

—⌒—

Tim floored the accelerator and shot past two police cruisers as he raced home to Pepper Plantation. When the trio arrived at the mansion, they made a dash for the great room. Tim grabbed the television remote control, Placenta uncorked a bottle of Veuve, and Polly flopped down on the sofa just as her not-so-secret crush, Anderson Cooper, was beginning his report on CNN.

The news was horrific. Cooper confirmed that television personality Thane Cornwall had been found stabbed to death in his bed. In addition, he confirmed that the alleged murderer was already in custody, having been caught literally red-handed by Cornwall's maid. Cooper read the name of the alleged killer. "Lisa Marrs."

"Who?" Tim said.

"No!" Placenta said.

"Surprise, surprise," Polly said. "She adored me."

"With Richard in the room, I wasn't exactly paying attention," Tim added.

"She had an edge," Placenta said.

"She hardly spoke," Tim said.

"My fans are usually harmless," Polly said.

The news report went on to say that Cornwall's maid had arrived at the estate and found Lisa Marrs in Thane's bedroom standing over the body.

Polly tossed back her flute of champagne in one long swallow and set the glass down for a refill. "Perhaps this Lisa girl was just in the wrong place at the wrong time. Richard sent her to Thane's house, she found the body, the maid came in, and everybody jumped to conclusions. Happens all the time."

As Placenta refilled Polly's glass she said, "To whom does this supposedly happen all the time? I've never been accused of killing anything more than an orchid."

Polly took a sip from her glass. "I mean, people believe what they *think* they see."

"Body. Blood. Weapon. Do the math," Tim said.

Placenta considered Tim's comment for a moment. She looked at Polly. "With me as the lone exception, most servants have Sundays off. I wonder what this maid person was doing letting herself into Thane's house on the Sabbath?"

"Perhaps she lived in," Polly said.

"Maybe she hated her boss, poked him with the shiv, then waited for someone else to show up so that she could point her finger," Tim said as he uncorked another bottle of champagne. "Call Richard Dartmouth to offer your condolences. If you don't comfort him, I will."

Like everybody else in the world, when it came to expressing the depth of her sadness—genuine or not—over another's loss, Polly felt ill-equipped and therefore procrastinated making such calls. However, Placenta punched the numbers on the telephone keypad and pushed the handset toward Polly. Before she could finish another fortifying sip of Veuve, Richard answered. "Dear, dear Richard, you must be devastated," Polly cooed into the microphone. After a beat she said, "It's me." She waited another beat and answered, "Um, Polly." She rolled her eyes. "Pepper. Thank God you're pretty, you silly man. Oh, you must be wracked with grief and guilt! No, of course I didn't mean *guilt* guilt. Only that you must feel a wee bit awkward having sent Lisa Marrs to Thane's house at the least opportune time." Polly covered the mouthpiece and whispered, "He's awfully defensive!" She continued. "Is there anything I can have Tim or Placenta do for you? Now tell me, exactly what happened? Why did Lisa murder Thane? What was her motive? Self-defense of course! Does she have a history of going wacko? Who will replace the inimitable Thane Cornwall on the show?"

During the time she and Richard spent on the phone, Placenta refilled Polly's glass twice. When Polly finally ended the conversation and disconnected the line, she said, "We dodged that bullet!"

"Bullet?" Tim said, pouring still another flute of champagne for his mother and himself.

"We've escaped having to go to Thane's funeral. He's being cremated, and apparently nobody wants to host a memorial service."

"You don't sound very sympathetic," Placenta snorted. "A colleague has been murdered. It could have been you!"

"Nonsense! Everybody and his dog adores Polly Pepper," the star said. "Anyway, you know I loathe funerals. Except my own. I mean the one that Tim, the most brilliant party planner in Bel Air, will create for me when the time comes. A long way off, to be sure. Don't forget the sobbing orphan children, skywriting, baying wolves, and bagpipes playing '*Pavane for a Dead Princess*.' Also, I've been thinking about producing a farewell video on YouTube. I want darling Nancy Meyers to direct. And Meryl Streep must do the voiceover!"

Tim kicked off his shoes and flopped onto the sofa, his legs resting on top of the coffee table. "So, what else did Richard have to say? He kept you on the line long enough."

"The dear does go on and on. People in grief tend to be thrilled that I call and patiently listen as they unburden themselves. It's one of my many natural talents. Curiously, he seemed more upset about having to break in a new assistant. Oh, and as far as Richard and the police are concerned, it's an open-and-shut case against Lisa."

Tim and Placenta became quiet. "Apparently, Lisa and Thane had been secret lovers, but he broke off the relationship just last night—"

Placenta interrupted. "So when Lisa went to his house, she probably begged for him to take her back. And when he wouldn't, she slashed him to bloody ribbons."

Polly looked at Placenta. "Do I do maid-type things? Then perhaps you'll let me tell the showbiz murder story. Yes, the maid claims to have seen everything. Of course, Lisa swears that Thane was already dead when she arrived at his house."

"Blaming it on someone else is to be expected," Placenta interjected.

"Lisa claims that she was just about to dial 911, but then Ophelia—that's the name of the maid—came upon the scene and locked Lisa in the bedroom with the body."

"Quick thinking," Tim said. "She could have been next on Lisa's hit list. How do the police know so much already?"

"Apparently, when the paramedics revived her—oh yeah, Lisa fainted when she couldn't escape—she confessed to everything."

"Everything but the murder," Tim reminded her.

"Everything but," Polly agreed. "Affairs lead to people getting hurt. God knows I wanted to kill your fathers often enough. It's not a stretch to pin the crime on a jealous ex-lover. Lisa's el-cheapo drugstore lipstick was not only on the bed sheets, but on the corpse, too. She knew the security code to Thane's house. And, best of all, her fingerprints were on the handle of the knife that she just happened to be clutching in her dainty little hands when she regained consciousness. In fact, her prints are everywhere throughout the house."

"That's a relief," Tim said. "You finally land another job, of course a dead body pops up, but this time you don't have to get involved because they nabbed the killer right away. End of story. Now you can concentrate on the show and have some fun. Plus, no more Thane to contend with."

Placenta muttered, "No Thane, no pain." Then she asked, "Who will they hire on such short notice to replace him on the judges' panel?"

"Richard's taking over," Polly said.

"Aha!" Tim pronounced. "Richard killed Thane in order to take his place on the show! Get it? *I'll Do Anything to Become Famous!*"

Placenta nodded. "He's certainly good looking enough to be on television."

"That's the silliest notion you've had since begging me to adopt Justin Timberlake," Polly said. *"I'll Do Anything to Become Famous* is Richard's baby. Daddies don't eat their young. Generally speaking."

"Perhaps after the first week's dismal ratings he needed a surefire publicity-grabbing headline. As a result of the news you'll have a larger audience and bigger ratings next week for sure," Placenta said.

Polly stood up and wandered over to the bar. "Anyone for *sevenths*?" she asked before opening a bottle of champagne on her own.

Tim and Placenta exchanged a quizzical look. "Polly, I'll do that," Placenta said. "I was joking about the dead guy being a publicity magnet for a larger share of the ratings. You're the only star for whom people tune in." Tim added, "Mother, I think it's time for your *boob-blee* bath. You're in shock or something."

Polly turned around. "I wonder if Toe Nail has an alibi."

Tim shrugged. "Why would he need one? There's a witness who saw Lisa kill Thane."

"How many times have I said, in Hollywood, nothing is ever as it appears to be?" Polly complained. "Don't forget that little matter of Toe Nail's threat against me. What if he realized that Thane would be a bigger prize after all?"

Tim and Placenta stood up while Polly slowly sipped her champagne. "Don't make this into something it isn't," Tim begged. "If Toe Nail or any of the other contestants had anything to do with this, they would have been boasting from coast to coast because it would mean that they really were willing to do the ultimate 'anything' to win fame. Please, Mother, for once, accept the facts and leave well enough alone."

"We don't necessarily have facts, we have allegations," Polly said.

"The police have the killer. Her name is Lisa Marrs. That's that," Placenta argued. "Now, I'm going to draw your bath. You'll soak until I call you down for dinner. Is that clear?"

Placenta hustled up the Scarlett O'Hara Memorial Staircase toward Polly's bedroom suite. Tim moved to the stereo system and slipped a CD of Julie Budd onto the carousel to give the room a lighter vibration. With "*Pure Imagination*" filling the air, Polly's thoughts of the death of Thane Cornwall slowly dissipated and she began to sway—either to the music, or because the champagne had gone to her head. Tim stepped in just in case and expertly waltzed her out of the room and up the staircase, where he left her in Placenta's hands.

Monday morning arrived earlier than Tim would have liked. Polly, however, was awake at seven, and dressed to the nines by the time Tim dragged himself from his bed at ten. When he found his mother, she was foraging in the gift-wrapping room, going through the closets filled with dumb presents that friends and fans had given to her over the past few years. Tim wandered in clutching a mug of coffee. "Looking for the Chia Pet that stingy Penny Marshall sent last Christmas?"

Polly gave up looking for something in one closet and opened another. "Where the hell did you put those black armbands from our *Ides of March* party?"

Tim set his mug down on a counter and opened yet another closet door. He reached for the top shelf and pulled down a plastic bag from Walmart. "We have these left over from your Karen Carpenter appreciation party."

Polly grabbed the bag. "Even better. Although they may be too small."

"For what?" Tim asked, not exactly eager to hear what his mother had on her mind.

"Just start the car, dear. We'll be late for rehearsals."

"You're not on call until Friday. Didn't you read any of the show's instructions? Judges aren't supposed to interact—"

"I'm only going in to offer condolences to the so-called talent," Polly said. "Surely, they'll need a comforting shoulder following the death of Thane Cornwall."

"Are you kidding? I can hear Munchkins singing 'Ding-dong, the Brit is dead!' Be realistic. Thane was one unpleasant guy."

Then a light dawned on Tim. He emitted a low moan and called out, "Placenta! I need you!"

Polly heaved a heavy sigh. "Am I not allowed to visit the grieving without you thinking that I have ulterior motives? You always get Placenta to take your side on everything!"

Placenta raced up the Scarlett O'Hara Memorial Staircase. When she reached the second-floor landing, she stood in the doorway to the gift-wrapping room and leaned her body against the doorframe, catching her breath. "What? Spider spray? Rat-traps? It's a little early for champagne, even in this house."

"A straitjacket," Tim said.

"The Bob Mackie, or that satin-lined leather thing with the buckle collar and two-strap crotch cinch?" Placenta paused. "Oh, I get it. You don't have to tell me what's on Polly's mind. I can read her like a fast food menu. There's not much up on the board, but she comes with fries and a Coke."

Polly looked at her son and maid. "I just want to chat with those little wannabes. What's wrong with that? Making a few inquires about their alibis for Saturday can't hurt."

Tim looked into his mother's eyes. "Tenacity is why you became a showbiz legend. That same determination is going to get you killed someday."

"Don't be a sissy," Polly harrumphed. "Anyway, you're probably right. The police apparently have the guilty party in custody. But what else have we got to do today? Just for kicks, let's run over to the Studio. We need to get moving. I want to be there before they all become sweaty and stinky from being rehearsed to death."

In Hollywood, even the movie studio security guards are usually as young and attractive as soap stars. When Tim rolled the car up to the gate at Sterling Studios, he was in luck. Someone in human resources had forgotten to dump the last geezer in town. The guard was actually old enough to be impressed by the fact that Polly Pepper was arriving on the studio lot.

"Ma'am, I've seen 'em come and go. Stars, I mean," the security guard said as Polly reached out through her open window to shake his hand. "But you'll be a legend for as long as people need laughter. That's a fact."

Polly was in heaven and played up her best character role: the humble yet ethereal supernova. "Dear, dear Jack," she said after catching a furtive glimpse of his name badge, "I'm only an international superstar because of darling people like you who continue to support me. Now, where shall we park?"

Jack looked at his list of authorized drive-on passes. He shook his head. "I'm afraid you're not on the list, Miss Pepper."

Just as Polly's frozen smile was about to melt, Jack shook his head and said, "These dumb assistants today, they can't even call in a simple drive-on pass for a legend. I swear, Miss Pepper, this industry is filled with screw-ups at every level. You just go ahead and park wherever you feel comfortable. I'll call ahead and tell 'em you've arrived. Where did you say you were going?"

Tim gave Jack one of his most winning smiles. "You are so right about the kids in the business today. One of 'em was even stupid enough to kill Thane Cornwall and get caught. I suppose you heard all about that."

Jack gave Tim a serious look. "Mr. Cornwall was a piece of work, wasn't he? Whenever he came on the lot, he didn't even bother to stop at the gate. No matter if you're Clint Eastwood or Robert Redford, everyone is supposed to stop at the gate. And Mr. Eastwood and Mr. Redford always stop! They're right nice gentlemen, too. But Thane Cornwall just drove on through without so much as a courtesy wave."

Tim continued. "Anyway, Mom, er, Miss Pepper, brought a cake for the kids on her show, sort of a condolence present."

Jack peered into the car.

"It's in the trunk," Tim lied. "We're going over to the set to surprise everyone. No need to call ahead. We know the way."

"Sure thing," Jack said, writing on his clipboard. He looked at Polly once again. "And isn't it just like you to think of others during their time of grief? I wish that someone would teach these new stars how to behave like you and Betty White!"

Studio B on the Sterling Studio's lot was easy to access. There weren't any security guards or thick-necked bouncers standing sentry at the doors, so Polly and her troupe waltzed in. They knew their way around and soon found the rehearsal room. A window in the door confirmed what Polly had hoped for, that all five contestants were together, going through a group dance routine with the in-house choreographer. Tim quietly held open the door as Polly and Placenta slipped in to watch from the sidelines. However, every wall was floor-to-ceiling mirrors, so their presence was instantly known.

When the choreographer stopped yelling at her charges for making stupid errors in a simple dance routine, she called for a ten-minute break. With disdain dripping in her voice, she said to Polly, "They're all yours, Your Highness." Then she flounced out of the room in a huff.

The moment the door closed, Polly applauded the contestants and gave them an enthusiastic ovation. "You're already stars!" she said. "Sure, this part is drudge work, but you'll find that it gets into your system and you won't be able to live without aching feet and the feeling that you're just not good enough. And of course the inability to hold down your dinner when the announcer calls you to stage is just part of the job. Oh, those were such good times for me. I miss all those mornings when I was put through the wringer by my choreographer. Sadist that he was, I adored his talent and dedication to making me look good."

As Polly continued pontificating about her past and the hard work it takes to make it in Hollywood, the five contestants slowly surrounded her, like a pack of jackals closing in on a kill. "But I'm not here to tell you all the things that you probably already know about me, or can easily find on Wikipedia, or my personal Web site, PPstarz.com. I simply wanted to express how sorry I am that we've lost one of our friends to the Grim Reaper. He appears out of nowhere, doesn't he? Mr. Reaper, I mean. One never knows when one will win the lottery ticket to heaven, or that other place."

"As in the case of Mr. Thane Cornwall," Toe Nail said with a surly curl of his upper lip. He stepped closer to Polly. "If you think any of us are sorry that he left the planet, you're mistaken. If you ask me, his departure was delayed long enough."

Polly looked into Toe Nail's eyes. "I'd like to believe that, in time, once we got to know Thane Cornwall better, he would have grown on us," she said.

"Like a fungus," Socorro said. "Thanks to Thane Cornwall, my entire family is being harassed and laughed at, in my own hood."

Polly shook her head. "I'd be upset too if I'd been nicknamed Taco Belle by a white man with an obvious prejudice against your lovely Mexican heritage. I agree, it was an insult, and Thane was extremely rude and heartless to call you that on national television. Not to mention that it's a trademarked name, and you could get into tons of trouble if you started using it without permission."

Socorro made a face. "I wasn't about to let that fool get away with it!"

Polly tenderly touched Socorro's shoulder. "Sticks and stones, and all that stuff."

Socorro shook off Polly's hand. "I know you're on his side, and you're going to say something stupid, like 'Thane may have been a self-absorbed, bigoted, Narcissistic, misogynistic, SOB, but nobody deserves the fate he got.'"

"As a matter of fact..." Polly said.

"Well, guess what, he did deserve his fate! I'm glad he got it," Socorro said.

"So am I!"

Everyone looked at rock-star-skinny Danny Castillo, who wore his goth costume of a black T-shirt, black jeans, and black eyeliner, accessorized with black spiked hair, and a silver safety pin piercing his right eyebrow. "The dude had it coming," he added. "I may not be the best singer in town, but he didn't need to tell the world that my performance of 'Wind Beneath My Wings' stank more than a coop full of bird-flu-infected pigeons!"

"True," Polly agreed. "And how prophetic of you to tell him that his dead body would stink more than your wind."

Miranda Washington cleared her throat, then leaned in closer to Polly. "You had an on-camera snit with Thane Cornwall yourself, Miss Big ol' Think You're Still a Star. So don't go looking at any of us like we're special or something."

I would never in a million years look at any of you that way, Polly thought. "I guess there isn't a lot of love lost between Thane and this dream team of rising stars. But you're not alone, dears. Someone disliked him enough to send him to an early grave."

"That Someone should have planned her revenge a little better, bless her heart," said Amy Stout. "When Thane suggested that I gargle with Drano to clean out my pipes, I knew exactly how I would have taken care of him."

"Any one of us could have done a better job of getting away with murder," Socorro added.

"Of course you could!" Polly said in her high-pitched squeal, which she had perfected in one of her most popular recurring variety show sketches in which she trips over Troy Donahue at the beach and goes berserk with excitement. Polly clapped her hands together. "Taco Belle, indeed!"

CHAPTER 6

—⁓—

Tim piloted the car down Sunset Boulevard. En route back to Pepper Plantation, he chattered about Danny Castillo and his Goth persona. "Even with that scary outfit, I think he's sort of, kind of, um, adorable. You've got to admit his singing voice is definitely unique."

"In a chanting-requiems-to-Satan-during-bloodlet-ting-human-sacrifice-rituals kind of way, unique," Placenta said.

"At least I could understand all the words to his song, 'Abra-cadaver'," Tim said.

"He's a potential murderer, dear," Polly called from the backseat. "Careful walking down the aisle with the Zodiac Killer." As she ticked off a list Danny's personality disorders, her cell phone's ring tone played "Puppy Love." Polly smiled and opened the device. "Is it you?" she purred.

"No, it's Hugh Jackman," Placenta said.

Polly giggled at something Detective Archer said; then she covered the mouthpiece and looked at Placenta. "Don't bother waiting up for me. If you get my drift."

"You're drifting a lot lately," Placenta cackled, and gave Polly a playful nudge with her elbow.

Tim looked into the rearview mirror to see a smug grin on his mother's face. She was famous, so even at her age she could potentially have all the beaux she wanted, but she was definitely smitten with Randy Archer. He looked at Placenta's reflection and said, "Let's make this maid's night off, and boy's night out! You and I are going club-hopping." Placenta gave Polly a haughty smirk.

As her Park Ward Rolls-Royce entered the gated grounds of the estate, and rolled to a stop at the front entrance, Polly said, "Don't stay out too late, dears. First thing tomorrow, we're visiting jailbird Lisa in her new six-by-nine Beverly Hills accommodations, which I've paid for with my inflated tax dollars. If she's guilty, that's the way Madame Guillotine falls. However, since I don't completely trust our judicial system, especially after that time that Rita Wilson's snarky little gardener uprooted my Italian cypress and the arbitration judge ruled in *his* favor, I want to hear the details of Thane's murder from Lisa's own lying lips."

Polly turned to Tim. "Hon, find out where Lisa lives— or rather, *lived*. After our little tête-a-tête in B.H., I want a tour of the place she may never see again. And you"—she gave Placenta a hug—"please be a doll and set up a luncheon for us and that young man that we saw Thane thrashing the first day on the show. Let's say tomorrow. Noon. The Polo Lounge."

Placenta turned to Tim. "There goes our fun night out!"

Polly entered the house and quickly ascended the Scarlett O'Hara Memorial Staircase. "Boo-blee time," she sang out. "I'm coming, Mr. Bubbles."

The family didn't see Polly again until she wandered back into the house at ten o'clock the next morning.

—❧—

As Polly led her troupe into the lobby of the Beverly Hills Police Station, and sauntered up to the front desk, Polly sang out to the policewoman with the Adam's apple, "I'm hee-re!"

"I win, boys," the policewoman said to her colleagues. Then she looked at Polly. "We all wagered bets on how long it would take you to show up after prisoner 7189B was booked. I'm only off by three hours and fifteen minutes," she said in her raspy voice.

"We've missed you too, Wilma!" Polly smiled brightly.

"Wrong Flintstone. It's Betty."

Polly snapped her fingers. "Drats! That's who I meant!"

"You may as well save your act for the next disaster telethon, TV Star Lady, 'cause no one, not even you, can see this prisoner."

Polly's smile remained constant, although her voice took on a vague edge of irritation. "How do you know I didn't just pop in to invite you to dinner at the plantation?"

The policewoman stood up from her desk and rose to her six-foot-plus height. "Promises, promises."

"Um, I absolutely did! I'll check my calendar and have Placenta give you a jingle."

"Sorry, Miss Pepper, but I have my orders," Betty said.

As Polly fruitlessly used all of her tricks and celebrity magnetism to convince the policewoman that she absolutely had to see and speak to Lisa Marrs, Tim met the gaze of another officer and wandered over to chat with him. In a few moments, Tim returned to his mother's side. He looked at Officer Betty and offered his most seductive smile. "Thanks for your time, ma'am. We'll be leaving." Tim took his mother by the elbow and guided her toward the front door. "I'll make sure that you're invited to dinner soon. I promise," he called back.

As Polly protested, Tim whispered, "Just hush for a few minutes."

As the trio exited the building and made their way back to the car, Tim looked at his watch. "Betty goes to lunch in five minutes."

Placenta cackled. "That cute rookie, Garrett—yeah, I saw you two, and I looked at his badge, too—promised to get us in to see Lisa?"

Tim smiled. "What good are blue eyes, dimples, and all those hours in the gym if I can't use 'em to get to home base? But we've only got twenty minutes!"

"Not bad son-in-law material," Polly said.

"All we need is a cop for Placenta and we'll have our very own Bel Air patrol unit."

Five minutes later, Polly, Tim, and Placenta were escorted down a long corridor toward the prison cells. When they reached Lisa Marrs's concrete room behind a steel door,

Officer Garrett knocked on the shatterproof glass. "Ma'am, Tim, er, Miss Polly Pepper, is here to see you." He then looked at Tim. "The Abbey? Seven o'clock?"

Tim smiled, his killer dimples revving the rookie's heart rate to NASCAR zoom-zoom. "Drinks are on me," Tim said.

Garrett then unlocked the cell door. "I'll be back in twenty. You have to be ready to run, or we'll all be in Poohville." He relocked the cage door and left the prisoner and her guests to their privacy.

Lisa Marrs looked unhealthily thin, and hadn't had a smear of makeup since being incarcerated. Polly opened her purse and withdrew a tube of concealer. She applied a dollop to her index finger and approached Lisa.

"What the hell?" Lisa backed up against her bed.

"Just hold still for a teensy weensy moment, honey. Your craters, er, pores are giving me the willies." Polly cautiously applied the makeup onto Lisa's face. "There!" Polly announced as if completing the final touches on a work of art. "Doesn't that make you feel like a million?"

"Oh yeah. I'm in hell, but I look good enough to date the homeless drunk in the next cell!" Lisa said. "Jeez, lady, you're as loony as Thane said you were!"

Polly was taken aback. "Then thank you for saving me from having to kill him myself!"

"I did not kill Thane Cornwall!" Lisa cried. "Why doesn't anybody believe me?"

"Maybe because you were caught in the act of doing the deed," Placenta said.

"But I wasn't! The maid came in *after* I found Thane. She doesn't even speak well English!"

"That makes two of you," Polly said. "Confess, dear. She saw you holding the knife," Polly declared. "You were the only wacko in sight."

"So what's your version of the story?" Placenta said. "You'd better make it interesting 'cause Polly Pepper's got a severe case of ADD, and the evidence is piled sky-high against you, babe."

"I've told everyone the same thing over and over!" Lisa implored. She was quiet for a long minute, then spoke. "Okay. Again. For the bajillionth time. I went to Thane's house because Richard Dartmouth sent me. You were there. You know that's the truth. I rang the doorbell forever. Then I decided to let myself in."

"If no one was home, why would you bother going inside?" Polly asked.

"Thane's Lamborghini was parked in the driveway. I figured he was there but ignoring me."

"If a person doesn't answer their door, it makes sense that they probably don't want visitors. Or are on the toilet," Polly agreed.

Lisa shrugged. "That's what I thought. But Richard would have killed *me* if I didn't drag Thane's butt to the meeting. He's not as tolerant of his assistants as he is of the stars he kisses up to," she said. "He hasn't even come to visit me, or sent me a note of support."

"Okay. So you're outside the house, and…" Polly said.

"I remember that the security system wasn't activated."

"It was daytime," Placenta said.

"Yeah, but Thane was paranoid about being burgled … or worse," Lisa said. "He kept the system activated twenty-four-seven."

"Of course, you knew the code because you'd used it often enough. Like the night before?" Polly said.

Lisa swallowed hard. "I suppose my affair with Thane is making news everywhere."

Tim sniggered. "I don't mean to laugh, but *Daily Variety* said, 'Psycho Secretary in Pillow Talk before the Big Chill.'"

"Then I'm probably as dead as he is."

"The media are having a blast playing up the jilted lover angle," Polly continued. "*The National Peeper* is concluding that yours is a case of being cast aside for a new play toy."

Lisa looked down. "That sums it up," she said almost in a whisper. "After we made love Friday night, the SOB told me I needed to join a gym."

"Yikes! That's insulting," Tim said. "Thane wasn't exactly God's gift."

"You can say that again. I got angry. I said I was leaving him. He laughed at me. He said that I was saving him the trouble of dumping me. He told me to get permanently lost." Lisa's voice broke as she cried.

For a moment, the entire jail cell was quiet. Then Lisa looked up and declared, "But he wasn't worth killing! I didn't do what they say I did!" She began to weep again.

Placenta withdrew a Kleenex from her purse and handed it to Polly to give to Lisa.

"We don't have many ticks of the clock left, honey," Polly said, looking at her Cartier wristwatch. "Fast-forward

85

this melodrama. You're trespassing in Thane's house. You see ... what?"

"At first, nothing," Lisa continued. "Nothing unusual, that is. I didn't want to startle Thane, so I called out his name a few times. As I wandered through the house and down the hallways, I kept calling his name. I even went into the backyard, thinking he might be in the pool. Then I figured he was probably in the steam room, or in bed with someone, so I went to his suite. It's way in the back of the house, where he might not have heard me earlier. The door was closed. As I got nearer I listened carefully. I didn't hear anything. So again I called his name. No answer. I knocked on the door. Nothing. I suppose I should have called 911 before going in there, but I never expected..."

"What?" asked Polly.

Lisa looked at Polly. "Thane was in bed. Facedown. Naked. The sheet drawn to his waist. Blood ... everywhere! At first I didn't do anything except try not to throw up. I guess I was in shock. Then I heard a noise and realized that whoever stabbed Thane might still be in the house. I saw a bloodied knife on the floor, so I picked it up for self-defense. That's when Thane's maid, Ophelia, came in. She looked at me. Then she looked at Thane's body. She said, 'Miss Lisa!' Then something in Spanish. She looked really frightened and slowly backed out of the room. When she got to the door she closed it behind her. I heard her scream, 'Miss Eva! Miss Eva! Nine-one-one! Nine-one-one!' I guess that's when I fainted."

"Miss Eva? The new significant other?" Polly asked.

"Thane's stupid Persian cat."

"Did you see anything that might suggest someone else had been there after you left the night before?" Polly asked.

"Besides a dead body? A butcher's knife on the bedroom floor? Bloody bedsheets? No." Lisa shook her head. "But it was damn odd that the security chimes weren't on. It's possible that Thane might have forgotten to turn the alarm system on, but he would never have been in the house— even if he had company— without the chimes that signaled whenever any outside door opened."

Suddenly the door at the entrance slammed open. Officers Betty and Garrett marched into Lisa's cage. With her arms folded across her chest, Betty looked first at Polly, then at Tim and Placenta. Finally she looked at Officer Garrett.

"They made me!" Garrett cried.

"Yeah, they're a really scary posse," Betty snarled. "Complain to the bartender at the Abbey. You'll have plenty of time to hang out there with your new friend 'cause I'm petitioning to place you on administrative leave!"

Garrett looked at Tim and shrugged. Then, with his thumb and little finger against his ear, he made the international sign for "Call me."

CHAPTER 7

—◦—

"Policewoman Betty has better developed biceps than Stallone on steroids," Polly said as they drove out of the Beverly Hills Police Station parking lot. "Remind me to hire her the next time we need the piano moved."

Tim drove the Rolls to Sunset Boulevard and turned left heading toward the Beverly Hills Hotel.

Polly looked around. "I thought we were going to Lisa's hovel."

"I called her landlady, she won't let us in," Placenta said.

Polly rolled her eyes. "Contacting her was a mistake. The surprise of finding Polly Pepper on one's crummy apartment doorstep is what does the trick. We'll tackle her later."

"That leaves more time for lunch with Michael McGrath," Placenta reminded her.

"Not another of Tim's *Dancing With the Stars* studs," Polly said. "How many of those talented men have you dated this year?"

Tim sighed. "This is the kid who worked for Thane. Remember? The guy who was ripped apart that first day?

You asked Placenta to set up lunch with him." "Drats! I need a nap," Polly complained.

Tim ascended the long driveway leading up to the hotel valet, and accepted a receipt ticket in exchange for the Rolls. A liveried attendant assisted Polly and Placenta from the backseat and made a great show of being overly solicitous because of the ritzy car in which they arrived.

As the trio entered the plush lobby of the world-famous hotel, Polly led the way to one of her favorite watering holes. Stepping into the room, she looked at the maitre d' and cried out, "Karl! *Grube mein freundl*" Polly accepted Karl's air kiss to each cheek and stood aside as he expressed the same gesture to Tim and Placenta. "The sultan has you working on such a lovely day! Ogre!" Polly said. "Tell him to go back to Brunei!" When Polly thought of the Polo Lounge, she thought of Karl (although she never knew his last name). A great and accommodating gentleman, he had been with the Beverly Hills Hotel as it had been bought and sold by one zillionaire after another. Now, after nearly fifty years working at what was affectionately known as "the Pink Palace," Karl continued to welcome stars, and subtly reject unaccompanied single men and women when he sensed that they were there to prey on his wealthy clientele.

"Your guest has been seated. Please follow me, Miss Pepper," Karl said as he picked up three menus and wended his way past tables of diners who all looked up and wondered if the elegantly dressed woman passing by was anyone of note. Polly's keen ears picked up several stray comments.

"Isn't that … ? You know her name … she used to be…"

"Don't look now, but I think Shirley MacLaine just walked by!"

"Who's the redhead with the lousy dye job?"

As Polly tried to ignore the peasants, Karl guided her to her favorite table. The freckle-faced young man whom she had last seen crying in the television studio stood up to greet her. Sotto voce, Polly asked, "What's his name again?"

"Michael," Tim reminded her.

"Sweetheart!" Polly called out, loud enough to cause the other diners to look in her direction. Then she offered her hand for him to shake while she palmed a twenty-dollar bill off to the *maitre d'*. "*Danka*, Karl," she said as he pulled out a chair for her.

Polly returned her attention to her guest. "You look so much more adult without red eyes and a runny nose!" she said to Michael as she patted his forearm. "That was such a horrid day for me, having to see you suffer so! By the way, this is my son, Tim, and our maid-slash-bff, Placenta." Polly looked up at a waiter who had appeared at her side. "Thank you, Lance. My usual would be lovely, dear. We'll all have the same."

As soon as the waiter departed to retrieve drinks for the table, Polly looked intently at Michael. "I guess this is a good news/bad news sort of day, isn't it? The good news, of course, is that you're having lunch with me, Polly Pepper. The bad news is that your boss, Thane Cornwall, is probably sitting in the big audition room in the sky with that *Dancing with the Stars* guy."

"Still alive," Tim whispered out of the comer of his mouth.

"Hardly possible!" Polly said.

"Good news after bad," Michael said as he adjusted his eyeglasses.

Polly nodded in agreement, just as the champagne cocktails arrived. "I'm parched!" she said. Not waiting for the others to be served, she quickly swallowed most of the champagne in her flute. "I'd better have another toot, pronto," she said to the waiter. Returning her attention to Michael, she said, "Did you hate Thane Cornwall enough to kill him?"

"A direct hit between the eyes," Michael said as he picked up his glass and took a long swallow. "Um, yeah."

"A confession? That was easy!" Placenta said.

"Not!" Michael said. "She asked if I hated Thane enough to kill him. Most people who knew the man would say yes. But that doesn't mean they'd actually do it! Could I? Yes. Would I? No!"

Polly finished her first glass of champagne just as the second one arrived. "Better keep the bubbles coming, Lance, dear," she said.

While Polly let the second serving effervesce easily on her tongue, Tim used the moment to cross-examine Michael. "You were assigned to be Thane's personal assistant. Did you ever see anything weird going on?"

Michael shrugged. "Be more specific. Everything in Thane's life was freaky. He had to have a new toothbrush every day because he was afraid of his own bacteria. He wouldn't handle money because he was terrified of where it had been. I took his car to be washed, and if there was so much as a streak on a window I'd have to take it back.

I even had to clip his damn toenails because he hated to touch feet—even his own!"

"A wee bit of OCD?" Polly said as she absently took another sip from her flute.

"I was hired by *I'll Do Anything to Become Famous,* and I was only supposed to be Thane's assistant for the show," Michael continued. "But he made me his personal twenty-four-seven slave. I don't know how I made it through the week. He was constantly yelling and screaming and threatening to fire me. But Friday night rolled around, and after the show I was still there. I started to think that maybe all the threats were just a bully control issue sort of thing. I was thinking that Thane was probably beating up on lesser people as a way of compensating for whatever inadequacies he felt."

"Why'd you put up with him?" Placenta asked.

"Why does anyone do anything in this town? A job. Money. To hang out with famous people. And I wanted to prove that I wasn't as weak as he said I was. Plus, I wanted to pitch him a screenplay."

"It always comes down to a screenplay," Polly deadpanned.

"I made my pitch," Michael continued. "He just laughed at me and said, 'That idea sucks more than anything I've ever heard. You're an idiot!'"

"I don't suppose there's a role for me," Polly said, straightening her posture.

"When did you last see Thane alive?" Tim asked.

"Friday night. After the show," Michael said.

"I left the studio at around eleven o'clock. When did you leave?" Polly said, looking into Michael's eyes.

Michael thought for a moment. "Yeah, that's about the time that Thane came to his dressing room and yelled at me for not bringing his black jeans. I did bring black jeans, but apparently they weren't the right black jeans."

"Who could tell?" Placenta said.

"Thane could," Michael said. "He called me a screw-up and told me to get his girlfriend on the phone."

"Lisa Marrs," Polly said.

Michael coughed a laugh. "That's what I thought as I picked up his cell and pressed the address book key and began to search for her number. He ripped the phone from my hand and said I was lame and as thick as a brick, and that I was as dense as Lisa and that I obviously didn't care about him because I hadn't paid attention to his illustrious personal life during the week. He said that Lisa was dangerous, and out of his life. He had someone new. Then he told me to bring his car around, and he tossed me his keys. When he came out of the studio soundstage, he was talking on his cell and didn't bother to say one word to me. I was completely invisible to him. He just got into the car and drove away. That was the last time I ever saw him alive."

"Who was his new flame?" Polly asked.

Michael shrugged.

"Any idea where he was headed?"

Michael shook his head. He paused and knitted his eyebrows. "Actually, before he closed the car door, I heard Thane yell at whoever he was on the phone with. He said that if they were serious about coming over, they knew the address, but that they better have a decent explanation—"

"Explanation?" Polly asked, biting her lacquered nails.

"Beats me. But the last words I heard were 'Over my dead body.'"

Polly was deep in contemplation when the waiter arrived to accept the group's luncheon orders. She pushed her chair away from the table, stood up, looked at Michael, and said, "Dearest, I know you'll forgive this ancient star. Sometimes I'm such an idiot. I just remembered that I have another engagement. Something with Miranda Richardson. She can be a keg of dynamite and the last one on the planet I want pissed at me. You stay and have lunch with Lance."

She looked at Tim and rubbed her fingers together, her not so subtle hint for him to give Lance a healthy tip.

As Tim and Placenta rose from their chairs and gave Polly quizzical looks, she silenced them with her eyes.

"Miranda better have some munchies, 'cause I'm about to faint from starvation!" Placenta said.

When they were once again in the car and driving down Sunset Boulevard toward Bel Air, Polly said, "Talk about low self-esteem. Why would an attractive and intelligent young man such as Morris—"

"Michael."

"—accept a job working for someone as mean as Thane Cornwall?"

"You heard him," Placenta said. "Some people will do anything to work in showbiz."

Polly said, "We have a saying in the theater. 'Actors are either trying to get into a hit show, or get out of one.' What if the kid was ticked off because Thane dismissed his screen-play idea and he wanted out of his job? That boy knows more than he's sharing. Take me to Lisa's place."

CHAPTER 8

—⁓—

Tim cautiously maneuvered the Rolls down Ogden Avenue in West Hollywood. The street was narrow, and made worse by the congestion of cars parked on both sides. Polly cringed and leaned into Placenta whenever another vehicle approached and squeezed past with less than a hair's breadth of space between them. "Is that Taboo you're wearing?" Polly said, making a face when her nose made contact with Placenta's breast.

Finally finding a parking place two blocks from Lisa's address, the trio set out and carefully made their way over sidewalks that were buckled from tree roots, and cracked from the thousands of imperceptible earthquakes that occurred each year. "This is it," Tim said when they arrived at the address. It was the most dilapidated apartment building on the already decrepit street.

"Naturally." Polly looked at the building. "New reality show idea: *I'll Do Anything to Burn Down My Crummy Apartment!*"

The trio walked up to the front door. A rusted sign said NO PETS. NO SOLICITING. NO VACANCY. NO HABLAR INGLÉS. MANAGER #1.

Polly pointed to a hand-printed piece of paper taped to the bank of mailboxes. "Office closed today."

"We'll just have to find our way into Lisa's crib by ourselves," Polly said. She looked at the labels on each mailbox. "L.M. number four," she said.

Tim backed away from the door. "Count me out," he said. "I visited a jail this morning. I will not become a permanent resident! I'm quite happy living in your mansion."

"Pooh!" Polly said. "Who's going to know, and what's the harm, if we take a teensy peek at Lisa's little ol' flat? You saw the sign. The office is closed, so the manager is probably away playing the horses at Santa Anita."

"How do you propose to gain access to the building without a key?" Placenta said.

Just then, the door opened and a young pregnant woman stepped outside. Polly caught the door before it closed. "The Lord provides," she whispered. Then, slipping into performance mode, Polly looked at Placenta and raised her voice. She announced, "Yes, I really do live here! It says so on the mailbox!"

"She's already reached the curb," Placenta said. "Get your butt inside before anyone else comes along." As Polly and Tim and Placenta scooted into the lobby of the building, they were all struck by how dingy the place was. The scent in the air was a combination of wet dog and gym locker. "Lisa's in a better place," Polly said, making a face as she looked around.

"Let's just get in and get out fast!" Tim demanded. "I'm hungry and I'm nervous."

"You just had lunch," Polly reminded him.

"A champagne cocktail may be lunch to you, but—" Just then the door to the apartment manager's office opened. "She's away, eh?" Placenta said.

"Who are you looking for?"

Polly stopped and turned around. Standing outside the apartment, a woman wearing a muumuu and who appeared to be in her early sixties gave the trio a suspicious look.

"Thanks, honey, but we're absolutely wonderful." Polly smiled. "Go back and watch *Ellen* or *Days of Our Lives* or—"

"You don't look like you belong here."

"Such a lovely compliment." Polly beamed.

"How did you get in?" the woman persisted with a harsh stare.

Polly thought for a quick moment. "My dear friend gave me her key and asked me to drop by to check on the cat."

"We don't allow pets," the woman said with a suspicious tone as she folded her arms across her chest.

Polly grimaced, realizing that she'd seen the sign that announced the pet situation. "I mean she wanted us to make sure that she didn't leave the iron on. She'll be away for a while. God knows our friend worries too much, but if it eases her concern while she's off visiting her sick mother in Rancho Cucamonga, then who am I to deny her some peace of mind?"

"What's your friend's name? All of my tenants are accounted for," the woman said. "One is away, but the only mother she's visiting is a prison matron."

Polly looked at Tim and Placenta. "Why would Enid fib and ask us to check on the cat, er, iron?"

"Perhaps you're the one who's lying," the manager said.

"Perhaps we're just in the wrong slum," Polly said, hands on hips.

"If you don't tell me who you are and why you're trespassing, I'll call the police."

Tim stepped forward, catching the woman off guard with his soap opera star good looks. As she nearly swooned, Tim smiled. "Please accept my apologies. My mother, Polly Pepper, was hoping the apartment manager would let her visit Lisa Marrs's unit. The poor kid's in jail and needs clean underwear."

Instantly the woman melted, looked at Polly, and held a hand to her heart. "Son of a…! Excuse my language … I thought you looked like Somebody," she said to Polly. "I can't believe that I didn't recognize you right away. You've changed a little. But the chin implant does wonders for you!"

Polly blushed.

"I used to watch your show every week," the woman continued. "Why don't you come back to television? I don't count that skuzzy new piece of doo-doo about kids who want to become famous. But I think that everybody would like to see you as Miss Midas again. Or Bedpan Bertha. I remember the sketch with Don Knotts. You were supposed to check his glands, but gave him a gynecological exam by mistake. Just thinking of it still makes me almost pee my pants!"

Polly immediately warmed to the woman, walked up to her, and extended her hand. "I'm Polly Pepper. With whom do I have the sincere pleasure of sharing this intimate moment?"

"Muriel," the woman said with a nervous chuckle. Polly thought of wet underwear as she reluctantly accepted the woman's outstretched hand. "I'm so embarrassed about lying to you. And here you are, so sweet to remember *moi*. Trust me, I'd love to be back on TV, Muriel, especially in a better show than the rip-off talent competition I'm stuck in. Alas, musical variety is dead. I have to take whatever work I can find. I know it's pathetic for my fans to endure seeing their national treasure in less than the highest quality engagements, but as they say, 'That's showbiz!' Nobody wants this poor, old, antebellum relic of an international icon anymore. There's no place for me. Isn't that the saddest story you ever heard?"

"Almost," Muriel said. "What's up with Lisa Marrs? She wasn't the sweetest thing on the planet, but I never thought of her as a killer. To think I rented an apartment to a madwoman! Why'd she murder that other judge on your show?"

Polly looked at Muriel. "We don't know why she went insane. But we also don't know for sure that she's guilty."

Muriel looked at Polly as though she was an imbecile. "Hell, it's all over FOX. Lisa was caught chasing that Thane judge person through his house. She had an axe. Or was it a chain saw? When she finally cornered him in the pool cabana, she chopped him into Kibbles 'n Bits!"

Polly and her entourage looked slightly amused. "Actually, I think she did it while he was sleeping in his bed. That is, *if* she did it."

"The *Peeper* said—"

"Oh, that rag!" Polly rolled her eyes. "How often have you read that I'm an alien from another galaxy? Those 'switched at birth' photos of me next to E.T. are abominable! I'd trust a Washington politician running for the White House before I'd believe a word they print in that waste of a forest."

Muriel nodded in reluctant agreement. "So you think she might not be guilty?"

"Hard to tell," Polly said. "But I'm hoping that clean underpants will bring her to her senses. Would you be a dear and let us into her apartment?"

Muriel looked defeated. "You know I adore you," she said, "but the police still have yellow barricade tape across the doorway. No one is allowed inside."

"But we were asked personally by Lisa Marrs, the woman who lives there, the one who has to endure those awful wool panties they issue to inmates. Delicate woman that you are, surely you cringe at the thought of the discomfort of wearing steel wool against your sensitive flower. Think of the rash!"

"When you do murder, you give up the right to Victoria's Secret satin and lace," Muriel said.

"Of course you're right," Placenta piped in. "But she hasn't been found guilty by a jury. Until then, she's not legally a murderer."

Muriel scoffed. "If she's in jail, then she's probably guilty."

"We certainly wouldn't want to get you into trouble with the police," Placenta said. "God knows you must have a difficult enough time with the city's chief health inspector." Placenta looked around. "Garbage in the hallway." She pointed to an overflowing bin. "Exposed electrical cords."

Polly and the others followed Placenta's gaze and looked up at the ceiling.

"Was that a darling family of kitties I saw a bit ago, or a pack of bubonic plague carriers?" Placenta bluffed.

Muriel frowned. "Are you trying to intimidate me? Extortion does not become a star of Polly Pepper's caliber." She looked at Polly. "I thought you were supposed to be a nice movie star."

"Mother would never do anything that wasn't lovely and nice," Tim said, trying to smooth over the sudden hostility in the air. "She wouldn't think of asking you to unlock Lisa's door and disregard the police's edict. However, if there was a way that you could let us simply grab a few of her undies, we promise not to touch anything else. And Polly Pepper is a clam when it comes to keeping secrets. Especially to the health department. No one would be the wiser."

Muriel thought for a moment. One could tell that she was weighing the possible consequences of helping a star, of whom she was genuinely fond, and doing something illegal. "Is your house in Bel Air really as grand as the pictures in *People* magazine?"

"We'll invite you over to see for yourself," Polly said. Muriel whirled around and reentered her apartment. Polly looked at her son and maid. "So much for being nice."

The door opened again and Muriel's arm reached out. She held a key for a moment, then let it fall to the ground. "Oh, my, I can't find my keys. I must have accidentally dropped them somewhere."

Tim retrieved the key from the doormat. "Thank you!" he whispered in a voice loud enough to be heard through the still ajar door. "Polly loves you. And so do I!"

"That wasn't so hard," Polly said as she led the way down the hall. "Now, where's number four?"

"My wild guess is that it's the one with the police tape and the sign that says 'No Entry! Trespassers will be prosecuted!'" Placenta pointed.

Polly looked around for anyone who might be watching and then rushed to the apartment door. "Strip away that nuisance tape, dear," she said to Tim, who nervously removed just enough tape to allow access to the lock, and for his mother and Placenta to squeeze into the apartment.

Once inside, the three looked at the one-bedroom apartment, which was clean, but crammed with furniture, a television, a computer, shelves containing hundreds of DVDs, and all the accouterment of home entertainment.

"What exactly are we looking for?" Placenta asked. "Real live skeletons in the closet?"

"Haven't a clue," Polly confessed. "Maybe something that the police overlooked. A publicity photo of Thane tacked on a dartboard? A voodoo doll? A copy of *Murder for Dummies?*"

As Polly and her troupe looked through drawers, under the bed, in the closets, and through the DVD and video collection, they found that Lisa Marrs had a meager wardrobe, was apparently addicted to Pringles, and that she had a penchant for Merchant Ivory films and old movie musicals. DVDs of *Singin ' in the Rain, The Bandwagon, Cover Girl, Show Boat,* and many others, were scattered everywhere. Polly picked up a DVD jewel case from a stack beside the television. "It's about time I watched this again!" she said. The title on the disc was handwritten. Polly read aloud, *"Anything Goes.* One of six." Polly placed the discs in her purse. "What?" she asked the questioning faces of Tim and Placenta. "I'm *borrowing* a movie. I haven't seen this oldie since Mitzi Gaynor coerced me and Bing Crosby to dinner and made us sit through ninety-two minutes of them and Ethel Merman and Ida Lupino in this god-awful piece of drivel!"

Polly was trying to close her small purse with its new bulky contents, when the trio heard the knob on the front door being turned and opened. They instantly sprinted into the bedroom. A familiar voice said, "Look everywhere. She said they were here."

Polly quickly opened a dresser drawer and pulled out all the underwear she could find. She clutched the garments in her arms and sang out, "Lisa will be thrilled!" A startled Toe Nail rushed into the bedroom accompanied by Thane's former assistant, Michael. "What the hell?" Toe Nail said.

Polly looked at Michael. "Sweetums, that was an awfully quick lunch! I hope you stuffed yourself!"

"I thought you were going to Miranda Richardson's," Michael said.

Polly looked confused.

Placenta stepped in. "Rescheduled."

Toe Nail looked at Michael with suspicion.

"They took me to the Polo Lounge this afternoon."

"And what a lovely time we had, too," Polly chirped. "We just stopped by Lisa's apartment to retrieve a few ladies' things for her." Polly displayed her armload of garments for Toe Nail and Michael. "What are you two doing here? Aren't you supposed to be in rehearsals?"

Toe Nail hesitated. "Lisa asked me to pick up…"

"Makeup?" Polly offered. "I'll bet the dear wanted her blushes and eye shadow and lipstick. And how lovely of you to stop by the jail to support our friend in need. When did you see our lost lamb?"

"Um, after rehearsals yesterday. Last night," Toe Nail corrected. "Yeah, she looks like hell. You would too, if you were a maniacal killer and were stuck in a hellhole like the Beverly Hills jail. Can't be easy to know you're on your way to the chair!"

"Imagine all those volts of electricity crackling along your nerve endings and baking your insides like a potato in the microwave?" Polly shivered. "Shall we wait for you to collect the stuff for which you broke into the apartment, and then we all leave together?"

Toe Nail and Michael looked at each other. "We didn't break in," Michael said. "The door was unlocked."

"We may take a while," Toe Nail said. "Then we've got to get right back to the studio. We'll see you at rehearsal on Friday."

Polly looked at Michael. "You certainly work fast, dear. One minute you're bossless, and the next—literally—you're working again. For Toe Nail! Bravo!"

A surreptitious look exchanged between Toe Nail and Michael was not lost on Polly or Tim and Placenta. "On that lovely note, we must be shoving off," Polly announced. "I promised Lisa that she'd have her panties ready by orifice inspection time tonight." She made kissy-kissy sounds at Toe Nail and Michael. "See you on set!" she called back as she stepped out of the apartment. "You little weasel," she muttered, just loud enough for Tim and Placenta to hear.

CHAPTER 9

—〜—

"Picking up Lisa's makeup? Give me a break!" Polly spat as she dumped the load of under clothes into Placenta's arms, then walked out of the building. "I may be dumb about a lot of things kids do today, but I'm not entirely brain dead. I clearly heard him say, 'She's the only one who could have *them*.' *Them* what? Blush? Bronzer? Lip-gloss? Not!"

"He lied about seeing Lisa last night," Tim added. "Visitors aren't allowed. Nor is makeup."

"We need to find out what they were really doing in Lisa's apartment," Polly said.

"Same thing we were doing, no doubt," Placenta said as she clutched the clothes and gingerly stepped along the uneven sidewalk. "They were looking for something. Something obviously important."

"And now they probably think that we were after the same thing," Tim said.

"We don't even know what it is," Placenta added.

"Something incriminating, of course," Polly said. "Or something to cover someone's hiney. Whatever it is, it's valuable. Otherwise a contestant wouldn't risk his shot at fame by breaking into an apartment that was sealed by the police."

"Not so fast," Tim said. "Don't forget, the show is called *'I'll Do Anything to Become Famous.'* And the grand prize is a 'get out of jail free' card if they win. Breaking and entering is further proof of Toe Nail's determination to win. Maybe they weren't really looking for anything. Maybe they just wanted to get caught for the appearance that Mr. Toe Nail would go to greater lengths than his competition."

The trio arrived at their car, and Placenta tossed Lisa's underclothes into the trunk. She withdrew a bottle of Veuve from the built-in refrigerator and they all settled into the plush leather seats of the vehicle and made their way back to Sunset Boulevard and the drive to Bel Air.

"And what's up with the little dork playing his sidekick?" Polly asked about Michael.

"I'd say he's helping the thug prove that he's the most nefarious, and thus entitled to be the show's winner," Placenta said. "After working for Thane, he probably has plenty of inside information."

"Inside information," Polly repeated. Snapping her fingers and knocking back what was left of the champagne in her glass, she sat up straight. "Of course! As Thane's shadow, he would know as much about the behind-the-scenes aspect of the program as Lisa did working for Richard Dartmouth. In fact, they probably knew where all the bodies were buried, so to speak! Methinks that Michael is helping Toe Nail to win. He may be a clever little rat with a lot more going on upstairs than he lets on. I wonder how much of his bumbling twit persona was a stunt to keep Thane from thinking he had a brain? Thane wouldn't have kept him around if he was a total bonehead."

"Assistants often know more than their bosses," Placenta agreed. "We collect a lot of bits of material, all of which could easily add up to lucrative feature stories in the *National Peeper*, or tell-all books."

Polly raised an eyebrow. "You know this from personal experience? I do keep some secrets."

Placenta grinned and stared Polly down.

Polly flinched. "Lisa and Michael both worked for the two most powerful men involved with the show. No doubt they had knowledge of things that were top secret. I suspect that Michael thinks that Lisa killed Thane for something that could potentially make a winner out of whoever knows the secret. I'll bet my star on the Hollywood Walk of Fame!"

Tim spoke up. "Michael said something at the Polo Lounge that just came back to me. Remember when he quoted Thane in his dressing room as saying that Lisa was trouble?"

Polly and Placenta exchanged looks.

"Maybe, as you say, Thane's death was more than just revenge from a spurned lover," Tim continued. "Maybe he knew something that someone else didn't want him to know. Something incriminating or illegal and the only way to protect their secret was to keep him silent forever."

"What could be so terrible that one would commit murder?" Polly said. "Unless Thane was trying to get that annoying actress who played Monica on *Friends* into another TV series."

Placenta held up her hands. "You're the one who's always saying that nothing in Hollywood is ever as it appears to be. But what if this is just obvious: a case of Lisa being dumped by Thane, and getting even with him for her battered pride?"

"No doubt Thane had plenty of experience with women who ended up hating him," Polly offered. "The jilted or rejected can do the most odious things in the name of retribution. When I discovered that your daddy had a crush on Florence Henderson, I sent all of his tuxedos to the cleaners and had the left pants legs altered three inches shorter. Men don't seem to check their formal wear until the night of a big event. Goodness, dear Flo was surprised the night he escorted her to the People's Choice Awards! Ha! That was one of my proudest moments!"

"So that's why Miss Henderson couldn't keep a straight face whenever we ran into her," Placenta said.

"And you thought I didn't have any secrets!" Polly said.

"If Thane had any concerns about what Lisa might do for vengeance, I doubt that he'd invite her over to his house," Tim said.

"We only have her word that she and Thane were together that night," Placenta said. "She very easily could have waited until he was asleep, entered the house, then wedged that knife between his shoulder blades while he was dreaming about Taco Belle and what mean and nasty things he would say to make her cry on the next show."

"But that's precisely what the police are saying," Polly said. "I may have been persuaded to go along with that, even after our visit with Miss Marrs. However, now that we know that Toe Nail seems, for some reason, to be interested in the crime, I'm not so sure the girl is lying. What if Toe is the nut job who pulled the trigger? Or, rather, pushed the blade?"

As Tim signaled to turn right and drove through the arched entrance to the Bel Air east gate, Placenta said, "I recall the rules of the show stating that judges were forbidden to initiate interaction with any contestant outside of the parameters of the program. But the rules didn't say that the contestants couldn't see the judges."

"You're splitting hairs," Tim said as he drove the car up Stone Canyon Road. "Judges and contestants together, contestants and judges. A great big no-no!"

"Technically," Polly said. "I'll check the manual. But for instance, if Danny came to me and wanted advice about his performance, it would be unethical for me to help, but it wouldn't exactly be against the rules."

"So here's an idea," Tim said to his mother's reflection in the mirror. "Hypothetically speaking, Toe Nail schemes to coax his way into a judge's life. He wants to get to the most important judge, so he befriends someone behind-the-scenes. In this case, Thane's assistant, Michael."

"Are you implying that I'm not the most important judge?" Polly said with wide-eyed annoyance.

"Michael, wanting to move up the Hollywood food chain, determines that Toe Nail has the biggest cojones of any of the other contestants and guesses that the guy has what it takes to win the game and go on to a showbiz career. He agrees to help Mr. Nail get in tight with Thane in exchange for Toe Nail taking him along on the next rung of the success ladder when he's the world-famous winner of *I'll Do Anything to Become Famous.*"

Tim pushed the remote control to open the gates to Pepper Plantation and entered the estate grounds. As he drove down the cobbled drive, Placenta chimed in. "Toe Nail had everything to lose if he was stupid enough to seek out Thane for anything. After all, it would only take one word from Thane to Richard Dart—"

"Oh my God!" Polly erupted. "That's why Thane's dead! Toe Nail played his own corrupt hand and lost. He got to Thane and offered something in exchange for winning the show. Remember, Michael overheard Thane talking to someone on his cell phone and saying that he better have a good explanation for something. It must have been Toe Nail, and Thane didn't go along with him. In fact Thane may have threatened to tell Richard Dartmouth about the scheme, so Toe Nail killed the bastard to keep him quiet."

Tim parked the car under the front portico. "And Michael's an accessory, 'cause he probably arranged for the alarm system at Thane's house to be off when his cohort arrived to do in the evil boss."

"I love being the one to hatch a conspiracy theory," Polly trumpeted. She turned to Placenta. "I'll have my champagne in the tub, please," she said as she stepped out of the car and headed for the front steps. "I'll work out this absurd scenario while I'm soaking."

Tim pushed the numbers on the alarm system's keypad. "The dam thing's not working again!" he complained as he opened the front door and stepped into the house.

In an instant, Tim grabbed his mother by the arm and pulled her out of the house where a familiar body lay on the floor in the foyer. Tim nearly knocked Placenta off the steps as he retreated. "Get back into the car! Now!"

— ⁀ —

Detective Archer made it to the estate before the SOS, Security Of the Stars patrol service, arrived on scene. He found Polly, Tim, and Placenta just outside the Pepper Plantation gates, locked in the safety of the Rolls-Royce. He tapped on the window and when Tim unlocked the door, Archer slid onto the front passenger seat. He instantly reached into the backseat to hold Polly's hand. "My guys'll search the place; then you can go back inside."

Polly squeezed Randy's hand. "The alarm system has been on the fritz. And speaking of system failures, we haven't had a sleepover in three nights!"

Detective Archer looked sheepish. "I've been in hell trying to find the perv who makes heavy breathing calls to Liza Minnelli. She's going nuts."

"Going?" Placenta said.

Polly looked at her detective boyfriend. "Before you start asking a lot of boring police questions, I'll tell you right off that yes, Tim set the alarm before we left the house. Yes, the security cameras were working the last time Placenta dusted the lenses. Yes, the gates were closed when we returned. If it hadn't been for Tim's quick thinking, I might be another 'Access Hollywood' real-life tragic ending!"

Detective Archer's cell phone rang. He answered and listened for a moment, then disconnected the call. He looked at Polly and Placenta, then turned to Tim. "How well did you know the contestant Danny Castillo?"

Tim shrugged. "He's weird, but cute. I mean, semi-talented."

Polly reached forward and playfully slapped the back of Tim's head. "Timmy's got a teensy crush on the little pasty-faced twit."

"Not!" Tim looked at Detective Archer. "You said, 'How well "did" we know Danny'?"

Archer hesitated. With a somber tone that none of the trio had ever heard in his voice, he said, "They found him in your house."

Polly was incensed. "That little weasel. He's not getting a good score from me this week, even if he sings like an angel! I'll break his neck before I see him advance to the final two!" She moved to get out of the car. Archer reached out his arm to stop her.

"An angel, maybe," Archer said. "But you won't have to reprimand him because he won't be performing."

"Damn right, he won't be! I'll press charges. Breaking and entering. Maybe killing that body in my foyer. Oh God, are we going to have ghosts haunting this place again?"

"Danny didn't kill anyone," Archer said.

"But Tim saw the body!" Polly insisted. In the silence that followed, she caught on. "Ohhhhh …."

CHAPTER 10

—◦—

Polly, Tim, and Placenta were escorted back to the mansion with Detective Archer leading the way. They passed armed officers standing as sentries at the front entrance, and others milling about the grand foyer, taking pictures and dusting for fingerprints. Polly tried to ignore two officers with nothing better to do than bitch about her famous house. "If I had this palace I'd definitely upgrade the window treatments," one wagged to the other.

"Time to shred the shag carpet, dearie!" brayed the other.

Polly rolled her eyes at Tim. "Other than Officer Betty, are there any butch cops in Beverly Hills?" When they arrived at the great room she asked, "What's that?" and pointed to an oversize garment bag lying on the floor, next to her floor-to-ceiling lighted glass shelves of Emmy Awards, People's Choice Awards, and every other imaginable citation for excellence as a star.

Tim put his arms around his mother. "I think it's a bag of Danny Castillo." He looked at Detective Archer, who nodded.

"Where are the EMTs? Who moved the body? What was he doing in my house in the first place?" Polly demanded. "Did he take anything? Was he alone? How did he die? Has this stupid show suddenly become one big scavenger hunt, where contestants freely walk into other people's private spaces to collect God-knows-what?"

"Maybe one of the contestants thinks one of the others killed Thane, so they decided to prove they could go one better by murdering you!" Placenta said.

Archer called another detective over to explain all that he knew about the incident. "We don't have a lot to go on, ma'am," said Detective Spencer. "You can see that your place wasn't ransacked. Either the intruder knew exactly what he wanted, or he was killed before he had an opportunity to make a mess. It's too early to tell."

"I wonder if he got his hands on the prize; then someone else came along, whacked him, and stole whatever the deceased had," Placenta added.

"And what might that prize have been?" Polly asked as she counted her Emmy statuettes. "Unless they wanted one of my pre-autographed photos, it doesn't appear that there's anything of value missing. And what would a contestant from *I'll Do Anything to Become Famous* possibly want from Pepper Plantation?"

"DNA for a voodoo doll is about the only thing of value around here," Placenta said to Detective Archer. "We don't keep a ton of money or jewels in the safe. A kid like Danny wouldn't be interested in Polly's autographed picture collection. Heck, he wouldn't even know many of the stars. They're mostly all from old TV shows anyway."

Polly stepped a little closer to Archer. "This may be silly and unimportant, but when we were going through Lisa's apartment, that boy Toe Nail and his new chum, Michael Somebody, popped in. When they saw us—"

"You were at Lisa's apartment?" Archer said with an edge to his voice. "We had an agreement."

"What would you expect me to do after our visit to her cell and ... um. Uh-oh."

"Of course you visited the suspect, too," Archer said, his words dripping with sarcastic displeasure.

Polly looked sheepish. "Let's not allow all the fun and excitement of having breaking news occur in my very own home spoiled just because curiosity got the better of me. Anyway, it was practically Placenta's fault!"

Placenta looked at Polly with the expression of a loyal friend being sold down the river.

"It's perfectly okay, dear," Polly said to Randy. "Tim met that adorable copper and just had to pay a visit to the jail where he worked." She looked at Tim. "Naturally, as the mother of the potential groom-to-be, I had to tag along as a chaperone. It was a total coincidence that Lisa Marrs was being held in the very same jail. When she came out for her exercise period we accidentally bumped into her. You couldn't expect me to give up a completely serendipitous opportunity like that to pay my respects and ask how the little angel is holding up in the Big House!"

Detective Archer took a deep exasperated breath. "You're a great actress. Tell me what you were doing at Lisa Marrs's apartment."

Polly looked at her wristwatch. "My goodness! It's way past Lush Hour! Who wants to be the first to pour Polly a drinky?"

Placenta hustled to the wine cooler, withdrew a bottle of Veuve, and filled four flutes. Even Polly was impressed by the speed with which her maid accomplished her most important duty. "Practice makes perfect. Cheers!"

Polly raised the glass to her lips and took one long swallow. Placenta stood at her side refilling Polly's glass.

Polly looked at the body bag. "Doesn't that thing belong in a refrigerator? I feel vaguely uncomfortable enjoying the fruits of the vine with Mr. Death's latest acquisition cluttering the room."

Detective Archer motioned for one of the police officers to remove Danny Castillo's body, then returned his attention to Polly.

"This is really all your fault." She pointed her manicured finger at Archer. "You haven't been around lately. I'm not responsible for what I do when you're not here! And don't come up with some lame excuse about Will Smith this or Vanessa Hudgens that."

Archer placed his flute of champagne down on the glass coffee table without having imbibed so much as a sip. "We were talking about Lisa Marrs. Specifically, you were about to explain what you were doing in her apartment. But why am I even bothering to ask you about it, since I suspect you'll do it again, despite inconvenient police signs forbidding access?"

"I swear, we didn't touch a thing," Polly said. "Except Lisa's underwear," Tim said.

"That's novel," Archer said.

"We needed a ruse for being there when Toe Nail broke in," Placenta said.

"Obviously, I can't vouch for what those two hoodlums did after we left, which was right away," Polly said. "But I suppose we sort of give Toe Nail and Michael an alibi. They were with us, in a manner of speaking. There's absolutely no way that they could have beat us back to the plantation, dismantled the security system, murdered Danny Castillo, and made their getaway before we came home."

Archer looked at his watch. "Unless they came here first. Then on to Ms. Marrs'. Next on my list is a visit to those two young men. We'll see if your stories match."

"They aren't 'stories,'" Polly said, emboldened by two glasses of bubbly. "You'll find that if they speak the truth, everything I've told you will be the same. But don't expect miscreants to be honest."

Randy Archer looked at Polly. "I'm not the bad guy. I'm just doing my job."

Polly returned her lover's look of regret. "Get your cute buns and badge out of here and do what you do best. Er, second best!" Then she whispered, "Make time for me soon."

Archer smiled and left the room.

"Is it my imagination, or did the handsome detective treat me like a naughty schoolgirl?" Polly asked Tim and Placenta, her annoyance rising. "So we slipped into a jail-bird's apartment while she was away. Big whoop. It's not as though she was coming back any time soon. And we weren't thieves … or killers! We even had a key!"

"Speaking of killers," Placenta said, "who do you suppose knocked off Danny Castillo? I'm shocked and confused and more than a little unnerved. What on earth did he ... and the killer ... want at Pepper Plantation?"

"Not her dated color scheme, that's for sure," one of the policemen who was supposed to be collecting evidence sniggered to another. Polly rolled her eyes, then made a face as an idea passed through her thoughts. She stared into the distance. "Color scheme," she said. "Scheme," she repeated. She looked at Tim and Placenta. "Okay. I know this is far-fetched. But what is the common denominator between Thane Cornwall, Lisa Marrs, and me?"

"The obvious answer is that you were all involved with the reality show *I'll Do Anything to Become Famous,*"Tim said.

"What about fame?" Placenta said. "You're a big name. Thane was making one for himself. And Lisa has notoriety."

Polly considered Placenta's words. "Some are born icons ... me, of course. Some achieve iconic status ... Thane ... sorta. Others are treated like icons-in-the- making if they work for a celebrity or do something stupid like becoming a prime suspect in a murder investigation of a sort of icon ... Lisa."

Tim looked at his mother with an expression of confusion. "I don't see any real thread there. Lisa doesn't belong in any category in which you or Thane would be listed for your achievements. The only thing she pulled off is scandal. Killing an audience, as you do, is one thing. Killing contestants' self-value, as Thane did, is another. But outright killing another person for real is ... well, it isn't anything to warrant praise or fame."

"I hate to play what-if," Placenta said. "But someone breaks into Thane's house and he gets whacked. Maybe by Lisa, maybe not. Then someone breaks into our home and doesn't steal anything, but may have been looking for a larger score, like taking out a bigger-name judge. You. Maybe it's a copycat killer. Maybe it's the same one. All I know is I no longer feel safe at Pepper Plantation."

Polly looked lovingly at her maid and best girlfriend. "Nothing will happen to me, or to either of you. I guarantee it. Now open another bottle and we'll toast to something like…" In a louder voice she said, "We'll toast to Beverly Hills' men in blue, who obviously watch too much Home and Garden Television's *Divine Design.*"

Two officers looked at Polly, then looked at each other and rolled *their* eyes.

Polly accepted a flute of champagne from Placenta and raised her glass to the two men. "Have you discovered anything interesting? Other than the fact that I have out-of-date track lighting on a cottage cheese ceiling?"

The more catty of the two lifted a plastic bag containing evidence. "As a matter of fact, Ms. Pepper, although this is police business, I'll offer you a little dish."

"Goody. What's that?" Polly asked, seeing little more than dust bunnies and strands of hair in the clear plastic sandwich bag.

With a pair of tweezers, the policeman pointed to what looked like a grain of white rice.

"We order in a lot," Polly explained. "Mr. Chow's is one my faves."

The policeman rolled his eyes. "Has anyone in the house broken a tooth in the past few hours?"

Polly used her tongue to feel around her mouth. "What about you two?" she said, turning to Tim and Placenta. "Anyone need to see *el dentista?*

When the response was in the negative, Polly looked at the policeman again. "So you're saying that the killer has poor dental hygiene?"

The policeman shrugged. "We'll be looking to interrogate someone with a chipped or broken tooth, that's for sure."

"Perhaps it belonged to Danny," Polly speculated. "He could have chipped it when he fell on my gorgeous sandstone tile."

"I'd say that was pretty unlikely," the policeman said. "We found what appears to be a portion of a tooth by your television." He pointed a few feet away to the entertainment center.

"Find the rest of the tooth, and I'll wager we find Danny's killer," Polly said.

The policeman looked at his wristwatch. "Oh, fudge!" he shouted.

"Late for another investigation?" Placenta asked.

"I'm missing *DOOL!*"

CHAPTER 11

—⁊—

The Wednesday morning edition of the *Los Angeles Times* featured a front-page story about the break-in at Pepper Plantation and death of reality show contestant Danny Castillo. The question on every radio talk show host's tongue was, why in the first place would an aspiring contender for a prize on a television reality game show break into the home of one of the judges? And in the second place, why did the contestant die in the famous mansion?

It wasn't enough that the media accurately pointed out that Polly Pepper wasn't in her home at the time of the young man's demise, and that she was in no way a suspect in his death. But the wags had to have their field day speculating about a possible relationship between older Polly and younger Danny.

Polly generally only made outgoing calls, so it fell to Tim and Placenta to field the media and their calling the house phone. "Miss Pepper's agent will be happy to answer all inquires," was their standard response to the parade of nosy newshounds who tried to get a statement from the television legend.

"Was Polly in love with the boy?"

"Did Polly give the young man a key to her house?"

"How does Miss Pepper feel about May/December romances?"

"Is it true that Polly is engaged to Daniel Radcliffe?"

When Polly was thrown off-guard by Gayle King, who somehow got hold of her cell phone number, she bellowed. "I'm not into boys! I mean, I want a man!" She paused. "You're confusing me. I meant to say that I date age-appropriate gentlemen. Hell, that boy Danny didn't even have any hair on his chest! No, I'm just guessing, for crying out loud. He was too young for me. Oh, go torture Jennifer Aniston!"

Polly finally accepted one call, when Placenta handed her a flute of Veuve and the cordless phone, and said, "Little Dickie Dartmouth."

Polly exhaled loudly, took a long swallow from her glass, and answered with a fake cry of elation. However, in a short moment, Polly was seated on the sofa, the color draining from her face, and a loud moan issuing past her lips.

"It's not fair," Polly said.

Tim and Placenta sat down beside her and tried to hear the other end of the conversation.

"But I'm the 'nice' judge. You're hiring who? You don't mean that pushy and intolerant little Miss Spray-on Suntan? *That* Trish Saddleback?" Polly said. "Is this because people are gossiping that I'm a latter day June Lockhart, sleeping with men younger than my son? I always said, 'Brava, June!' I suspect that one week's suspension will turn into two and three and four! Then the program will be over! I'm being punished because some loser parvenu broke into my home and had the disrespect to get murdered here."

Placenta reached for the bottle of champagne that rested in the ice bucket on the coffee table. As she refilled Polly's drink, the star's tone changed. "Oh dear, my agent, J.J., will be crestfallen. He's such a fan of me being on the show."

Polly smiled as she listened to Dartmouth for a moment. "Don't believe every little ol' thing you've heard about J.J. Temper? Nonsense! He's a precious pussycat. At least to me. It was just a coincidence that Sharon Stone, Greg Kinnear, and dear Jane Seymour all had near death experiences shortly after one of J.J.'s little, shall we say, *episodes*. Don't let my being unfairly treated by you and Sterling Studios keep you from answering when J.J. rings. However, you might want to wear earplugs. And if you're on antianxiety meds, you'd better take an extra couple of doses. Oh, and call your therapist. And your mommy."

Polly hung up the phone and stared into space. "I'm out of work for a week! I didn't do anything wrong, but I'm suffering the consequences of what those delinquent heathens, otherwise known as contestants, do in their spare time! If that walking pincushion Danny wasn't already dead, I'd rip out all of his piercings!" After another long swallow of champagne, Polly sat back on the sofa and stared at her shelves of Emmy Awards. Soon, Tim and Placenta could read a look of peace crossing over Polly's face. She turned to Placenta and lovingly grazed her cheek with her hand. "You know that I love and adore you." Then she looked at

Tim. "Dearest, dear man," she said as she leaned over and enveloped him in her arms.

"Oh, damn," Placenta sighed. "It's time for another game of 'Meet the Murderer.' I smell another dinner party with a cast of killers stuffing themselves at our dining room table."

Tim gave Polly a stem look. "You've forgotten again that judges aren't allowed to associate with the contestants."

Polly beamed. "I'm no longer a judge! Therefore, I'm free to mingle with whomever I please!"

"Randy will be furious," Tim said.

Polly shrugged. "He won't know because he isn't invited. Now, for the place cards. Calligraphy, of course. Taco Belles, Toe Nail, Amy Stout, Miranda Washington ... is anybody else still alive? We shouldn't leave Michael out of the fun. They'll all be thrilled to have dinner at our famous home." Polly looked at Placenta. "Saturday. Seven o'clock. Formal." She then turned to Tim. "Come up with a fun theme, sweetums. Something lavish, with Hollywood stars. Oh! A séance! Dead stars! How lovely would that be! I've wanted to get Karen Carpenter and John Denver back for ages! Or maybe Petula Clark!"

"Alive," Placenta said.

Tim added, "You'd better summon Anna Nicole Smith and Heath Ledger. I don't trust those kids to know that anyone existed before P. Diddy or Puff Daddy, or whatever he calls himself these days. If they'd ever heard how great Karen or John were, they wouldn't have the guts to open their own vocal cords in public."

Polly nodded. "Speed-dial someone for me, and hand me your phone, hon," she said to Tim.

Tim did the dialing, and just as Polly predicted, each of the invitees was eager to visit Pepper Plantation. They may have been unsophisticated teens, but because the facade of the mansion had been used as the exterior location shot for the popular sitcom *For Closure,* about a once-rich family trying to come to terms with the fact that their dead daddy's mansion is being taken by the bank, the kids acted as if they had been invited to the Cedars Sinai emergency room on a day when more than three former Disney Channel child stars were ambulanced in for overdosing on reality. "We're just as eager as you are, dear," Polly said to Taco Belles, who demanded that Polly send a car to pick her up. "I wouldn't treat my guests with any less outpouring of my well-known largesse."

By the time Polly, Tim, and Placenta were settled in to watch *Colbert,* their party plans were in place. The guest list was complete. It now fell to Tim to organize a memorable evening, and to Placenta to visit her favorite online cooking service and order a meal that would give the *I'll Do Anything to Become Famous* contestants an idea of how a real, live, living legend dines.

It was unusual for Polly to be unable to sleep. Regardless of how little she may have worked or played during the day, a nightcap of champagne (after an entire evening of champagne) almost always calmed any fears or insecurities she may have felt at bedtime. Tonight, however, in the darkness of her room, thoughts about her career, her relationship with Randy, and the deaths of Thane Cornwall and Danny Castillo bombarded her. She couldn't help believing that there was a connection between the two murders. Surely it couldn't be a coincidence that Thane's and Danny's life-lines were scheduled to end at roughly the same time? Did Danny kill Thane? Had he come to Pepper Plantation for a second judge? But then who killed Danny? Were there perhaps two or more killers among the contestants who were vying for the first-place prize on *I'll Do Anything to Become Famous*? And drats, would her agent J.J.'s bombast kill off any future chances for her to work with Richard Dartmouth and Sterling Studios?

Polly tossed and turned, until she finally gave up trying to sleep. She sat up in bed, rested her back against the padded headboard, and stared into the semidarkness.

In the abyss of her master suite, she could make out the silhouettes of the fireplace, her dressing table, a fake ficus in the comer, her computer desk, and the chaise by the window. Polly sighed and scooted down once again to attempt sleep. The instant she set her head onto her pillow and closed her eyes, Polly thought she saw a hint of light ricochet off her window. She froze.

You're just tired, Polly reassured herself. *A car passed by the house. No, we're too far back on the estate. Headlights never reach this far. Plus, this room doesn't face the street. An airplane? A helicopter? That's it.* She closed her eyes again. Just as she was about to roll over and hug her pillow, another flash of light startled her.

Polly eased herself out of bed and cautiously made her way toward the window. A light moved through the garden. She quickly backed up and reached for the security alarm pad next to her bed. However, it wasn't illuminated, which meant it was inactive. She pushed the panic button anyway. Nothing. She raced down the hall to Tim's bedroom, roused him from sleep, and told him to call 911.

Tim went to the window and saw nothing more than the solar lights that outlined the garden walkway. However, Tim knew that his mother wasn't an alarmist and therefore he turned to his own security system keypad next to the bed and pushed the code for emergency service.

"It's no use," Polly said. "The alarm isn't working."

Tim looked at the keypad, then at his mother. "Yes, it is."

Polly looked at the lighted numerals. "Mine isn't on."

Just then, the telephone rang. It was an operator from SOS. "We've received a signal indicating an emergency."

"We have an intruder," Tim said.

"What is your password?" the operator said.

"PP4U," Tim replied.

"No shit," the operator chuckled. "A car is on its way."

"I'm calling Randy," Polly said, and reached for Tim's cell phone. Although the room was dark, she could see the illuminated face of the screen.

Suddenly, a human form appeared in the doorway. Polly looked up and shrieked, "JesusJosephandMary!" She held her hands to her chest and took a deep breath. "Placenta! You scared the hell out of me!"

"What's going on?" Placenta asked.

"Polly saw something in the garden," Tim said.

"Not something," Polly corrected. "Someone. Walking around with a flashlight."

Now it was Placenta's turn to become agitated. "Why didn't the security lights go on? Where's that freakin' SOS when we need 'em? I told you we should switch to Mayday!"

Tim handed his cell phone to Polly. "Call Randy. I'll go check all the doors." He made his way to the hallway and down the stairs.

As Tim descended the Scarlett O'Hara Memorial Staircase, he heard the chime of the front gate intercom. He went to the front door and pushed the Talk button. When he was assured it was the security company, he pushed the button to open the main gates to the estate. Still, he wouldn't open the door to the mansion until he was certain that the guards were legitimate. "Check the grounds," Tim said. "My mother saw an intruder walking through the back garden."

Tim felt safe enough to turn on the lights throughout the house and outside, as well. If someone had trespassed on the property, the commotion would surely have scared them away.

It was nearly 2:00 a.m., and Polly and Placenta joined Tim in the great room of the house. "I can't reach Randy," Polly said. "He always keeps his phone on. Not a good sign when you can't reach your boyfriend twenty-four-seven!"

"Don't go there," Placenta advised. "He works hard. He's probably zonked out and didn't hear the ring tone."

Soon, the SOS security detail was once again at the front door. This time Tim invited the two men into the house, and led them to the great room. After introductions, and Polly apologizing for not looking her movie star best, a handsome Hispanic guard, impressively dressed in a stiffly pressed khaki shirt with faux police and military-style badges sewn onto the sleeves and pockets, explained that although he and his partner had covered every comer of the property, they failed to find any trace of a gate-crasher. "If anything, including a raccoon, had wandered onto the property, the alarm would have been triggered," the guard assured Polly.

"It's not working properly," Polly said. "At least the keypad beside my bed isn't functioning."

The guard looked sheepish. "Look, because I'm a huge fan of yours, I'll be honest. SOS sucks. I could get fired for telling you this, but I know that our system has been experiencing intermittent communication failures, especially here in Bel Air."

Placenta gasped. "Are you telling us that we're not safe in our own home? We spend a fortune for security, and now we hear that it's not working."

"Everyone says to hire Mayday!" Tim said.

"It's working," the guard said. "It's just not working all the time."

"I'll stay here until the system is once again operating," the guard said in a clipped military manner. He looked at Tim and smiled. "Sir, may I see you outside for a moment?"

Tim looked at his mother and Placenta, who were in a deep discussion. "Someone was on the estate, and I think they're after me!" he heard Polly say as he followed the security guard out of the room.

Once in the hallway, Tim looked at the guard's badge. "Raul." He smiled. "Thanks for getting here so quickly. But what's with the signal breakdown? I hate to say it, but it looks like there's some truth to the rumor that SOS stands for Shit on a Shingle. "

"I've heard 'em all," Raul said. "'Switch Our Service' being my personal favorite."

"We're safe now, right?" Tim asked.

Raul smiled. "If you mean the house, yes … and no."

Tim's smile grew wider. "So every night we may have an emergency and you'll have to keep coming back?"

Just then, Randy Archer rushed into the house and bellowed, "What's going on, and who's in charge?"

Raul squared his shoulders and looked defiantly at Archer. "I'm Officer Cervantes, with SOS. And you are?"

"Taking over!" Randy said. "Beverly Hills Police Department. A *real* policeman. You can go now."

Tim looked at Randy. "What's with you? This man's done a great job of securing the area and protecting us."

Randy looked at Raul and shook his head. "I'm sure you did an awesome job. But I'll take things from here."

Tim and Raul shook hands. As Raul was leaving the house, Tim sprinted to the front door. "Um, here's my card." He reached into a drawer in the granite-top foyer sideboard and lifted out a business card holder. Raul looked at the engraved card. "I'll e-mail you." He met Tim's eyes. *"Hasta luego,* man."

"Was I interrupting something?" Randy asked when Tim returned to his side.

Tim exhaled in resignation. "Polly's in the great room."

When Randy arrived at Polly's side, he gave her a tight hug and asked her to tell him what she had seen from her window.

"A light," she said. "Someone was walking around with a flashlight. How did you know to come over?"

"Your number came up on my missed call log. I got here as fast as I could. You wouldn't call at two in the morning unless it was something important, so I called ahead for backup."

Polly smiled. "Then you're not angry with me?"

"How could I stay … Let's talk about what you saw. It's a bit breezy tonight. Is it possible that the wind moving the leaves on the trees could have made it appear that the glow from the garden lights was moving?"

"I saw what I saw," Polly said.

"But the security system wasn't breached," Randy continued. "If someone had gotten onto the property, the alarm would have sounded."

"It's not working properly," Polly testified. "I went to press the Panic button and it was off. Tim's was fine, but not mine."

Randy signaled to one of the police officers standing by the doorway. "Check all the quadrants in the house, and the security boxes as well."

"It's no use," Polly said. "That cheap-o security service we have is on the fritz."

Placenta poured a glass of champagne for Polly. "Anyone else?" she asked. "Polly doesn't make stuff up, except her date of birth. If she saw someone on the property, it wasn't from the DTs."

Randy agreed. "I have no doubt that someone was here. But how did they get in? Even if the alarm isn't working, the gates are locked, and the hedges are so high and thick, who could get through? First Danny and the person or persons who killed him. Now someone trespassing in the middle of the night. I don't like it. And I don't like you being here alone."

"I'm hardly alone," Polly said. "However, if it'll make you feel any better, I'll let you bunk with me for a few nights."

Randy smiled. "That would make me feel just fine."

"No pressure," Polly said with a grin. "You could share space with Tim again, if I snore."

CHAPTER 12

—⌇—

Friday morning dawned, and the residents of Pepper Plantation moved into the day with much lethargy. Polly shuffled to the outdoor breakfast table at half past ten. "What time did Randy leave?" she asked Placenta as she sipped a Bloody Mary. Soon after, Tim wandered down to the patio and greeted his mother and Placenta with a groan. Placenta, too, was tired and took her time pouring the coffee and serving her famous scrambled eggs with cream cheese, and a side of hash browns. When the family was served, she sat down at the table with them and sprinkled Tabasco sauce over her eggs. "I want a man around the place," she said.

Both Polly and Tim made guttural sounds that seemed to say, "Who doesn't?"

"I mean a security guard," Placenta continued. "Someone who'll patrol the grounds day and night."

"A retired old codger? Someone who always dreamed of being a policeman, but never made the force? A deluded nut who lives out his fantasy by wearing a uniform and sidearm?" Polly said. "I don't think so!"

A Talent For Murder

"I was thinking more along the lines of hiring the UCLA gymnastics team," Placenta said. "We would feel safe, and at the same time live our fantasies." She looked at Polly. "You keep jeopardizing our lives by playing with freaks and felons. We need more protection than a faulty alarm system or a besotted detective."

"I agree with Placenta," Tim said. "The gymnastics part anyway. But seriously, I think we do need someone around here twenty-four-seven. This week has been weird, and last night was scarier than when Bea Arthur came over."

Polly looked out through her sunglasses and gazed at her manicured estate. The pool water was shimmering and bees were drifting among the roses and snapdragons and peonies. She loved the privacy and the silence of her property. "With a stranger around, I'd have to be Polly Pepper in my own home. I can't keep that up all day long."

"Celebrity guards sign confidentiality agreements," Placenta encouraged. "If you behave like the Beckhams, they can't run to the *Peeper* and spill their story for big bucks."

"But their nanny did just that!" Polly raged. "So did Rob Lowe's chef! Big celebrities like me can have their staffs sign confidentiality agreements, but who wants to go through the pain and expense of suing household help?"

Polly sulked. "Fine," she said. "But I don't want any part in the selection process. Just find someone who won't blab all our secrets to Oprah!"

Tim looked at Placenta. "Let's get on this right away. I know the perfect candidate."

"Amigo Sanchez cannot be our guard!" she said. "Neither one of us needs the distraction."

"I can at least have lunch with him and get a few references." Tim drained his coffee mug, grabbed two slices of bacon, dragged his napkin across his mouth, and stood. "Time for my ablutions. Have to make a good impression on potential employees."

"It's supposed to be the other way around," Polly said.

As Placenta scraped up the rest of her scrambled eggs with her fork Polly complained, "This'll shoot my budget all to hell. I almost can't afford the gallons of Veuve that flow through our veins, let alone add someone to the payroll. Personal safety takes a backseat to personal satisfaction."

"Look at it this way, I'm cheap labor," Placenta said. "I haven't had a raise in five years, so you're probably actually saving moola even if you hired two guards."

Polly rolled her eyes. "If people would just stop trespassing and falling down dead around this place, we'd be fine." From the corner of her eye she caught a glimpse of something moving in the distance amid the pygmy palms and tall hedge that divided her property from Kenny Rogers's estate. "What the hell ... ?

Placenta followed her gaze to the end of the yard. "I'm calling 911!" she said as she reached into her apron pocket for her cell phone.

Before her trembling hands could turn the device on and let it find a satellite signal, two rugged but filthy-looking men wearing work boots, jeans, and orange vests approached the patio. One called out, "We're lost."

"Damn right you're lost," Placenta said. "This is private property. How'd you get in?"

"Sorry. DWP. We were checking the underground cable. Who knew that rich people had their own personal access to the sewer?"

Polly was suddenly excited. "I have my own hole?"

"What's a maintenance utility hole doing in our backyard?" Placenta asked, looking from one man to the other.

"A what?" Polly asked, bewildered. "Placenta, get these interesting men some coffee."

"A manhole," one of the men said to Polly. "They're not just for sewers, the holes, I mean. We're working on the city's cable lines. Everyone in the area is experiencing outages. I guess you rich people in Bel Air have problems, too."

Placenta gave the men a quizzical stare as she poured two cups of coffee. "Cream? Sugar?"

"Black is good," both agreed.

Polly took another sip of her drink and stood up. She started to cross the patio toward the grassy yard from which the men had appeared. "How long have I had my hole?" she asked as the men followed her. "I've never seen it. Never knew it existed."

"It's pretty well covered over," one of the men said to Polly. "It's possible that even your gardener hasn't seen your hole." Both men looked around and admired the huge manicured estate. "This place reminds me of that house they once showed on that old show *Lifestyles of the Rich and Famous*," one said to the other. "Wait a minute." The man stopped and looked at Polly. "Are you? Is this?"

"Holy moly," said the other man. "Are you ... Polly Plantation?"

"Pepper," Polly corrected, "Polly Pepper." She smiled her most winning international icon smile and started to offer her hand to shake, then thought of where the man had been working. "Do you make it a habit of popping up through celebrity holes?"

Both men looked contrite. "Your opening isn't marked on our map, so we just wanted to see where it led. Really pretty place you have here."

Just then, Tim returned to the patio. He was at first concerned by the two men escorting his mother and Placenta into the garden and sprinted to their side. Polly introduced them, and explained that they were fixing the electrical cable in the neighborhood.

"Can anyone get in here from the manhole?" Tim asked.

Both men shrugged. "If you know where it is."

"Then it's possible that someone gained access to the estate without the alarm going off," Polly said. "That could be how Danny got in here without SOS racing to the scene."

Both men looked at each other, and then at Polly. "This is where that reality show guy got knocked off yesterday," one said to the other. "Wow! You must've freaked when your boyfriend got wasted."

"He was *not* my boyfriend," Polly said. "I hardly knew the young man."

"Sometimes that's more fun." One of the men grinned. "I say, go for it, lady! You're not half-bad looking for your age."

"I don't go for anything," she said. "I mean, I'm involved with someone. Oh, hell, why am I explaining myself?"

"Could Danny Castillo have somehow known about the manhole and used it to access the estate?" asked Placenta.

"Unlikely," the men agreed. "Hell, like I said, it don't even show up on the DWP map. We discovered it by accident."

When the troupe arrived at the location of the manhole, Polly was thrilled. "Let me see!" She took a flashlight from one of the men, and aimed it down into the blackness. "Where does it go? Can I get to the beach from here? Maybe we can use it to avoid traffic, or from having to pass by Jackie Chan's ugly old place down the street."

"Yeah, you could get around down there," one of the men said. "If you don't mind rats and spiders and snakes and raccoons and two-headed slime monsters."

Polly shivered. "I guess we'll just keep closing our eyes when we have to drive by Bill Shatner's place." She turned around to go back to the house. "Be sure to seal it up tight when you leave. I don't want zombies wandering up my hole."

"I don't mean to be rude," Placenta said, "but I think you gentlemen should go back to work and take care of business. I'm sealing this thing off for good."

As the men descended back into the dark pit, one said, "Don Johnson has a hole too. But trust me, you don't want to see it."

When the manhole cover was replaced, Tim helped Placenta rake leaves and dirt over the lid. Then they moved a wrought-iron park bench over it to both conceal its existence and make it more difficult for anyone—or anything—to gain access to the estate. "We still don't know if this is where the person who Polly saw last night got in," Tim said. "Like the guy said, it's not even on their official map. If someone had been in the sewer last night, it's unlikely they'd know that it led to Pepper Plantation."

"I won't dismiss anything," Placenta said. "Now get on with your date. I'll feel better once we know that a guard is standing by. And FYI, tonight we're having buffalo wings and champagne while we watch *Famous*."

"Polly still wants to watch the show, even though she's been dumped?" Tim asked.

"We should all know how the contestants are doing since they're coming over tomorrow night. Oh, crap!" Placenta said as she realized the dinner was only a day away. "We'll have to do vegetarian. If I served Mexican, Taco Belles would think I was making fun of her. And God knows who's allergic to what. I wouldn't want to kill anyone off with all the peanuts they use in Thai food."

Tim gave Placenta a hug. "There's never a dull moment around Polly, or Pepper Plantation," he said before leaving for lunch with his SOS date.

CHAPTER 13

—⁊—

Fifteen minutes before *I'll Do Anything to Become Famous* was scheduled to air, Polly, Tim, Placenta, and Tim's new friend, Raul Cervantes, seated themselves in the media room and balanced trays with plates of buffalo wings and coleslaw on their laps. For the benefit of his guest, and to add to his own allure, Tim explained that his mother had been a judge on the show they were about to watch, but that she had been temporarily replaced because one of the contestants had been discovered dead in this house. "Right in the foyer, where you first came in," he boasted to Raul. "The program is crummy, and the ratings for the first show stank, but with all the notoriety about a dead judge and a dead contestant, the television audience should be huge this week."

Placenta popped a cork from a chilled bottle of champagne and passed it on to Tim, who filled Polly's and Raul's glasses, then his own.

"Shush," Polly said. "It starts right after this guy on the Lavitra commercial gets laid." Moments later, the screen was filled with the handsome face of Steven Benjamin, who was welcoming the audience to the program. He joked about how quickly stars come and go in Hollywood, and tried to jest about Thane Cornwall and Polly Pepper not being available for this week's broadcast. "One is gone but not forgotten," he said. "The other is mostly forgotten but not entirely gone." He laughed at his own lame sense of levity, then welcomed the two new judges, Richard Dartmouth and Trish Saddleback, and returning judge Brian Smith.

The television camera practically glowed when it focused on the handsome face of Richard Dartmouth, who smiled and nodded his head in artificial humble appreciation for the enthusiastic ovation from the studio audience. "I wouldn't be here except for the very sad fact that one of the great men in our industry, Mr. Thane Cornwall, was killed shortly after the last broadcast," Richard said. "I know that everyone who saw the show last week was impressed by Thane's rich contribution to the program. We'll all miss him. But we know that he would want the show to continue, which is why our producers and Sterling Studios decided to keep the contest alive. By the way, I'm not replacing the irreplaceable Thane Cornwall. I'm simply keeping his seat warm."

"Be wary of young and handsome Hollywood producers," Polly said. "That one's a wolf in Abercrombie & Fitch clothing."

"I wouldn't mind him preying on me," Placenta said.

Camera number two found Steven Benjamin solemnly nodding. "Indeed, Thane was someone I'll never forget." He instantly switched gears and broadcast a wide smile. "Tonight we also welcome the equally lovely and overbearing—and I mean that with all sincere admiration—the talented Trish Saddleback!"

As applause erupted from the audience Polly spat, "Motor mouth. I can't wait to hear what she has to say about the contestants' lack of talent."

The camera captured a smiling and radiant Saddleback. She looked into the camera and said, "Polly, if you're watching, I, too, am just keeping your seat warm." Polly harrumphed. "Damn, I wanted to hate her, but now I can't!"

Steven Benjamin explained that owing to the untimely demise of Danny Castillo, the number of contestants had dwindled down to an even four. "But before we begin this week's competition, we'd like to pay tribute to Danny with this short clip."

The screen was suddenly filled with images of Danny Castillo from the cattle call audition in which each of the final six contestants had been selected. The visuals of Danny goofing off, making faces at the camera, and then launching into a song made Polly and Placenta audibly sigh. More behind-the-scenes footage showed Danny at his makeup mirror punking out his hair and adding black eyeliner around his eyes, and black polish to his fingernails. A clip of Danny's performance from the debut show flashed onto the screen, followed by Thane Cornwall excoriating him after his performance of *"Abra-cadaver"* Danny simply stood before the judges and didn't show any emotion. When Thane was finished ripping him apart, Danny bowed and moved backstage.

"Whoa!" Tim said when the film clip switched to Danny in his dressing room. Danny was out of control, screaming and breaking furniture. He threw a chair into the vanity mirror and yelled, "You're a dead man, Thane Cornwall!"

The camera returned to Steven Benjamin, who looked surprised. "I'm sure the good folks at Sterling Studios are cooperating with the investigation into Thane's murder. I'd say Danny is a good place for the police to start! We'll return after these messages."

Cars. Diets. Sissy Spacek in Depression Era rags for a *Hallmark Hall of Fame* weeper. "Side effects may include…" As commercials played on the screen, Polly, Placenta, Tim, and Raul commented on the first few minutes of the show. They all agreed that a tribute to a murder victim probably shouldn't have included his last rant.

"You may hate your mother, but at the funeral you only say nice things," Raul said.

"Timmy loves *his* mother!" Polly said.

"Of course Tim loves you," Raul said. "Everybody loves you."

"Welcome to the family!" Polly said, and patted Raul on the cheek.

Placenta added, "One has to wonder why they chose to put in that clip. D'ya think the editor or director or someone wanted to throw suspicion for Thane's death clearly on Danny Castillo? The kid's dead and so not around to defend himself."

"A good imitation of that scary Rush Limbaugh guy on that radio station I avoid," Polly added. "Anyone with his anger issues needs his meds—oh, wait, didn't I read that Rush was an addict? Poor baby. What he needs is a long session on the couch. If I were investigating Thane's murder, which I'm not, at least not officially, I'd be looking at Danny too. Smashing that makeup mirror was not a good move. Seven whole years of bad luck! Or in his case not quite seven days."

"Quiet," Placenta said. "We're back to the show." Steven Benjamin continued the broadcast as if nothing had changed from the previous week. "It's oldies night," he said, giving the audience a heads up that they probably wouldn't know any of the songs. He introduced Miranda Washington, who walked down the tall staircase and found her place center stage with a microphone headset taped to her cheek. To a cheering audience and a rapt panel of judges Miranda began to sing *Someone to Watch Over Me*.

Fifteens seconds into the song Polly blurted out, "My God, I can actually understand the lyrics!"

Tim, too, was mesmerized. "Ella Fitzgerald would be thrilled with her delivery!"

The group watched with surprise and delight as Miranda ended with a plaintive "... oh how I need ... someone to watch over ... me."

Polly and her troupe cheered along with the audience. "Damn! The one night someone shows promise and I'm not there to gush!" Polly said.

The contestants who followed Miranda each failed to reach her level of achievement. Toe Nail sang "My Cherie Amour," and by the time he reached the boring "La la la la la, la la la la la" ending, Polly found herself slipping into Thane mode and trying to come up with words that, without destroying Toe Nail's practically indestructible ego, would convey she thought he sucked.

Unfortunately, the shimmering costumes worn by Taco Belle and Amy Stout did nothing to camouflage their hopelessly inadequate vocal abilities. Taco Belle and Amy, singing "Save the Best for Last," and "The Morning After," respectively, showed that it's not easy to be Vanessa Williams or Maureen McGovern. They didn't have "it." And the judges tore them apart.

After another long series of commercials about bladder control issues, restless legs, and a cure for vaginal itch, Steven Benjamin returned. "The night isn't over yet," he said. "Despite any contestants' lack of stage presence and talent, winning the competition doesn't hinge on how well they performed, but on how far they'll go to reach the top. Let's bring out our contestants and let the judges begin their interviews!"

Taco Belle was the first to face the trio. Steven said, "Let's begin with our lovely Trish Saddleback."

The camera focused on Trish. "You were darling!" Trish began. "I see a lot of talent in you, more than in some of my colleagues with whom I argue every day on *The Shrews,* or the pathetic guests we invite on the show. So, tell me, Ms. Belle, hypothetically, you're driving down the 405 freeway. The traffic is hell, as usual. You're late for an audition for a movie with Meryl Streep. The job, which your agent says is practically yours, will completely change your life. You're crawling along looking at your watch and screaming something vile that includes taking the Lord's name in vain. Suddenly, sweet, dear Jesus Christ the Lord Almighty Himself appears in your side-view mirror. You shout, 'Glory and amen!' You figure that you're being divinely guided to the audition!

"But just then, that eighteen-wheeler with an unsaved and asleep-on-the-job redneck trucker who's been kissing the bumper of your junky '85 Honda for the past ten minutes crawls into the driver's seat with you and changes your plans. In the last instant of your unaccomplished and futile little life, do you ask Satan to drag the sleeping driver who is responsible for your early demise to hell? Or do you take one last peek in the mirror at the smiling and benevolent face of our dear Lord and thank Him for the thousands of joyous, if fruitless, auditions that reaped nothing more than a nonspeaking atmosphere role in *High School Musical 12: Pimples and Puberty*?"

Taco Belle stood with her arms folded and her mouth hanging wide open.

"You only have a minute to answer the question," Steven prodded.

Taco Belle sighed, pursed her lips, shook her head, and said, "I'm sending that freakazoid trucker who drove over me, and my dreams, straight to an eternal vacation on the Lake of Fire! He'll be roasting on an open flame forever. Ain't nobody getting away with keeping me from starring with Meryl Streep! Who is this sorry-assed trucker, anyway?" she asked. "I have a mind to drag him out of his cab right after this show and have the Blessed Virgin make sure he doesn't ruin any other dream of mine!" Polly stared at the screen as Taco Belle went on her tirade. "She's serious."

Trish Saddleback looked annoyed at Taco Belle. "Please calm yourself, dear. There is no trucker. It was a fictional scenario. Except that dear, sweet, *Republican* Jesus is always in your mirror, guiding you. Welcome to *Hellywood!*

While Tim, Placenta, and Raul laughed, Polly steamed. "Isn't there supposed to be a separation between church and television? Who does St. Saddleback think she is, touched by an angel?"

"This is exactly what Sterling and the network want, Mother!" Tim said. "It's a show that caters to the same demographics as *American Gladiator* and female mud wrestling. Go with it. Have fun. The contestants don't really mean what they're saying. They just need the voting audience to think that they'll climb over bodies to get ahead. It's what they expect from wannabe stars."

Steven Benjamin thanked Taco Belle, and summoned Toe Nail back to center stage to face the judges. It was Brian Smith's turn to interview a contestant. "Heya, bro," Smith said. "Awesome good song. Did an awesome fine job. But let's get serious for a moment."

Polly nudged Placenta.

Brian said, "Celebrities are known for saying pretty lame things sometimes. Remember Anna Nicole Smith, who said of suicide bombers, 'Doesn't that hurt?' Or the lame guy who said, 'If we're not supposed to eat animals, why are they made out of meat?'

"Now, let's say that you win this competition and become famous. Alex Trebek invites you to appear on *Celebrity Jeopardy*. It's the Final Jeopardy round and you've wagered a fortune on the category Classic American Playwrights. The answer is, He wrote *Cat on a Hot Tin Roof.* Say something stupid that you'd regret seeing on Google and YouTube for the rest of eternity. Prove to us that you're dumb enough to be a big celebrity."

While the audience giggled at the idiocy of the question and, by association, the man posing the question, Toe Nail stood looking at Brian trying to figure out whether the judge was calling him stupid or if Brian was in earnest. Toe Nail instantly decided to reply with a response that would sound like Paris Hilton trying to sound profound.

Toe Nail shook his head and rolled his eyes. "Would you repeat the *Jeopardy* answer, please?"

"He wrote *Cat on a Hot Tin Roof.*"

"Who is Dr. Seuss?"

A few snickers could be heard among the audience of mostly young adults, but it seemed that few understood what Toe Nail had revealed about his wit.

"Thank you, my man," Brian said as Toe Nail moved off the stage. "But I think you should have gone for an incorrect response. You were supposed to say something you'd regret."

Steven Benjamin made a show of slapping himself on the cheek in a mock effort to return to the moment. Then, with a large smile, he said, "Let's welcome back Amy Stout!" He turned to Richard Dartmouth and said, "She's all yours."

Richard smiled. "Oh, if only that were true." The audience made wolf calls. Richard held up his hands to quiet the crowd and said, "I'm no Thane Cornwall…"

To which Amy smiled and said, "Amen!"

" … but I have to say…" He paused for dramatic effect. "…That I think Thane would have said something like 'Your performance tonight made me think that crawling into a cage of skunks would be preferable to the stench of your voice.'"

Amy's smile vanished.

"But that's not what I would say," Richard said. "Now. For your interview question. You're on a date with our lovely host Steven Benjamin …. That's not too hypothetical, is it, honey?" he said with a wink and a sideward glance at Steven. "Instead, let's say that you're on a date with … me…"

Camera number three caught Steven Benjamin looking bewildered and angry.

" … and you're hit on by the head of production at Twentieth Century Fox. Who do you screw … I mean, what do you do … to get ahead?"

Amy took a deep breath. "First of all, been there, done that. I'd have an affair with both of you. Turn out the lights and maybe there wouldn't be much of a difference. If I were on a date with you, and even if the impossible happened and I fell in love with you, when a bigger fish comes along, I have to go swimming. I've only been in Hollywood a little while, but I see the wives and girlfriends of stars and movers and shakers all looking for the next step up the ladder to security and social status. I would do what they do."

Polly sighed and held out her champagne flute for a refill. "Raul, darling, in your work you must see a lot of Bel Air *ladies,* and I use that term loosely. How do they catch their rich husbands? Larry King's easy, but what about the others?"

"Just as this Amy girl says." Raul nodded. "They're always on the lookout for the guy who needs a diversion from his family and career. At least that's how they start out. Men are pretty much easy targets. And if the woman's sexy enough, and cunning enough, there's not much the present wife or girlfriend can do. Although, whenever I hear about a young so-called actress gone missing or discovered dead, I think it's probably the work of the wife who had her husband tailed and then got rid of the competition with professional help. Happens all the time."

"In my day, we only had to worry about other stars interloping," Polly said. "Sedra Stone, may she rest in peace, took not one, but two of Tim's daddies from me. But at least she was from the same social circle. Well, sort of. I think she killed a few people on her way to destroying my heart. But today, they let almost anyone into this business. Just look at the riffraff on this show! I'm loath to say this, but mediocrity rules."

Steven Benjamin looked into the camera. "And we're back. After one more interview question, it will be up to the voting viewers to decide who stays on after next week, and who gets the axe!"

"More blood," Polly said.

"Without further ado, welcome back Miranda Washington!"

Miranda made her entrance down the long flight of stairs that graced the stage and wandered up to the microphone and the panel of judges.

Steven Benjamin said, "During the commercial break the judges decided to let Richard Dartmouth have the final question for the evening. Do you feel lucky?"

"No, but what can I do?" Miranda said.

"At least you're honest," Richard said, "which is no way to win this game, but have it your way." He stared at Miranda for a long moment. "Everybody has a dark side to their personality. Some otherwise very nice people suddenly snap and kill a noisy neighbor. Or the quiet guy at the office gets one e-mail too many and shoots his colleagues. If you were this close to being famous, but someone smarter or more talented … or younger got in the way, what would your dark side reveal?"

Miranda pursed her lips and rubbed her nose. "I've got a mean streak a mile long, all right," she said. "I sent my dumb-ass boyfriend to the ER for constantly leaving used Kleenex around in piles. I suppose if I were faced with someone about to steal my limelight, it would be like they were taking a parking space I'd been waiting a long time for. If they pulled into my fame space, I'd have to whup their sorry butt. Ain't nothin' gonna keep me from winning this game, and becoming the famous person I was meant to be. I've got dreams, and I mean to make 'em come true. My voice alone will take me where I'm going."

"All the way to the unemployment office," Polly said. "Yikes! What a lousy show! I may not go back, even if they ask me!"

Just as Placenta was about to turn off the television, Steven Benjamin looked into the camera and said, "Join us next week when one of our contestants will say adios to all their dreams of becoming famous. And we'll have extra security on hand, just in case a poor loser takes aim at one of our wonderful judges. Don't forget what we, who have important Hollywood jobs, always say, 'When the going gets tough, the tough take out their rusty razor blades and carve up. anyone who gets in their way!' See you next week!"

Placenta turned the lights on in the media room as Polly stood up and yawned. "It's time for a nightcap," Polly said, looking at the four empty bottles of Veuve left on one of the chairs in the room. She put her arm around Raul's waist and said, "Are you sober enough to drive, or shall I ask Placenta to dust off the sheets in one of the guest rooms?"

"Mother ...," Tim warned. "Go to bed. *We'll* see you in the morning."

—❧—

"I had another dreadful night," Polly complained when she arrived at the patio breakfast table Saturday morning. "Which one of our friends does a commercial for sleeping pills? I'm getting desperate. Kelsey?"

"I think he's irritable bowel syndrome," Placenta said.

"Cybill?"

"Menopause."

"Whosy Whatsy, from *Northern Exposure.* "

"Janine? Nah. She used to do a commercial for that dry-eye disease. I think it's off the market like the stuff that Dorothy Hamill hawked."

"Well, what does Sally sell? She always looks young and well rested. She must have a pill!"

"Osteoporosis, I think. Just go to Dr. Feel Good. He'll prescribe anything you want," Placenta said.

"Drugs are too damned expensive! I just want a sampler to get me through an afternoon nap," Polly lamented.

"Tonight's important, and I'm going to be a wreck if I don't get some shut-eye!"

"Speaking of tonight, Tim has hired a guard to keep us safe from those murderous contestants you've invited to dinner."

Polly looked up from sipping her mimosa. "What's his name?"

"Sandy."

"As in hunky Orange County surfer? Leave it to my Timmy."

"As in Sandra. Tim hired a female security guard."

Polly rolled her eyes and poured another mimosa from a juice pitcher. "If she's anything like Officer Betty down at the jailhouse, I feel safer already." She looked around, then glanced at her wristwatch. "Speaking of Tim, he's got a ton to do before tonight. He can't sleep the day away."

Placenta cleared the breakfast table. "Timmy's long gone. He and Raul … no, he didn't spend the night … were meeting for coffee. Apparently, Raul has access to the files that SOS kept on Thane Cornwall."

Polly took another sip of her drink. "Sounds a tad unethical. I knew I liked that young man. I'll bet he knows the secrets and mating habits of every celebrity in Bel Air." She paused. "If SOS has a file on Thane, surely they have one on us! That's not good."

Placenta tossed bits of a blueberry muffin to a few sparrows that had flown into the yard. The birds pounced on the meal and hopped around looking for more. "You won't have to worry about SOS until after Tim and Raul stop seeing each other. Right now, Raul is in the 'Let me impress you' phase. He'll volunteer classified information just to keep Mr. Perfect hanging around. He's the one who recommended the new security guard."

Polly huffed. "When things cool down, I'll have to get the poor boy fired, so he doesn't take revenge by letting any of Pepper Plantation's secrets out! Oh, I hate playing the bad cop! And speaking of cops, or at least security personnel, when does this Sandy person begin?"

"Noon. She's coming to meet you, and to start patrolling the grounds. She'll be working in twelve-hour shifts, along with a partner."

Polly stood up from the table. "I'd better put on my Polly Pepper face," she said, tightening the belt around her bathrobe. "I'll be in the shower if anybody needs me." She left Placenta to continue cleaning up the breakfast dishes.

At eleven-thirty, Tim entered the house and greeted his mother with an air kiss to her cheek. "It's been a very productive morning!" he said as he poured a glass of lemonade for himself. "Raul is amazing! He got us into the SOS confidential computer files and we had a blast checking out George and Tom and Keira and Kevin and Elton. I felt like a snoopy nurse at Cedars!"

"Anything useful … for when Angelina calls to dish?" Polly asked. "What types of records does SOS keep? Guests to Thane's home? Telephone calls? The time of day when he activated his security system?"

"Thane had their super celebrity protection package," Tim said. "They watched the house twenty-four-seven. In addition to the regular remote alarm service, they patrolled the property with drive-by service once every half hour. And get this! They had a two-way intercom connection. Raul said that without clients knowing, the guy who owns SOS monitors what goes on in their homes. He's got months of recordings on some of the biggest stars in town, including Thane Cornwall!"

"Oh my God," Polly said, shocked. "We're definitely changing to Mayday!"

The chime at the front gate sounded. Tim looked at his watch. "It's our new security detail. Your very own armed response team!" After confirming who the visitors were, he pushed the intercom button to release the entrance gates. Within a minute, he was introducing his mother and Placenta to Sandy Sanchez and Dak Ditson.

Polly reluctantly put on her professional face and instantly ingratiated herself into the lives of the two women. Dak was old enough to be Sandy's mother. The women were military professional. They "Yes, ma'am"ed and "no, ma'am"ed and never cracked a smile or let on they may have been impressed by Polly Pepper. Indeed, as they rattled off the list of celebrities for whom they had served, Polly was merely one of many notable names.

Polly, Tim, and Placenta listened with trepidation as the pair of guards explained how the estate would be operated under their care. It was made clear that no one was allowed to exit the grounds or reenter without first notifying the guard on duty and signing in on a minute-by-minute log. Also, visitors, including close friends, would be screened before being admitted to the property, and scrutinized throughout their stay, in order to ensure that not only the family would be safe, but also the contents of the house.

"We *do* expect to be addressed as Sergeant Sandy and Officer Dak. We don't expect to be your friends," Dak explained in a clipped military tone. "We're here with one mission, to secure the residents and property from unwanted and potentially hostile intruders."

Polly and her troupe could only nod in agreement. "Do we get any time off?" Placenta asked.

"We are not here to make you comfortable with us," Sergeant Sandy stated. "We'll be watching you as closely as we watch your video monitoring devices. Get used to it."

Polly looked at Tim, who shrugged his shoulders as if to say, "Sorry. I didn't know the Gestapo was moving in."

Sergeant Sandy looked at her wristwatch, then nodded to Dak. "Enough small talk. Dak will return at midnight. In the meantime, I've got a job to do." Sergeant Sandy saluted Polly and with toe to heel, she pivoted 180 degrees and marched away.

Polly looked at Tim and made a face. "How can we have any privacy with the SS keeping their eyes on us? I may as well stay in bed all day!"

"Alone!" Placenta added.

Tim shrugged. "She came highly recommended by Raul."

"Then why aren't they still working for all those B-list celebrities?" Polly said, and walked away in a huff.

"Give her a fair chance," Tim said. "She just might save our lives!"

Placenta put her hand on Tim's shoulder. "As a matter of fact, with the lowlifes who are eating at our table this evening, I'm very happy for the added protection. What the heck is your mother thinking when she invites killers to the house?"

"We don't know that one of tonight's guests is a killer," Tim said.

"Someone's out there killing judges and contestants on that sucky show," Placenta said. "Every single one of the people she's having over tonight had a motive to kill Thane Cornwall. And opportunity, too, I suppose. Do me a favor. Run back to your new friend and have him check out the file of Thane Cornwall for the night of his murder. See if there's a recording of what went on in the house. Maybe there's a record of someone other than Lisa Marrs being there. Oh, how about a tape from the intercom? Something that proves that one of the kids didn't do the deed. I'll feel much better knowing that Toe Nail, or Miranda or Taco Belle or anyone else I'm serving, isn't going to carve me up."

"We already checked. So did the police," Tim said. "Thane's security system failed that night. The cameras, too."

Placenta heaved a heavy sigh. "Life's too short to worry about death."

Sergeant Sandy stationed herself at attention outside the front entry gates to Pepper Plantation, imagining herself at the gates to Buckingham Palace. As each guest arrived she insisted on two forms of identification, plus contact with the main house to confirm that the name on her clipboard matched the master guest list that Tim kept by the front door.

When Toe Nail finally got through the checkpoint and entered the mansion, he opened his sports coat and boasted to Polly, "The chick in the pants didn't catch this!" He showed off a large knife sheathed in leather and attached to his belt.

Well-trained hostess that she was, Polly offered a hearty laugh and a hug. "She's new at the job. I've planted a dozen WMD and she hasn't found a single one. So much like that dummy in the White House, but not quite as moronic!"

Soon the invitees were all in attendance and Tim was serving drinks. Polly, dressed in an elegant aqua-colored silk back-zipped dress with a ruched bodice blouse above a darted skirt and a matching beaded jacket, circulated among her young guests. As they each asked questions about the grand house, wanting to see exactly where their co-contestant Danny Castillo's body had been discovered, Polly became more comfortable with the group. Everybody loved the house, and seeing the display of Emmy Awards, People's Choice Awards, and other symbols of Polly Pepper's fame, made each even more impressed with their hostess.

"So, which way was his head twisted?" Taco Belle asked when Tim escorted her to the place where Danny was found. "Did it look like the priest who got thrown down the stairs by Satan in *The Exorcist*?" she asked.

Tim assured her that no, the body looked like Danny had just gone to sleep.

"That's not what I heard."

Tim and Taco Belle turned to the sound of Amy Stout's voice, and found that she and Miranda Washington had joined them at the scene of the crime. "Thane's assistant, Michael, said Danny looked like he was staring at a ghost."

Tim cocked his head. "I was here, he wasn't."

Amy shrugged. "Are you calling him a liar?"

Tim was taken aback. "I'm just saying…"

At that moment, Michael joined them. "Who's a liar?"

"Apparently, you are," Miranda said.

Tim shook his head. "We were just talking about finding Danny's body right in this spot, that's all."

Taco Belle took another sip of her champagne. "And Mr. Rich Boy here said you lied about how the body looked when they found it cold as ice on the granite floor."

Tim was incredulous. "I didn't say anyone was a liar. I just described what I saw, and you said that's not what Michael saw. And the floor's not granite."

Michael squared his shoulders. "I just reported what I heard, that's all. Toe told me what it looked like."

Miranda put two fingers to her lips and blew an ear-shattering whistle. "Yo! Toe! Over here!" she demanded.

Polly, who had been speaking with Toe Nail about the lack of sadness felt by almost everyone over the death of Thane Cornwall, followed him into the foyer where the others were gathered.

The center of attention, Toe Nail was surrounded by his co-contestants and the Pepper Plantation household. "Whassup?" he asked.

Miranda said, "Our host says you're a liar."

Tim gasped. "I never said that. In fact, I never said anything about anybody lying about anything."

Amy Stout joined in. "Michael said Danny's body was a twisted wreck, with his eyes popping out of his head, like he was being attacked by zombies. But Tim here disagrees. Michael told us that you saw the body. So now you're being called a liar. Whatcha gonna do 'bout that?"

Toe Nail looked at Michael with smoldering eyes. Then he looked at Tim and shrugged. "I was just guessing, that's all. It's like I used my imagination and thought of what a dead body that had been strangled would look like. I never said I actually saw Danny all busted up and looking any special way. How could I? This is my first time in this ritzy crib."

Michael drank the rest of his glass of champagne and said, "So now I look like a liar, 'cause I believed what you said you saw."

"Sweetums!" Polly interrupted. "Dead bodies in Bel Air look just like the ones found on Sunset Boulevard or in Laurel Canyon. They're just dead people. You see them all the time on *CSI,* so what's to imagine? I think it's time that we all skedaddle into the dining room, that's what I think. We'll all feel less hostility with full tummies. I know I will!" Polly tapped her three-carat pear-shaped diamond ring against her champagne flute. "Placenta has a very special menu planned for this evening. Hop to it, ladies and gentlemen," she said, leading the way to the formal dining room.

Place cards at each setting identified where Polly had determined each guest would be seated. With Polly at the head of the table, Tim and Placenta pulled out chairs for Miranda and Amy and Taco Belle, while the men seated themselves, giving no indication that they knew anything about dinner table etiquette.

Tim joined Placenta in the kitchen and began serving the soup course. Polly was the first to be served, followed by the women, then the men. "Start, start, start," Polly encouraged, before Tim and Placenta had finished placing all the bowls of squash soup before their guests. "You'll die when you taste this," Polly said.

As Toe Nail slurped soup from his spoon, and Miranda looked around to make sure she was using the right utensil, Polly added, "Speaking of dying, I think we can all understand why Mr. Thane Cornwall came to his end, but why do you suppose our sweet Danny was done in?"

"Typical dinner table conversation at Pepper Plantation?" Taco Belle asked as she patted her lips with her cloth napkin. "I've heard about your famous parties."

"You aren't far off," Polly said, "but perhaps we should save such talk for dessert."

As everyone oohed and aahed about the starter course, Michael asked his hosts, "What'd you think of the show last night?"

Polly took a sip of champagne and said, "I thought that Miss Jesus-in-the-Mirror motor mouth was actually quite acceptable as a judge."

Taco Belle noisily dropped her spoon into her bowl. "She made fun of me!"

Amy Stout declared, "You got off a hell of a lot better than I did with Richard! What the hell was he doing making up such a vulgar quote from Thane? 'The stench of my voice'? What was that all about?" She coughed into the palm of her hand and tried to smell her breath.

"He was just saying what he thought Thane might say," Toe Nail said. "I'm the one who got hit between the eyes by Brian! He said I was stupid!"

As Polly finished her soup and placed her spoon in the bowl, she looked up, rested her elbows on the table, and intertwined her fingers. Her diamonds shone under the light of the Waterford crystal chandelier. "You're all reading negative ideas into the judges' questions. I'll admit their queries weren't very good, but I don't believe the judges were at all as hostile as you've led yourselves to believe. They don't need to be analyzed like a dream in which you discover yourselves tying your honey-slathered mothers over a hive of African red ants. God knows I don't give advice—"

Placenta nearly spat up her soup.

"—but I'll tell you that in all my years as an international celebrity and icon, I've found it's best to eliminate the negative and focus on the positive."

Placenta wiped up the soup spittle from the front of her dress and said, "For instance, it would be negative of Polly to say she's positive that there's a connection between the deaths of Thane and Danny."

"I think so too," Toe Nail said. "We all do. That there's a connection, I mean. It's too freaky that two people involved in the same show have died within days of each other. It's been a whole week since the last one went, but that doesn't mean that the killer is through with us. The show has bad karma, and you know what they say, everything comes down to money. I think there's a killer producer on the loose. Last night's big ratings proved that the publicity from murders worked."

"Hold that thought," Placenta said as she stood up and retrieved the soup bowls. Tim joined her in the kitchen to serve the main course.

While placing chicken breasts stuffed with fontina, artichokes, and sun-dried tomatoes on eight plates, Placenta whispered, "That Toe Nail isn't as stupid as he looks. I think he's on to something. The producer connection, that is."

"If he's right, and the ratings do reflect all the freebie publicity, then we're looking at Richard Dartmouth as a possible killer," Tim said. "Oh, but please, dear God, don't let Polly catch on. She'll have another potential murderer over and we'll have to play this same game with him."

"Polly's not a complete idiot," Placenta said. "She'll add two and two and at least come up with three." She picked up two plates and moved toward the door to the dining room. "I'll take these to Michael and Toe. Don't forget to add the sodium pentothal bearnaise sauce."

When once again everyone was seated and making yummy sounds with each forkful of food, Polly announced, "I'd like to propose a toast," raising her champagne flute. When everyone else had set their silverware down and lifted their own glasses, Polly closed her eyes as if in prayer. "To dear Thane Cornwall and lovely Danny Castillo. Your friends and fans miss you. We, at this table, are particularly sad that you aren't here to join us, but we know that you're both in a better place than Hollywood, which isn't exactly all that's it's cracked up to be anyway, especially if you're just a tart-tongued judge and a minimally talented contestant on a bottom-of-the-barrel television show that takes advantage of youthful dreams and capitalizes on America's thirst for blood, and challengers' devotion to winning a competition at all costs."

Polly drew a breath and continued. "I remember how Lana Turner tried to sabotage me when I had my first screen test at Metro. I was supposed to play her precocious step-daughter in a movie that never got made. She wanted an established actress for the role. So Lana, dear killer Lana, in her inimitable way, made sure that the cinematographer didn't light me well. She also made certain that I had the wrong script pages. But did I take my anger out on that luminous legend? I did not. And when the morbidly obese but still darling star who played Perry Mason, and that crippled Ironside guy on television, came on my show and refused to learn the choreography for a sketch about wheelchair waltz competitions that my darling writers had spent weeks perfecting, did I expose one iota of his secret gay life to any of my friends in the media? Assuredly not!"

Polly waited just long enough for the guests to think that the sermon might be over. Wrong. "So, you two darling men of the theater, or at least of pop culture and television, I propose a toast to you and send our most powerful thought vibrations for your killers to be identified, and brought to justice. I am doing all that I can in my limited capacity as a living legend to ferret out the loathsome creature or creatures who perpetrated these crimes and deprived both of your beautiful bodies from drawing another breath and being with us at this fine and expensive antique dining room table with the professionally starched and ironed linen tablecloth that was given to me by Rosalind Russell on the occasion of my marriage to Mr. Pepper number one. You'd love the food and drink, I'm sure, and the company of others here who are just as determined to succeed in show business as both of you were.

"When we all meet in heaven, I'll be sure to bring along a case of my favorite bubbly, and we'll have our own little celebratory reunion and I'll regale you with reports of all that you missed out on just because someone decided you were dispensable. Trust me, dearest dear men, the planet is not the same without you. We miss Thane and his cruel behavior, which led everyone who didn't know the real Thane Cornwall, the one that lived way deep down a couple hundred layers beneath the surface of your strident exterior, to misunderstand you and to not know that you were just a human being with the same frailties as Caligula, and with just as much obvious need for attention. Your lack of a bridle on your tongue was a wonderful thing that most people couldn't tolerate, but that didn't stop you from being exactly who you were. As inconsiderate and spiteful as you appeared to be, I know that at your core was a volcano that wanted very much to be smothered out with cotton candy and lemonade, and to no longer cause pain and suffering among the masses."

Polly dismissed her guests' yawning and continued. "Oh, Danny. Dear, sweet, all those tattoos and piercings, Danny. Your bravery, at standing up to those who dismissed you as untalented and tried to beat you down with hurtful words, was no match for the real Danny Castillo. Yes, like Thane, on the surface you appeared to be a tough cookie. But on the inside you were a marshmallow. I think we all know this.

"So why, dear boy, did you have to invade my home and get yourself murdered? Oh, you sweet thing, with the voice of … well, a better voice than Alvin the Chipmunk … why did you get into this trouble? Did you know something about the murder of Thane Cornwall that you were trying to prove? Did you suspect that there was something at Pepper Plantation that might claim the innocence of Lisa Marrs? Oh, my dear Danny, if only you could come back for an hour and tell us everything you know about the case, and your last day, hour, and minute of life. Oh, to be in a position to offer you a glass of champagne and a hug. I'm among those who will always miss you. Thankfully, after a few days and no more than a month, you'll fade dead away. Still, I know that whenever I see a nipple ring on a man, or a lovely wall that's been defaced with graffiti, I'll think of you and the way you chose to decorate your living temple of the Lord."

Polly stopped for a breath. Then she sighed and said, "I'm not hungry anymore."

By now, the food was cold, but the guests were fired up. "I'd say cheers and amen, but I wasn't a fan of either Thane's or Danny's," Miranda said. "Thane's death wasn't a bad thing. Danny, I'm not too sure about. But the fact that he got himself killed while trespassing at Pepper Plantation, well, he was obviously up to no good." Amy Stout raised her glass. "I, too, would like to propose a toast."

As groans issued from the other contestants, Polly smiled at Amy. "Of course, dear. If Thane and Danny are paying attention, they'll certainly appreciate your thoughtful words."

Amy cleared her throat. "My toast is to Richard Dartmouth, for selecting me for this competition in the first place, and to Steven Benjamin, who has given me a lot of encouragement." She paused. "I also hope that Thane and Danny suffered horribly when they got murdered! The knife couldn't have gone deep enough to find Thane's nonexistent heart! And, if what I heard is true, that Danny choked to death on his own body-piercing studs, it wouldn't have tasted metallic enough for him! We all eventually get what we have coming to us."

Everybody at the table appeared stunned. Amy took a long swallow from her glass of champagne, smiled, and said, "What's for dessert?"

"A double scoop of acrimony with a venom glaze," Placenta said.

Polly, astonished, looked at Amy and asked, "How did you know that the cause of Danny's death was from choking?"

Amy shrugged. "Someone said so."

CHAPTER 14

—⁓—

"Can't the maid clear the table?" Polly said to Placenta as soon as their guests had left the house. "Oh, wait," she sniggered, "you're the maid! Timmy, give Placenta a hand."

With a harrumph from Placenta, and a roll of the eyes from Tim, the two began their chores. "Indentured servitude," Placenta griped.

When the dining room was once again in perfect order, and the dishwasher filled with china and silverware, Tim and Placenta joined Polly in the great room where she was engrossed in her favorite HGTV program, *Decorating for These Folks is Murder.* Polly was comfortably seated on the sofa, with her legs out-stretched and her back resting against the padded arm of the couch. "It's curious," she said when a Lowe's home improvement store commercial interrupted a homeowner who had booby-trapped his dining room with a carpet over a wide hole in the floor and was lying in wait for his designer.

"What? That Amy knew so much about the death of Danny Castillo? I had that thought too," Tim said.

"No. Well, yes," Polly said. "But I was remembering the video clip they showed of Danny on last night's show."

"That was one sick-looking swayback pony he was photographed on as a kid," Placenta said.

"Hmm ," Polly agreed. "No, I mean, where did they find that footage of his dressing room tantrum? He wouldn't have done that if a cameraman was present. A hidden camera? If there was one in Danny's room, there must be one in every dressing room."

Tim rubbed his tired eyes. "That would be totally unfair and probably illegal. It's a dressing room, for crying out loud. Like a bathroom. Things go on there that you wouldn't want Peeping Toms to see, let alone viewed by the entire world."

"Hell, they'll throw anything up on YouTube these days," Placenta said. "Remember those bully teen cheerleaders who videoed themselves dismembering a rival cheerleader, specifically to play on the Net?"

"I'd be mortified if a camera was trained on my lace and frills," Polly said. Then she put her hand to her mouth. "Suppose my dressing room had a hidden camera, too! Jeepers creepers! I don't think privacy exists anymore!"

Placenta poured herself a glass of Veuve and plopped down on the twin sofa opposite Polly's. "Wait a darned minute! I think we're all missing the bigger picture. If each dressing room had a hidden camera, there's a chance that if one of the show's contestants is responsible for Thane's or Danny's deaths, we might find some clues on the tapes."

Tim nodded. "Maybe a tape or two captured someone plotting beforehand, or confessing after the fact."

Polly rolled her eyes. "Who'd be stupid enough to talk about doing murder, especially on tape?"

"Um, try a Menendez brother," Tim said. "Those idiots confessed to their shrink that blasting the bloody smithereens out of rich mommy and daddy was about greed. Dr. Lobotomy recorded the whole thing. It's not out of the realm of possibility that if one of our contestants had a dirty secret, they might spill the beans to a confidant. Especially if they didn't know anyone else was watching or listening."

Polly was deep in contemplation. "If there are hidden cameras, and if anyone said anything incriminating on tape, surely the person who keeps that stuff on file would have called the police. First we have to prove that hidden cameras exist. If they do, I can't imagine who would let us see the coverage. Not Richard. As the show's producer, he'd probably be the one who set up the video traps in the first place."

"Lisa would know," Placenta said. "Any good assistant has the dirt on everything that goes on in their boss's office."

"Okay. Tomorrow we go back to the studio and take a look around," Tim said. "We'll thoroughly check out your old dressing room. Surveillance devices are so dam small these days, they could be planted anywhere."

Polly began to fret. "Good grief, if there's a tape of me saying such awful things about Thane the night he died, I might be accused of killing him myself."

"'Hollywood isn't big enough for the two of us' could be misconstrued," Tim agreed. "Especially when you artfully decorate the dressing room mirror with a lipstick circle

175

around Thane's name and a line through it, like a no-smoking sign," he added.

"No problem. I smeared it away," Placenta said.

"If it was on tape, it's forever," Polly complained.

"Tomorrow's Sunday," Tim reminded her. "The show is dark on Sundays. There's no one to let us in for a reconnaissance."

"Plus you're in exile," Placenta added.

"That old security guard, Jack, likes you," Tim said. "Bring him a box of Krispy Kremes and he's bound to be putty in your hands."

Polly smiled. "I'm charming enough without adding to his weight problem. But it's worth trying to get into the place, I suppose." She was silent for a moment. "While we're at it, can anyone tell me how anyone came to the conclusion that Danny choked on body-piercing accouterment?"

"I'm stumped," Tim said.

"Ya got me," Placenta added.

"Ooh! Ooh!" Polly said, sounding like a straight-A student begging to answer a question in class. "Wait. I've solved it! Danny broke into our house and one of his ear studs, those hideously big things that looked like rivets that gang members wear, fell out of his lobe. He bent down to retrieve it, and discovered that the backing had rolled behind the sideboard in the foyer. Needing both hands, he put the stud in his mouth as he got down on his hands and knees to get the other piece, something startled him. He took an unexpected deep breath, and he sucked the stud into his esophagus. Voila! One dead body!"

Tim and Placenta looked at each other, silently agreeing that Polly was either a genius or a nut ... mostly the latter.

"And why did he break in?" Tim asked. "I suppose he wandered in looking for the annual meeting of the Official Polly Pepper International Fan Club?"

Polly gave Tim a stern look. "You're the one who thought he was cute. You probably gave him a key to the place!" Polly stopped teasing her son. "I've seen Danny's dead body in my mind's eye every waking moment since yesterday. There he was, on our floor, clutching his throat with his black-polished fingernails. And he was missing his right ear stud. I can see it clearly. I hated that stud. The one with the black widow spider! Gives me the creeps just to think about it."

"Brava!" Tim said, impressed by his mother's skills of observation. "In that short amount of time that you saw the body, you noticed he was missing his ear stud. Wow! So maybe he died exactly the way you described it. That still doesn't tell us what he was doing here in the first place. And trust me, I did not give him a key!"

"The alarm system didn't go off," Placenta said.

"Because the system failed," Tim reminded her. "He was obviously here for a good reason. I'd like to believe it was simply a stunt to make the judges and voting audience think that he was doing something nefarious in order to score the most points on the show."

Placenta slapped her knee and then stood up. "We can spend the rest of the night making these ludicrous speculations. I'm hitting the sack. I'll save my own foolish theories until after we check out the dressing rooms at Sterling Studios tomorrow."

—⁓—

Tim signaled to maneuver the Rolls-Royce up to the Sterling Studios gates and stopped at the guard kiosk. "Uh-oh," he said, before rolling down his window and making eye contact with the security guard. "Where's Jack?" he asked a sullen twenty-something in a dark blue uniform, holding a clipboard. The guard looked at Tim without a smile and tried to peer through the smoked windows of the expensive car.

"Off on Sundays," the guard responded. "Whassup?"

"Just dropping my mother, Polly Pepper, off at *I'll Do Anything to Become Famous*. Studio B."

"They're not working today," the guard said.

"I know. But she left her purse here after the show the other night. We'll only be a moment."

Just as the guard knitted his eyebrows, the back window rolled down and Polly reached out her hand. She looked at the guard's name badge and called out, "Jimmy? Is that you, dear?"

The guard was taken aback. "Have we met?"

Polly smiled. "It almost seems so, the way Richard Dartmouth goes on and on about you." She silently prayed that he wasn't new on the job.

"Mr. Dartmouth knows who I am?"

"Of course, sweetums! And my dear friend Jack, your adorable confrere, who I would have chastised for not being here to greet me, but I see that he left me in your capable and talented hands. By the way, dear man, and I don't mean to embarrass you, but I envy your girlfriends having such seductive eyes to stare into. How on earth did you get them to be so green?" Polly fanned herself as if she were blushing and about to faint.

As Jimmy wrote Polly's name on his clipboard, Polly asked, "By the way, has Mr. Dartmouth arrived yet? We're supposed to meet to discuss my return to the airwaves."

Jimmy stopped writing. "I thought you were here to retrieve your purse?"

"Oh, that too," Polly lied. "My Timmy doesn't always get his facts straight." She leaned forward and smacked her son on the back of his skull. "Do you, dear?" she said through gritted teeth.

After hesitating, Jimmy nodded and handed a drive-on pass to Tim. "Display this in the windshield," he said. "You can park wherever you like. When Mr. Dartmouth arrives, I'll let him know that you're here."

Polly reached farther out the window to shake Jimmy's hand. "You're a living doll. I'll be sure to tell little Dickie Dart … er, Richard Dartmouth how helpful you've been. *Ciao, bella!*"

As Tim passed through the famous studio gates and made a left down Tina Louise Lane, he cried out, "Oww! You didn't have to hit me so hard!"

"So sorry, darling," Polly apologized. "It was for a good cause. My purse, please."

As the car passed by the Louella Parsons Fountain, and found a parking space on Donna Reed Circle, Polly looked around wistfully. "I know this is a stinky show, but I do enjoy being on a studio lot."

When they arrived at Studio B, they breathed a collective sigh when they discovered that the door was unlocked. Inside, it was deathly quiet, and they automatically spoke in whispers. "First, your dressing room," Tim said as they walked through the dimly lit stage. Once there, Polly looked at the door and found that her name had been covered over. Obscuring her name was that of Trish Saddleback. Without thinking, Polly reached up and automatically peeled away the tape to reveal her own name. She rolled Saddleback into a ball and tossed it across the corridor. "Now we can enter," she said.

Slowly opening the dressing room door and flipping on the light switch, Polly whispered, "Don't they lock anything up in this place? If my purse is missing, I'll sue."

"On what grounds?" Placenta said. "It's an imaginary purse and it's in a make-believe place. Now start looking for surveillance devices!"

While Tim pulled the emergency flashlight out of the socket next to the makeup table, and dragged a chair to the center of the room, Polly and Placenta looked in various plants and vases of flowers. They pulled out a love seat to examine the wall behind it, and then looked for wiring that may have been hidden next to the doorframe. "I saw this once in a spy movie," Polly said. "At the end, the guy who didn't know he was being watched found his whole apartment bugged. The KGB or CIA had done such a great job of hiding the cameras and microphones that this poor slob never noticed anything for years."

Just then Tim said, "Oh, oh!"

Polly and Placenta turned to see Tim standing on tiptoes and peering into the dark space behind the acoustic ceiling tiles. He ducked down from the space and replaced the ceiling tile. With a finger to his lips, he cocked his head toward the door. Together the trio silently left the room. When they were once again out in the hallway, Tim whispered, "Don't look around. Just follow me and return to the car. Act naturally. Don't rush, just move with purpose."

"Why? What's—"

"Shush!" Placenta said. "Do as Tim says."

When they were once again in the car, Tim said, "When we get to the gate, I'll tell the guard that you heard from Dartmouth and the meeting was canceled. Then I'll tell you what I've found. Again, just act as though nothing is wrong."

"What *is* wrong?" Polly pleaded.

"Whistle, or something," Tim said. "Act nonchalant."

Finally out on the street again, Tim looked in the rearview mirror and found Polly's and Placenta's inquiring faces. "We're in trouble. Polly was right about hidden cameras. The room was bugged. Everything that we said or did when we were on the show was probably recorded. In fact, there's a motion sensor. It's set to go on automatically when there's activity in the room. No doubt they have us snooping around today. Surely the hallways have cameras too. There's no denying that we were here."

"Oh, sweet Jesus!" Polly said. "This is all my career needs, a breaking and entering rap!"

CHAPTER 15

—✍—

As Polly's Rolls-Royce traveled down Sunset Boulevard toward Bel Air, Placenta whined, "Why can't you be an average international living legend? Like Doris Day? Or Shirley Temple?"

"Oh God, save me from average anything!" Polly whined with equal petulance. "And you know better than to lump my extraordinary Doris with anyone mediocre! Now stop complaining and dial Officer Betty at the Beverly Hills Police Station. I want to let her know we'll be arriving soon."

Tim let out a loud moan. "You're dragging us back to the station? It's Sunday. A day of rest! You didn't get much of anything from Lisa before. What makes you think she'll have a new tune to sing?"

Polly ignored Tim as she accepted the cell phone from Placenta. She reached forward and tapped it on Tim's shoulder. "Tell her she's invited to dinner. But don't say when. As for why we're seeing Lisa again, have you already forgotten what we found in my dressing room this morning? We need to find out what she knows about this!"

—〜—

Officer Betty grabbed her hair and made a mock primal scream when Polly Pepper sauntered into the lobby of the police station. "What did I ever do to you?" Betty said. "You must be my reward for being a serial killer in a previous life."

"I don't expect hero worship, but I'm really a lot of fun … when I'm not knee deep in dead bodies." Polly reached out and grazed Office Betty's cheek. "We should have a girlfriends' sleepover and play dress-up. You'll love my Bob Mackie's. And I have a wonderful product that would help with your five o'clock shadow."

"Heaven help me." Officer Betty made an unflattering noise with her lips as she got up from behind her desk. "This way," she said, cocking her head for Polly and her family to follow her. The group moved to the steel door behind which the prisoners were held. Betty pushed the button to automatically unlock the door. "No more than twenty minutes," she said as she led the way down the corridor to Lisa's cell.

When the group arrived together Betty called out, "Company's coming!" She unlocked the cell door. "Can you spare a minute?" she chuckled to Lisa and ushered Polly and her troupe into the tiny room. "Help me out here. I needed a break from Madame Movie Star."

When Officer Betty was gone and the foursome were making idle chatter about what it was like being in jail, what the latest news was about Thane's murder investigation, and how the ratings of *I'll Do Anything to Become Famous* had rocketed the show to the number-one spot for its time period, Polly dropped a bomb. "I can understand someone wanting to kill Thane, but poor Danny…"

Lisa looked confused. "Danny Castillo? What about him?"

Polly looked at Placenta, then at Tim, and back to Lisa. "I've always heard that jailbirds were more tuned in to what's happening on the streets than those of us who are solid law-abiding citizens."

Lisa looked blankly at Polly. "This isn't Folsom. I don't have a fink who keeps me in the loop."

"Danny's dead," Polly said.

Lisa gasped. "What happened? Who did it? This might prove that I'm innocent!"

"Why would you assume it was murder?" Polly asked.

Lisa shrugged. "I didn't say that I thought anything. You said you 'could understand someone wanting to kill Thane, but poor Danny…' What was I supposed to think?"

"You asked, 'Who did it?'" Polly reminded her. "Danny's death could have been an accident, but you assumed that he was killed. Why?"

"I suppose I'm getting used to people dying in suspicious ways whenever you're around," Lisa said.

Placenta cackled and nudged Tim. Then, for a long moment, there was silence in the cell. Placenta looked at the cinder block walls painted gray, and Tim looked at the combination toilet and washbasin. Polly continued to look at Lisa.

Finally, Polly said, "Danny's death looks like an accident. But I'm not so sure. He died at Pepper Plantation. He broke in while we were visiting your apartment."

"My apartment?" Lisa said. "What the hell were you doing there? Who let you in? What did you find?"

Polly folded her arms across her chest and took a solid stance. "What did you expect us to find?" she asked.

"Nothing."

"We didn't find *nothing*."

Lisa looked at Polly, then refocused on Tim and Placenta, then back to Polly. "What are you going to do about it?"

"There's nothing to do," Polly said.

"Why? Because I'm in here, and now you hold my keys to the kingdom?"

"If you say so." Polly had no idea what she was saying, or to what Lisa was alluding, but she sensed that if she just played dumb, Lisa would reveal something important.

"You know it's like having a treasure map," Lisa said. "But it won't do you a bit of good unless you know where X marks the bloody spot, so to speak."

"You don't say." Polly played along.

"You need to fit all the other pieces together."

"Placenta solved the Rubik's Cube once. She's helping me out on this one," Polly said. "Don't underestimate us."

"Okay!" Lisa said, shrinking away from Polly. "But don't say I didn't warn you! There's much more than what you see. Ask the young wunderkind producer Richard Dartmouth to explain why he secretly tapes everybody." When Polly didn't blanch at the mention of video surveillance, Lisa knew that Polly was on to her. "I guess it's all for the best. You might even catch a killer ... or two."

At that moment, Officer Betty arrived. Detective Randy Archer was right behind her.

It was late afternoon. The Los Angeles basin was an oven. Although the sky above looked clear, one had only to gaze to the north, to where the Hollywood Hills were supposed to be, to see that the air was actually dense with smog. Usually, the high daytime temperatures in L.A. cooled off at night. However, the forecast was for an evening of hot air blowing in … from the steaming police detective Randy Archer.

As the cadre moved out of the police station and into the parking lot, Polly tried to ease the tension. "Don't stress about things you can't control. This is our second anniversary!"

Detective Archer, Tim, and Placenta each gave Polly a puzzled look.

Polly sighed. "Two dead bodies since last week!"

"Some people go a lifetime without having even one!" Archer bellowed.

"Exactly!" Polly added. "So by now you must realize that I can't help it if I'm a death magnet. And there's nothing you can do about it."

When they all arrived at Polly's car, Tim pushed the button on his key fob to automatically release the door lock. Randy reached for the griddle-hot handle and pulled the door open. Placenta and Polly settled into the backseats and let their respective windows down to release the hot air from within. As Randy stood beside the vehicle and looked at his girlfriend, who seemed unaware of the dangers to which she exposed herself, he smiled.

"Now, that's the look of the man I adore," Polly said, reaching out to hold Randy's hand. "You'll feel a heck of a lot better when you get your clothes off … to go swimming,

I mean. Follow us home. Placenta won't cook on a hot night, and Tim thinks that barbecue is beneath his elevated level of living. So we'll have something delivered from Wolfgang. A nice cool pool awaits my hot police detective."

Polly finger-waved to Randy, then raised her window as Tim backed the Rolls out of the parking space. "Move this coach before he has a chance to catch up," Polly called to the front seat. "Then get us over to Michael's apartment, pronto."

Tim and Placenta both whined, "Polly!"

"Just go!" Polly demanded.

"We don't even know where he lives," Tim said. "That's why they invented cast and crew contact lists," Polly said, opening the storage compartment behind the front passenger seat and holding up a sheaf of papers. She scanned the first page, then turned to the second. "DeLongpre Avenue! Lisa thinks we have a treasure map. I'll wager that Michael, having worked for Thane, knows what the hell she's talking about."

Placenta looked out the passenger window and hummed for a moment. "Anyone else might have simply asked Lisa what she meant. But no, some other people have to pretend that they're know-it-alls." She looked away from the traffic and gazed at Polly. "You're like a man who's lost but won't ask for directions. Would it have been so hard to say, 'Duh! What the hell are you talking about?'"

Polly looked at Placenta as if she had never seen an episode of *Miss Marple*. "And let the potential killer think we're clueless? How could I pose such a silly question to Lisa, when she all but tells us that Danny Castillo was murdered by the same person who killed Thane!"

Tim looked at his mother through the rearview mirror. "It is weird that she assumed Danny's death was intentional," he said, and picked up his cell phone.

"What are you doing?" Polly asked.

"Letting Michael know that he's about to have unexpected guests," Tim said.

"Unexpected is the operative word!" Polly said. "Put the phone down, talk to that nice Google Lady, and never underestimate the power of surprise."

In twenty minutes, Polly's Rolls-Royce was traveling along Fountain Avenue, approaching LaBrea. A voice from Tim's Google Maps said, "Turn left at the next signal." Tim moved into the left-hand turn lane and when the light turned green he slowly entered the intersection. A long line of cars coming from the opposite direction made their way past the Rolls, before Tim turned the wheel and proceeded up La Brea. He followed Google Lady's directions and turned again onto a decrepit street lined with stucco apartments and run-down early twentieth century Hollywood bungalow-style houses. "Oh God. You're paying for an expensive security detail at the house, but didn't think to bring her with us!"

Polly ignored the remark, although she, too, was uncomfortable driving down this street. "Um, that's the one," she said, pointing to a two-story house with all the curb appeal of the homes featured on her second favorite HGTV show, *Divine Demolition!*

Remarkably, Tim found a place to park a half block away, and the trio gingerly made their way to the address on the cast and crew call sheet. At the walkway leading to two steps and the front door, Polly, Tim, and Placenta looked at each other and offered expressions that said, "Real people actually live here." Then, together, they proceeded up the steps. The front door was open, but an old wood-framed screen door kept the flies and Jehovah's Witnesses out. Tim knocked.

After a second series of knocks, a young man, who appeared to be in his late teens and was wearing a perspiration-soaked T-shirt, came into view. He looked at the well-dressed strangers on the front porch and asked, "Prize Patrol?"

The threesome outside smiled their most charming smiles. "Do you see flowers and balloons? We're friends of Michael's. Is he in?"

"What's he look like?"

"Um, five-nine. A hundred and twenty. Glasses."

"The skinny guy?" the young man said. "I think he's here." He unlocked and opened the door, and allowed the visitors to enter.

The smell inside instantly accosted their nostrils. "Burnt kitty," Placenta guessed.

"Spam," Polly said. "We ate that crap when I was a kid. I'll never forget the stench."

"I'm gonna puke," Tim said.

"Mike's place is over there," the guy who'd let them in said, pointing toward what appeared to be the living room. A large army surplus blanket was draped over a clothesline strung up to divide the room.

Tim looked at his mother as he led the way. When they were close enough to see that the khaki blanket was quite old and had been a steady meal for moths and silverfish, Tim called out, "Michael?"

"Honey, it's us," Polly added.

Just as they reached the blanket they heard Michael's voice. "Wha? Who?" He drew the blanket along the clothesline and revealed himself, and his bed, which was just a recliner chair with plastic milk crates for an ottoman. "What the … ?"

He looked mortified. "If I'd known that you were dropping in, I would have put up the Laura Ashley."

"I told Tim to call in advance, but he never listens," Polly said with genuine empathy. She had spent her entire childhood doing everything possible to keep friends from finding out that she and her mother lived in a single room in Hollywood. "We'll leave."

Michael shook his head. "Why bother? You came all this way from your mansion in Bel Air to my place in Flea Town. Let's have a tea party."

Placenta put her hands on her hips and said, "Excellent idea! But we're having it at the plantation."

Polly looked at her maid as though she'd lost her mind. "Wait…" she began to say, but caught Tim's look. " … um, of course. We've got dozens of extra toothbrushes. And Tim can loan you a clean pair of underpants. Come."

Although Michael attempted to back away from three pairs of arms that suddenly reached out for him, he quickly gave in without a struggle. "Er … kidnapping is a federal crime."

"Living in a room made of blankets ought to be," Polly countered.

When they were all settled in the car, and heading up to Sunset Boulevard, Polly looked at Placenta and held her hand. Her eyes said, "You go, girl!"

CHAPTER 16

—⁓—

The sun had long ago set over Los Angeles, but the heat still blanketed the city. Polly and Placenta, sitting at the poolside patio table sipping flutes of chilled Veuve Clicquot, watched the men horsing around in the water. The jubilant ruckus made everyone euphoric. Polly was delighted as she watched the easy camaraderie between Randy and Tim. And Michael's cannonball jumps off the diving board gave Polly a sense of childhood glee. She glanced at Placenta for a moment and heard her best friend and maid making a sound that she interpreted to be either appreciation or condemnation. "What?" she asked.

"Men," Placenta said without taking her eyes off the pool. "Look at those bodies. And I'm not being weird about Tim, I've known him since before he was out of the womb."

"I know exactly what you mean," Polly sighed. "I've got eyes too. All men are attractive in one way or another. Michael's twenty-one. Timmy's twenty-seven. Randy's fifty-two. No matter what age, they're all good looking, and we could eat 'em with a spoon. Well, Michael and Randy, anyway."

"Look at us," Placenta sighed. "If Michael's mother saw that we're lusting after her son's tattoo of Che Guevara, she'd call child protective services!"

"That's the problem," Polly said, "he's not a child. And the big surprise is that underneath his dorky clothes is a sexy man. Whodathunk?" After a moment, Polly looked back at Placenta and said, "We're pathetic. We're both very good-looking women. Heck, I've got a police detective boyfriend, and you had a date with Tom Hanks's doctor's best friend six months ago. We're not exactly out-to-pasture. As soon as we figure out who murdered Thane Cornwall and Danny Castillo, I'm taking us both to *The Oaks at Ojai* for a full spa week! We'll fool around with every masseur in the place!"

"Better come up with a killer pretty soon." Placenta smiled. "If I have to look at these gorgeous half-naked men in my own backyard much longer, I may have to drown just for the CPR."

Polly sighed in agreement, and as she reached for the champagne bottle from a silver bucket on the table, she saw a beam of flashlight moving across the wide acreage. "Here comes our security detail extraordinaire. Time to get into Polly Pepper mode. Jesus Christ."

When Sergeant Sandy arrived at the patio she gave Polly and Placenta a formal nod and reported, "The estate is secure, ma'am."

Polly offered a wide smile. "That's absolutely lovely. You're taking such good care of us. I almost feel guilty that we're having all the fun on such a hot night. Please feel completely comfortable about taking a swim. In fact, take off that hot shirt and let your body breathe, dear! Those wet patches under your arms must be very uncomfortable. As you said, the place is secure. No paparazzi!"

With wide eyes, Sergeant Sandy looked at Polly, Placenta, the bottle of champagne, and the men in the pool. "Officer Dak will be along shortly to relieve me," she said. "I'll take a cold shower at home." She then leaned in closer to the two women and whispered, "Be wary of the boy you brought home."

Polly and Placenta looked at each other, then turned back to Sandy.

Without her employer asking for details, Sergeant Sandy volunteered, "When the young man was at your dinner the other night, he and that Miranda girl scuffled out back by the little cottage behind the grove of orange trees. I was making my rounds while everyone else was at dinner."

"They excused themselves, along with Taco Belle, to go to the bathroom," Placenta said, remembering a time when the two had left the dining table together.

"Pardon me, but Taco Belle is an insult," Sergeant Sandy said, adding PC Police to her job description.

"Which is why I'd never set foot in one of those cheap-o food places," Polly said. Placenta and Sergeant Sandy stared at her. "Oh, you mean the name of our pretty Latina contestant. It was Thane Cornwall's mean nickname. But it sorta stuck."

"Never mind," Sandy said. She returned her thoughts to the night of the dinner party. "Michael and Miranda were fighting over something that the young woman had in her hand. As they struggled they lost whatever it was. It was pitch-black over there, and they practically ran into me as they were searching for it. Then they gave up and returned to the dinner table."

Placenta said, "Why didn't you tell us this before?" Sergeant Sandy took a deep breath. "It's in the daily report that I handed in."

"Who reads those things?" Placenta huffed.

"Which is why I'm telling you now," Sandy said with a touch of exasperation.

"So what were they fighting over?" Polly asked. Sandy looked back at the pool to make certain that she wasn't being overheard. "It looked like a DVD. When I searched the grounds close to where the altercation took place, all I found was a disc jewel case."

Placenta remembered, "Raul, our gardener, found a DVD. I stashed it with the others."

Sergeant Sandy looked anxious. "I should take a look at it. To make my report as specific as possible."

"It's lost among a bunch of other DVDs and CDs with missing covers," Placenta said. "I'll take a look for it in the morning."

"I'm only offering a verbal account of what I witnessed because the young man is a guest in your home and you should be aware that he may be prone to hostility," Sandy said in an officious tone.

Polly nodded. "That's the name of the game. Well, almost. He worked for one of the dead judges on that new reality show *I'll Do Anything to Become Famous*. It's considered a requirement that all the players ... and perhaps staff ... have a history of ... shall we say ... strong personalities. We'll keep an eye on him."

Sergeant Sandy placed her cap back on her head of severely pulled back hair and gave a two-finger salute. "Back to my rounds. I can take the disc now, if you'd like. Save you an extra chore come tomorrow."

"I won't forget," Placenta said dismissively.

Sergeant Sandy looked at Polly and bid goodbye with a curt, "Ma'am." She looked at Placenta and again said, "Ma'am." And then she walked into the darkness.

Once again, the cacophony from the pool enveloped the atmosphere and Polly and Placenta turned toward the roughhousing. Polly stood up and Placenta followed her. They walked to the edge of the pool, its water choppy from all the splashing and diving. "Which one of you is Shamu?" Polly called out.

"Join us!" Randy yelled over Tim's and Michael's laughter and sloshing water.

"Too wet!" Polly called back.

"It's called water," Randy yelled out.

"Can't ruin my new do," Polly added, patting her hair. "We're going inside for another bottle. You boys keep playing. Shall I fetch Tim's ducky?"

"We'll join you in a little while," Randy called out as Michael made another cannonball dive and displaced enough water to quench an entire drought-ravaged village in Africa.

Walking back to the house as casually as they could, Polly said, "Where did you put that damn security report?"

Placenta said, "It's in the top drawer of the sideboard in the foyer!" They both raced through the house, and when they arrived in the front hallway, Polly pulled open the center drawer of the table and retrieved a manila envelope. She tore it open and found three pages of notes on lined white paper. She handed the pages to Placenta. Polly withdrew a smaller envelope from within and ripped that open. An empty DVD case fell to the floor. Polly bent down and retrieved it. She squinted to read the handwriting on the thin plastic box. *Anything Goes.* 4 of 6," she read.

"It's that old movie you *borrowed* from Lisa," Placenta said.

"So what was it doing out in the yard?"

Placenta shrugged. "Tim was probably playing Frisbee with the gardeners again."

Polly grimaced. "He's got to stop teasing Fernando! Where did you put Lisa's other discs?"

Placenta turned and walked down the corridor toward the great room. Polly followed and when they were at the custom built-in DVD library shelves they scanned the jewel cases to no avail. "I couldn't find the damn case, so I slipped the disc into one of the others from Lisa. Perhaps Miranda tried to pilfer a memento from a legend's house and Michael tried to get them back for us," Polly said. "That's how it ended up in the backyard."

"She doesn't seem the type to care about old third-rate movie musicals," Placenta said as she moved to the other side of the cabinet. There, in a catchall drawer, she sifted through a large number of DVDs that hadn't been returned to their proper slots in the cabinet. "Ah!" she said, picking up the other discs in the series marked *Anything Goes.* She counted out, "'Six of six. Two of six. Three of six." In a moment she had accounted for all the other discs. "What would Miranda have wanted with an old movie musical with mostly dead stars anyway?" she asked, handing the discs to Polly.

"Perhaps she has a sweet tooth for Mitzi Gaynor."

"Who doesn't?" Placenta mocked.

"I haven't even had an opportunity to watch these yet. And why the hell doesn't that sucky film fit on one disc?" Polly said. "Six sections? Absurd!"

Polly thought for a moment. "Here's a great idea! Tomorrow, let's have a flick fest! We'll show Michael what Hollywood musicals used to do for the soul."

"Escapism during the Great Depression," Placenta said. "Michael's not exactly cultured. I'll bet the house that *High School Musical 3, Mamma Mia,* and *Hairspray* are the extent of his understanding of the musical genre."

"*I'll Do Anything* … is back in production tomorrow," Placenta reminded her. "He'll be doing gofer stuff until after the show on Friday."

"We'll watch the film ourselves," Polly said in a huff. She slipped the last jewel case in the six-chapter series into the alphabetized nook of the DVD shelf. "Maybe ol' Mitzi'll come over and watch herself with us. She's always good for a few drinks and a naughty laugh or two."

"Who's naughty?"

Polly and Placenta were startled by the sound of Michael's voice. Standing in the great room wearing nothing but a wet pair of Tim's swimming trunks, Michael grinned when he saw the two women absorbing him with their appreciative eyes. "Tim asked me to grab another bottle of champagne, if that's okay."

Placenta turned around and walked to the wine cooler. She withdrew a bottle of Veuve and handed it to Michael. "Save some for us. We'll follow your puddles and be along in a jiff."

Michael was about to leave when Polly said, "*Anything Goes. I'll do Anything ...* Kinda similar titles, when you stop and think about it."

Michael gave her a quizzical look. "Yeah. I guess. Like *CSI: Miami* and *CSI: New York*." He turned and walked out of the room.

"Of course, he's right," Polly said. "For a moment I had a silly notion that there might be a connection between our show and the old film."

"One stars Bing Crosby. The other stars Taco Belle. Yeah, there's a connection. They both have big ears," Placenta said.

"Never mind," Polly said. "Let's go help the men pop their cork."

By the time the men stepped out of the pool and wrapped themselves in beach towels, Placenta was serving snacks. Michael looked at Polly and asked, "Why are you being so nice to me? I mean, I appreciate your generosity and hospitality, but why me?"

"Because I couldn't bear to see you living in that squalor!" Polly said. "If it were a proper boardinghouse, with your own room and a bed, instead of little more than a tent, it wouldn't have been so dreadful. But for crying out loud, who is the landlord, and how many tenants does he have? And, if you don't mind me asking, what is he charging?"

"I found the place on the bulletin board at the community college. The rent of two hundred fifty dollars a week is steep, but it was the best I could do right now," Michael said. "There's, like, ten guys living in the house."

"You're paying a thousand dollars a month! You could find a decent apartment for that price!"

"Not without a first and last month's rent in advance. I don't have the money."

"The slumlord is raking in the dinero!" Placenta said. "I suppose you all share one bathroom."

Michael nodded his head in despair. "One stall shower. Newspapers for a bath mat. And the roaches! They keep me awake at night. I can hear them scurrying around the kitchen, which is close to where my part of the living room is. I know they're plotting to eat me."

"Couldn't you find a roommate in a better part of town?" Tim asked, looking around his mother's house and feeling more fortunate than ever.

Michael sighed. "Too expensive. I'm here to be a screenwriter. It's tough now, but someday I'll be one of your neighbors. I'm sure of it."

"What about getting a better job?" Placenta asked. "You seem like a smart young man. I'll bet you can find something over at Brooks Brothers, or Barney's."

"I've been looking," Michael said. "When I finally landed the assistant job on *I'll Do Anything* ... I thought I was definitely on my way. I mean, working with a famous celebrity like Thane Cornwall, even though he was a mean son of a bitch, I had my foot in the door. It doesn't pay much, but the experience is more valuable than eating three squares a day. I had to find a cheap place to crash, and that's where I ended up."

Placenta tsk-tsked. "You were buddy-buddy with Toe Nail, why couldn't you two pool your resources and move in together?"

"The guy's a killer," Michael said.

Polly gasped.

Placenta's eyes grew wide with intrigue.

Randy said, "Let me get my tape recorder."

"No. Not a death row inmate kind of killer," Michael said. "Just your average watch-your-back hard-boiled thug who's on his way to fame when he wins the contest. The only reason he had me hanging around was to use me. He thought that since I worked for Thane, and now Richard, I'd be helpful in finding the treasure. That's why we were in Lisa's apartment."

"Treasure?" Polly said.

Michael was quiet for a long moment. After a sip from his glass of champagne he looked Polly in the eye and said, "Rumor has it that someone connected with the show … probably one of the judges … has the Holy Grail. So to speak. There's something, somewhere, that when found, will be the key to winning the contest. At least Toe Nail thinks so."

Polly gave Michael a hard look. "Where did Mr. Nail get such an idea?"

"This isn't a scavenger hunt," Tim added. "The contestants are supposed to show how desperate they are to become famous by doing extraordinarily egregious things. How could something as simple as finding this treasure or whatever it is help? And who told Toe Nail about this in the first place?"

Michael shrugged. "Me, I guess. The day before Thane died I overheard him talking to Steven Benjamin on the phone. I remember he said, 'You'll never find it. But whoever does … 'big money,' as they say on *Wheel of Fortune.*'"

Polly took another swallow from her glass. "That doesn't mean anything at all. So what? You overheard part of a one-way telephone conversation. You don't even know what the heck they were talking about. They could have been talking about buying a vowel from Vanna White!"

"Except that Lisa said something to me earlier that I didn't give a second thought to at the time," Michael said. "It was after one of the bajillion instances when Thane reduced me to tears for something, I don't even remember what it was. Lisa happened to come along right afterward. We talked for a while; then she said she had to rush to do an errand for her boss. She said, 'You think you've got troubles? You're in clover compared to some other people associated with this stupid show. If those idiotic contestants would just keep their eyes open, they wouldn't have to do much to win the game.' Then she looked down at a black zippered purse that she was holding. She clutched it tight to her chest and sang, 'He knows when you've been bad or good, so be good, for goodness' sake!'"

"Here we go again," Polly snorted. "All of these cryptic comments out of context! 'Santa Claus Is Coming to Town?' In August? Not unless Oprah drops a new Rolls down my chimney."

Michael sighed. "I'm really sorry," he said. "You guys are being so great to me. I just thought maybe that information might come in handy. It's probably nothing. But then…"

Polly and her clique looked at Michael.

"With a couple of dead bodies, there might be something to the rumor," he continued. "I mean, why would Danny come to this house and wind up a corpse? And why would Thane get whacked? What if someone was looking for something that really exists? First at Thane's, then here? Two people died at judges' homes. If you'd been home, who knows what would have happened?" Michael picked up his wristwatch, which he'd laid on the table before diving into the pool. "I'm calling in sick tomorrow. I need to get used to this place. Now I'll hit the sack."

CHAPTER 17

—✍—

After air kisses from Polly and a firm handshake from Randy, Michael followed Tim and Placenta back into the house. They ascended the Scarlett O'Hara Memorial Staircase to the second level of the mansion and wandered down the east corridor. As Michael passed a gallery of memorabilia from Polly's long and illustrious career, he tried to remain indifferent. However, when he saw an autographed photo of Gilda Radner he stopped in his tracks. "Did your mom know her?" he asked with awe.

"Gilda was one of Polly's best friends. They idolized each other," Tim said. "She was on Mom's show a lot." He pointed to another photo. "There they are at Carnegie Hall. They sold out the whole place."

For the first time since meeting Polly and her clan, Michael was truly impressed. "I didn't know that your mother was all that famous," he said. "That idiot Steven Benjamin introduces her as 'a legend from the last century,' so I thought she was a nobody, like a lot of judges on reality shows."

Placenta chuckled. "Trust me, Polly won't let you leave the house without knowing exactly how famous she used to be, er, is. Every overnight guest to the plantation gets the same parting gifts: a promo bumper sticker from her short-lived career as an AM drive-time DJ." He pointed to a framed photo of her Rolls-Royce with a colorful sticker on the back that read *PP In Your Car!* "You'll also receive the superdeluxe boxed DVD collector's edition of classic sketches from *The Polly Pepper Playhouse*. Watching those discs, you'll be so tired of seeing old stars like Linda Lavin, Kim Darby, Cesar Romero, and Nancy Wilson, your eyes will be bleeding.

"I've heard of Cesar," Michael said. "My folks took me to a fancy restaurant when I graduated from high school, and it was on the menu."

"Not unless you went to McCannibal's," Tim laughed. "He's not a salad. And not a Roman emperor either. He was an old-time movie star. Dead now, but a big heart-throb in his day. Anyway, Mom had a crush on him when she was a little girl, so when she got to be important and famous she had him on her show."

Although Placenta had passed this gallery of photos every day for years, it had been a very long time since she had taken a close look at the pictures. "There's Martha Rae," she said, pointing to a framed photograph of Polly and Martha onstage holding hands raised in the air. "Oh, and Johnny Carson," she said, pointing to another picture. "That's Shirley MacLaine and Bob Newhart on the couch next to her."

"Wow," Michael said. "Polly was once a little girl who grew up and made all of her dreams come true. I don't know why Thane hated her so much."

Tim looked at Michael. "Thane hated everyone. Mom didn't take it personally."

"For some reason, he had a special dislike for your mother," Michael added.

"She never did anything to him," Placenta said.

"Some people don't need a reason for not liking some other people," Michael said. "I think he thought that Polly was too sweet to be real. I've found out today that he was so wrong! But you're right, he didn't have much of anything good to say about anyone. Except…"

"You mean there was one person on the planet to whom he wasn't a nasty so-and-so?" Tim asked.

"Who was the lucky dog?" Placenta encouraged. "I'll bet it *was* his dog!"

"He didn't have one," Michael confirmed.

"Then his own mother?" Tim said. "Even serial killers love their mothers. They kill 'em, and cook their organs, and stuff 'em like a taxidermied deer head over the mantel, but they still love 'em, in a queer sorta way."

Michael whispered, "Steven."

Tim and Placenta gave Michael a confused look.

"Steven Benjamin," Michael said. "Thane used to worship the man. They were best buds when I started working there. Then something happened."

"All those mean on-air innuendos hinting about Steven's sexuality weren't just for fun?" Placenta said.

"In the beginning they were on the phone together and at each other's homes all the time. Never one to give credit where credit was due, Thane actually admitted that Steven was entirely responsible for getting Richard Dartmouth to hire him as a judge in the first place. They had a weird relationship."

"Were they having an affair?" Tim asked.

"Nah," Michael responded. "Thane was a totally straight dude. And Steven has a really hot babe for a wife. She's a famous model from England. Thane and Steven just got downright nasty with each other."

"What happened?" Placenta asked.

Michael shrugged. "One day it's kissy-kissy; then suddenly there was genuine hatred between them. Thane wouldn't take Steven's calls."

Tim pondered the situation. "Maybe Thane came on to Steven's wife?"

"Nah. I think it was a business thing," Michael said. "Or maybe it was the hate mail that started pouring in. There are tons of crazies out there. You know the type. A lot of people have nothing better to do than comment on what they see on television. They like a certain star, in this case Steven Benjamin, and if anyone says anything against them, they go ballistic. One of my jobs was to copy the hate letters that Thane got each week, before sending the originals to Sterling's legal department."

"Were there threats against Thane's life?" Placenta asked.

"Sure," Michael said, as if that were a no-brainer. "But it's hard to take anyone seriously when they write in all lowercase letters, spell everything phonetically: 'Sycotic. Saten.' And beg that for the sake of his soul, Thane had to mend his evil ways or go straight to hell. There was only one letter that I knew bothered Thane."

"A threat?" Tim asked.

"I never got to read it. It was from Steven Benjamin and marked 'Personal. For Thane Cornwall's Eyes Only.' Come to think about it, they had their falling-out at that time."

As the trio walked farther along the corridor, Polly and Tim glanced at each other. "And we're here," Placenta said, stopping outside a multipaneled oak door. "'The Vanessa Williams Success-is-the-Best-Retribution Room.' Hope you don't mind the collage from her starring role in that infamous layout for *Penthouse* magazine." Placenta opened the bedroom door and led the way into the guest suite.

Michael suddenly turned around and drew Tim into a tight hug. After a long moment, he let go and said, "Let me die in my sleep tonight. I never want to wake up from this dream."

Placenta chuckled and continued to play docent as she pointed out all the amenities of the suite. "Flat-screen television and plenty of DVDs. Wet bar. Computer. Balcony overlooking the garden." Then she escorted Michael into the bathroom. "Steam room. Rain shower. Jacuzzi tub. Electric toothbrush. Bubble bath. Intercoms in all the rooms. If you need anything push the green button and someone will answer." She pointed a stern finger at Michael. "Don't even think of using it while I'm trying to sleep! I've laid out all your clothes," Placenta said. "A pair of Tim's pj's is under your pillow. We keep buying them, and he just wears the same old T-shirt and boxers! Breakfast is at eight. Nighty-night."

Tim said good night too, and followed Placenta out the door. When they were far enough down the hallway, Placenta whispered, "We've gotta tell Polly about Steven and

Thane. Hurry, before she passes out, or Randy hauls her up to her room."

When Tim and Placenta were once again in the great room, they pounced on Polly. In their haste to report what Michael had said, they stumbled over each other's sentences.

"Thane ... secret ... Steve," Tim said, trying to speak while catching his breath.

"No!" Placenta scolded. "Letter ... Thane ... Mean..." she wheezed.

"Kissy-kiss..." Tim said.

"Friends ..."

Polly looked at Randy, who was in mid-pour of champagne into her glass. "Either these two have just had simultaneous strokes, or they need a padded cell," she said. Then looking at her son and maid, she said, "What the hell are you two babbling about? Here," she said, handing her glass to Tim, then giving Randy's glass to Placenta. "Drink up and calm down."

Making a face as she drank the entire flute of champagne, Placenta said, "Too warm."

Tim, too, finished his bubbly in almost one long swallow. Then he looked at his mother and said, "Thane had a crush on Steven Benjamin."

"I knew he was gay!" Polly said.

"They were just pals," Placenta replied.

"They hated each other's guts," Polly countered. "Michael told us that all that animosity between Thane and Steven was relatively new. They once were very close."

"Once, I had a secret love," Polly began to sing an old Doris Day song. "Gay!"

"Mother!" Tim parried. "Thane was a hetero hound. And Steven's apparently married to a hot babe! Michael thinks a disgruntled fan killed Thane."

"Not so fast," Placenta said. "Thane got tons of threatening letters from Steven's fans and people who didn't like the way he treated contestants. That doesn't mean someone followed through."

Randy cleared his throat. "As a matter of fact, whenever a celebrity gets killed we always consider the possibility of a loony tunes fan doing the deed. I've personally read some of Thane's fan mail. There's zero shred of evidence to support a theory that a freak-o Steven fanatic did the job."

"Damn it all!" Placenta said, pulling the champagne bottle out of the ice bucket and pouring herself another glass. "Just when we think we've got a clue, you go and throw cold water on our theory." She took a sip from her glass. "As a matter of fact, I didn't really think that Thane was killed by a fan. I'm still intrigued by that so-called trophy or treasure idea. Something that supposedly holds all the secrets."

Tim nodded. "Yeah, I'll wager that the killer thought that one of the judges had possession of it. They got to Thane first. Then they came here. If Brian winds up dead, we'll know that we're on the right track."

"However, if someone wrings Ms. Saddleback's neck first, we won't know if it's our killer or just someone who's tired of her whiny right-wing 'Jesus for President' voice ringing in their ears," Placenta said.

"I'm not sure that I buy that trophy theory either," Polly said. "What is it, the Maltese Falcon, for heaven's sake? And I'm Sam Spade!" The room was silent for a moment. Then

Polly added, "We've been dreadful hosts! It's been a week since our last dinner party!"

Tim moaned, and Placenta sighed.

"It's time we invited the dear Brian Smiths and Steven Benjamins over for a light repast," Polly said. She looked at Tim. "Call up Bob Mackie and make an appointment for Michael to be fitted for a tux." Then she looked at Placenta. "Use the leftovers from last week's soiree. They'll never know the difference. I'm going to bed." She held out her hand for Randy to take.

CHAPTER 18

— ❧ —

During the pre-dinner party staff meeting in the dining room, Polly told Sergeant Sandy to relax her security rules for the night. She made it clear that she didn't want them to suffer the humiliation of anyone being patted down and detained while their immigration status was being verified. "These people are my guests and they should feel as comfortable in my home as I do in Mark Harmon and Pam Dawber's."

Placenta said, "You wouldn't feel so comfy and cozy if Pam knew how much you lusted after her husband."

"Nonsense!" Polly spat. "Pam isn't an idiot. She knows how I, and bajillions of others, feel about Mr. Mark. Pam's a darling who cleans up my drool, and Timmy's, too, without any fuss."

Tim looked around the table, which he and Placenta had set with Polly's most elegant china and Waterford stemware. "Place cards," he replied as he retrieved small Post-its-size Crane stationery on which he had hand-inscribed their guests' names in calligraphy. He placed Polly's card in its

PP-monogrammed crystal holder at her place setting, then set Placenta's at the opposite end of the table. "Where do you want me to sit tonight?"

Polly nibbled on her thumbnail as she tried to picture where each guest should be seated. "Um, I'm placing you and Michael in the middle on either side of the table. Steven and Brian will be on my left and right, respectively. We'll seat their wives next to you and Michael." Starting at her place, and going around the table, Polly pointed with her index finger and said, "Girl, boy. Boy, girl. Girl, girl. Boy, boy."

Placenta frowned. "It's supposed to be boy, girl, boy, girl, all the way around."

"Screw Miss Manners," Polly said. Then she looked at her wristwatch. "Holy moly! They'll be here in two hours. I'm nowhere near ready!"

As Sergeant Sandy left the dining room and headed back to complete another circuit around the estate, Polly flew out of the room and headed toward the Scarlett O'Hara Memorial Staircase. "What am I wearing?" Polly called back to Placenta. "Oh, and any luck with getting Patricia Arquette to do her 'Medium' shtick after dinner?" she yelled to Tim.

As Polly ascended the staircase, Placenta was immediately behind her and said, "You'll be in a smart cocktail dress. The silver one you wore to Star Jones's divorce party. And no, Patty wasn't available. At this late notice we'd be lucky to get the 1-800-Dentist guy suggesting root canal specialists."

"That should make everybody eager to drink the Kool-Aid," Polly snapped as she walked down the corridor toward her room, undressing as she went along, and passing each garment item to Placenta. "I'll have to be entertainment enough."

Shortly after seven o'clock, Sandy's voice crackled through the intercom system. In every room, the residents heard, "Please be advised that a party of four, consisting of Mr. and Mrs. Steven Benjamin, and Mr. and Mrs. Brian Smith, has arrived. Their ETA at your doorstep is ... one, one thousand. Two, one thousand. Three, one thousand. Ding-dong!" Just then the doorbell rang.

Gathering with her family in the foyer, Polly patted Tim's cheek and smiled at Michael as she straightened his black clip-on bow tie. Then she twirled around in her cocktail dress and said, "Anything hanging out that shouldn't?"

"You were wise to go with the pearls," Placenta assured Polly.

Polly frowned and said, "Don't forget to return my emeralds before you go to bed!"

Tim opened the double entry doors.

As the guests entered the mansion, they oohed and aahed at the fabled home of Polly Pepper. The mistress of the manor graciously accepted a bottle of red wine wrapped in colorful cellophane and ribbons from Brian, and a bouquet of Casablanca lilies from Tiara Benjamin. Polly cooed to her guests, "You shouldn't have, but I'm glad you did." Then she handed the tokens off to Placenta. After initiating hugs and reintroducing everyone to each other, Polly called out, "Follow the leader," and led the way to the formal sunken living room. Tim politely waited to be the last in tow.

As Michael had done the night before, the new arrivals tried to maintain an air of indifference; however, they were unable to conceal their obvious awe at being in a residence that always made the top ten lists of both dream vacation destinations and fantasy final resting places.

"Sit! Sit!" Polly graciously encouraged.

As her guests settled onto the sofa and deep chairs facing the large stone fireplace, Polly stood under a special amber pin spotlight in the center of the room and displayed a dazzling smile, which showed off her large teeth and famous overbite. "I was just about to indulge with a teensy drop of champers. May I ask Placenta to serve the same to you? Or perhaps a martini? A Black Dahlia? Something stronger. A Slovenian Sphinx?"

Brian's wife said, "I'll have whatever you're having, Miss Pepper. The *National Peeper* says that your champagne arrives via armored truck, so it must be good stuff."

"Don't believe everything you read about me in that gruesome rag, dear," Polly laughed. "And please, drop the Miss Pepper routine! I'm just Polly! And I'll call you…" For an instant Polly was stumped. Then she quickly ad-libbed, "Well, I refuse to call you Mrs. Smith. You're not a frozen pie!"

To Polly's infinite gratitude, her guest said, "I'm just plain ol' Lyndie."

"Plain is too far from the truth!" Polly enthused. "You're as beautiful as Michelle Obama!" Then she turned to Tiara Benjamin. "I saw that famous Chanel ad that you did for *Vogue*. The one where you were holding a flute of champagne in one hand, and the Hope diamond in the other.

You were licking the stone as if the facets tasted better than a chocolate-covered strawberry. Mmm. My kind of dessert! I'll guess champagne for you, too, dear?"

"Brilliant!" Tiara said with a lilting British accent. "Stevie'll have the same, won't you, Kitten?"

"Ditto for me," said Brian as Placenta, having anticipated the orders, appeared in the room with a tray of champagne flutes.

She served Polly first, and when she offered the last glass to Steven she grinned and said, "And one for— 'Kitten.'"

When everyone was served, Polly announced, "A toast! To our darling new friends, who honor us with their presence at Pepper Plantation this evening. And to Thane Cornwall, who obviously can't join us, but is certainly here in spirit." Everyone was stone-faced. Just as Polly and her guests were about to place their lips to the rims of their glasses, Polly added, "And to Trish S. Thank you for being too busy speaking to the NRA's 'Aim for Jesus' seminar to join us!" She then sucked up half of the champagne in her glass and held it out for a refill. "Lovely," she sighed.

Steven Benjamin clinked his glass against Tiara's and savored a small sip. "And to Polly Pepper and her famous generosity. We appreciate your invitation, and we know that Michael over there is thrilled to be staying in this beautiful mansion. Word's gotten around." He looked at Michael and added, "You clean up pretty good, kid."

"I guess every man looks good in a tux," Michael preened.

Polly smiled. "We're delighted that he's with us. Tim needed a playmate, Placenta needs more cleaning chores, and I needed to feel wanted since Richard Dartmouth obviously doesn't plan to include me on the show anymore."

Brian raised his glass. "Richard's a douche bag."

All eyes in the room instantly turned toward Brian. Until this moment, his reputation for being well mannered nearly matched Polly Pepper's. He added, "If you think Thane was a miserable prick, and God knows he was, you should see Richard Dartmouth in action. He makes me wonder if the killer got the right judge."

"He is pretty evil," Steven agreed as Placenta appeared with a silver tray bearing her famous salmon tortilla appetizers. Steven accepted a cocktail napkin and selected a wedge of the offering.

"Thane was a lunatic, no two ways about it," Michael said. "Yeah, Richard's scary too, and I know for a fact that his assistant, Lisa, was desperate to find another job, before she got tagged as a killer. But he's nothing compared to that temper-throwing, malevolent Darth Vader I slaved for."

The sounds issuing from the others in the room seemed to confirm Michael's assessment of the dead talent. Tiara nodded vigorously, as Brian shook his head in disgust. Lyndie Smith made a face and rolled her eyes. "I've heard all the horror stories from Brian," she said. "Thane was particularly vicious to my man. All those insults about being a former Pip. I would have strangled him, if I were Brian."

Steven, too, nodded. "Richard can cut steak with his tongue, but Thane would gnaw through concrete without breaking a tooth."

Polly looked at Steven. "I was under the impression that you and Thane were dear friends. I thought that all that onstage ribbing was just to add a little spice to the evenings. It's a damn shame when relationships fizzle."

Steven took another sip from his glass and shrugged. "A friend is someone you can count on. Not so with Mr. Thane Cornwall. You try to do a friend a favor and he stabs you in the back."

"Literally," Tiara said.

Polly took another long swallow from her glass, then stood. "I'm starving! Let's have num-nums!" Relief among the guests was palpable. As Polly conducted the train of people toward the formal dining room, she said, "If you don't like sauteed beaver on a bed of sea moss, blame Placenta. She was in charge of the meal." Her guests gave each other looks of horror. "I'm teasing, of course!" Polly trilled. "But I hope you like your porcupine, tartare."

While still laughing uncomfortably, everyone arrived in the dining room. As the guests found their appointed places, Tim gallantly helped his mother into her chair. "If you'll excuse us for a wee moment-o, we'll be back in a jiff," he said as he and Placenta retreated to the kitchen. When they returned bearing trays of soup bowls, Polly was already holding court. "John Wayne, too! I swear!" she laughed, obviously telling her old story about the time the screen legend appeared on *The Polly Pepper Playhouse,* and arrived for rehearsals wearing nothing but a mink coat. "Trust me," she continued, "there's a reason why some men are called 'cock of the walk.'"

All were served, and Tim and Placenta took their seats. "First this simple starter. Cream of hibiscus soup. Then we'll go on to plain of Provencal chicken with olives, tomatoes, and red peppers. And I shan't propose another toast or offer grace," Polly said to the relief of all. "Let's just enjoy our meal and the time we have together. We'll forget about the dreadfulness of Thane being murdered in his bed, and that poor Danny boy took his last breath right here in this hallowed house. Oh, we forgot to show you the spot where he died! How thoughtless of Placenta!"

She looked at Tim. "Make a note to place a black wreath to mark the spot."

Polly then looked at Brian and said, "After dessert we'll have a look-see and play twenty questions about how you all think he came to expire in my lovely home."

"Left for dead on a cold marble floor! I wonder what his last thoughts were?" Tim said.

"Probably how exciting it was to die in a spot once featured in *Home & Garden* magazine," Polly said. "Start eating!" she implored, picking up her spoon. "Don't let my running on at the mouth keep you from enjoying the soup while it's still hot!"

By the time the second course was served, the camaraderie was easy. Everyone at the table heaped praise on Polly, even as Placenta patted herself on the back for being able to follow the recipe. "Oh, the competition and feuding that go on behind the scenes of a television show," Polly said. "If fans ever knew the truth! Don't you agree?

"I clearly remember when Laura Crawford … you remember that little witch who was part of the company of regulars on *The Polly Pepper Playhouse* … had the freak accident of a number-one hit record with some stupid country song about a woman in a poor mining town. She wins the big state lottery but refuses to take the gazillion-dollar prize because the man she loves—some grimy mole who works a thousand miles down in a hole—would feel bad that she could afford to buy the whole damn mountain while he only earned a few bucks an hour. She was retarded! Oh, the idiot woman in the song too!"

Polly looked at the disillusioned faces of Tiara and Lyndie. "What? The song? Oh, I know she massacred it."

"You just burst my bubble about sweet Laura Crawford," Lyndie said.

"Sweet?" Polly said. "So sorry, dears. I thought it was common knowledge that the real Laura Crawford— baby voice and dimples and all—is a major freakazoid! She wanted my job! Seriously! That little inept Eve Harrington thought she had talent and could carry an entire show. Ha!" Polly stopped for another sip of champagne. "Here's a little secret. One of the other regulars on the show … I'm not naming names … but this person was known for his or her comic genius, and equally sullen attitude … was plotting to have the lovely and talented Laura Crawford eliminated from this world. Of course, when I discovered what was up, I had to intervene."

"Yeah, because she was popular and the ratings would have tumbled," Tim said.

"Every show I've ever worked on had a Laura Crawford," she sighed. "I thought that Thane Cornwall was ours, but now I suspect it was either one of the contestants or, more than likely, Lisa Marrs, as the police are saying."

"I'm still shocked," Lyndie Smith said. "I mean, I only met Lisa Marrs once, and I confess she seemed to have a lot of ambition, but I would never have suspected that she was a killer. As for the contestants, I find it hard to believe that anyone would want to be famous badly enough to kill for it."

"You've never wanted to be famous, so you don't know the extremes to which others will go for success," Brian Smith snapped at his wife. "You don't know what it's like being somebody, and then have it all end, but you keep trying to get the celebrity back. Some people would kill to live in a big house like this one." He looked around the elegant room. "You set the bar on success in your life pretty low."

Shocked, everyone looked at Brian, and then at Lyndie, who was mortified.

Lyndie picked up her champagne glass and took a long silent swallow. When she set her flute down on the table she turned to Polly. With a calm and reassuring voice she said, "I never had an ego that demanded everybody pay attention to me. As for setting the bar too low, perhaps Brian is right. I should have expected that the man I married would never humiliate me in public."

There was a good reason why Polly Pepper was considered a gracious hostess. Not only were her parties fun and entertaining, but also she had a great talent for making even the most distressing social situation seem of little consequence. She now put the full force of her powers to work. She raised her champagne flute to Lyndie and said, "At last! I have a new lifelong friend who knows that fame and fortune are hardly all they're cracked up to be. Those poor kids on the show think that getting their names in the newspapers will solve their self-esteem issues. Only therapy, and a lot of drugs, can do that! Am I right, Lyndie? Or am

I right!" Polly looked around as all glasses, except Brian's, were simultaneously raised to her.

"Hear! Hear!" Placenta said. "What good is fame unless it comes with a poop load of money? Preferably in euros. God knows the U.S. dollar is in the crapper!"

Brian looked at Lyndie. "It was the champagne speaking. I'm never rude in public. You know me. I'm sweet. I make brownies to bring to work!"

"Tell it to Michael Richards," Lyndie said.

Tiara turned to Lyndie and said, "I love your brownies. Sometimes Steven brings a few home. But there's no use in pretending that you don't do the baking! With all the time that Brian and Steven spend at the studio, neither has time for anything domestic."

Lyndie managed a slight laugh. "Brian's actually a very good cook. And since he only has to go to the studio on Fridays for the show, he has plenty of time to stir up Rice Krispies treats … if nothing else."

Tiara gave Steven a searching look and said, "I guess the hours are a lot different for the host. Stevie's never home."

Polly exchanged curious looks with Tim. "*I'll Do Anything to Become Famous* clearly would have been the ideal show for me," she said. "Working just one day a week was swell. And the money was pretty great. That schedule could have given me time to earn a few bucks and still volunteer in the psoriasis ward at Cedars."

"I suppose that being the host of a show is much more time consuming than judging the contestants," Tiara said. "Sometimes Steven doesn't get home until well past the time I've gone to bed."

"Ah, the hours one keeps in order to maintain a level of success," Polly agreed. "If I have one regret it's that I worked all the years while Timmy was growing up. But I had my career. I couldn't let family get in the way." She looked across the table at her son. "Do you hate your legendary mommy for being away so much of your childhood?"

Tim rolled his eyes. "We've had this conversation a bajillion times," he said to the room. "Sometimes Polly thinks she should have stayed home and baked cookies for my Cub Scout troop. Trust me, if she'd baked anything, there would have been fatalities!"

"Speaking of fatalities, I hope we've seen the last of 'em. Among our group, I mean." Michael reached for the champagne bottle resting in an ice bucket on a stand to the side of his chair. "Four contestants remain. I remember Thane telling me that answering stupid questions was not going to produce a winner. The one who found the right key would easily trample the other competitors."

Steven Benjamin gave Michael a lethal look. "Actions speak louder than words, eh?"

Michael shrugged. "During one of the few times that Thane actually spoke to me, rather than scream, he said, 'Sterling Studios better have their accidental death and dismemberment insurance policy premiums paid up.'"

Polly shifted in her chair, and the others at the table leaned forward as if to better hear what Michael was saying.

"What's that supposed to mean?" Brian Smith asked. "Did Thane anticipate his death or Danny's?"

Michael continued. "I think he just knew that there's no place in Hollywood for losers. He predicted that Richard

224

Dartmouth had inadvertently, or maybe not so inadvertently, created a diabolical show. He said that as each contestant tried to outdo the others in the despicable-deed-to-succeed department, there would be a domino effect of everyone trying to outdo the others, and someone was going to get hurt. Or worse. But he also said that if any of them had brains, they'd figure out the one thing that would bring them the big prize."

Tiara Benjamin clasped her hands together and leaned her elbows on the table. She looked at her husband. "I remember Thane saying precisely that, before you two had your—"

Steven interrupted. "I'll bet he never expected to be the one that a contestant used to win the game. It's obvious that one of the kids killed him. Any wager that it was that scumbag Toe Nail?"

Michael countered. "Toe Nail is definitely serious about becoming famous in Hollywood, but I wouldn't bet the house that he's a killer. He looks the part of a maniac, but I don't believe that murder is his bag."

Brian Smith cleared his throat. "I wouldn't be surprised if Richard Dartmouth, the producer himself, got rid of Thane."

In an instant, everyone else at the table simultaneously said that was absurd, idiotic, stupid, wild, and …

"Actually, Richard shouldn't be ruled out as Thane's murderer either," Steven said. "Not only did he not want Thane on the show in the first place, he didn't waste any time filling Thane's job with his own butt in the judge's chair."

"Steven's the one who convinced Richard to give Thane a shot in the first place," Tiara said. "I remember that Richard was definitely opposed to Thane. He wanted someone who was already a big star in America. Someone that the audience demographic would tune in to watch. Isn't that right, Kitten? Steve and Thane were friends … used to be friends … from way back when they were both working for the modeling agency that represented me."

Steven said, "Thane was the publicity marketing director when we first met. I was starting out as a model and we became friends. I know that things didn't end well for us, and I'm sorry as hell that we didn't make up before he died. Of course we all want whoever killed him to be caught and executed. He or she should die the way Thane did."

Polly took another long swallow from her champagne flute. "What would Richard's motive be for doing away with Thane?" she asked. "Why not accuse Taco Belle? Or Amy Stout? It seems to me that they're the ones with more reason. Oh, and Miranda, too. Thane treated them all so shabbily on live network television."

Steven shook his head. "I'm just saying … I'm taking a wild guess," he said. "Sure, the others are just as high on the list of suspects, but the way Richard behaves … like he's the man with golden cojones."

As Placenta stood up to clear away the plates, she said, "If you ask me, they probably have the killer in jail right this minute."

Tim stood up to assist, and picked up his mother's empty plate. He added, "The Beverly Hills Police Department has made a few errors in the past, but all fingers still point to Lisa."

"Mine, too," Steven said. "She's probably guilty. After all, she was caught on the scene. She had the weapon. And a motive. She was a jilted lover."

Polly raised an eyebrow. "Then I'm guilty, too."

Tim and the others around the table looked at their hostess curiously.

"Guilty of being a poor judge of character," she said. "I liked Lisa Marrs. I even liked Richard Dartmouth. And I don't have a real problem with any of the contestants. So don't come asking me for an opinion on who killed Thane or Danny. I'm simply not equipped."

Tim nodded. "Mom has many talents. Feminine intuition is not one of them, unless it's the next fashion trend. Dessert?"

CHAPTER 19

—⁓—

"Not one of our better dinner parties," Polly said as she stepped out of her heels and plopped her tired body onto the sofa in the great room. She held out her glass for a refill. "Where's Michael?"

As Tim refilled his mother's glass with a cold bottle of Veuve, he said, "We should've had the 1-800-Dentist guy after all. As for our so-called guests, we go to the trouble and expense to feed and entertain a possible killer, and he or she doesn't have the proper etiquette to offer their wrists for handcuffs. I'd say it was a wasted evening. Michael went to bed."

Placenta joined Polly on the couch and slipped her shoes off, too. She rubbed her tired feet. "I'm with Tim. You drag those stiffs to our home, they guzzle our champers and chow down on our vittles. What do we get in return? One broken Waterford goblet, more stains on the tablecloth than there are on the reputations of Disney teen stars, and a stopped-up toilet. Who the hell doesn't know you can't flush those paper guest towels?" Polly took a small sip from her glass.

"You both whine too much," Polly continued. "Look on the bright side. So we lost an expensive glass. The gash in Tiara's hand didn't require stitches. And the cleaners may hate to see you coming with that nearly ruined heirloom tablecloth, Placenta, but when you explain that Joy Behar and Meghan McCain were here for dinner and had a little disagreement, they'll be thrilled to see famous laundry from Polly Pepper. As for the plumber, we'll get Timmy's favorite sexy drain opener here tomorrow. He'll be happy for the Sunday overtime, and Tim can help by holding his snake. So it's a win-win for all of us."

Suddenly, the door to the great room creaked open and everyone quickly turned their heads. Michael stood there wearing Tim's pajama bottoms and a white muscle shirt over his slight frame. Polly exhaled loudly. "Ovaltine time?"

Michael smiled. "I just wanted to say good night. I didn't mean to eavesdrop, but I heard all the positive things you just said. You really are as nice as everybody says."

"Skip the obvious, dear," Polly said. "Tim, pour another glass for our guest."

As Tim reached for a champagne flute from the cabinet behind the bar, Michael came into the room and settled onto the twin sofa opposite Polly and Placenta. He took a small sip from the glass that Tim handed to him, then made a face. "It doesn't mix well with Listerine."

"Next time, gargle with champagne. No chemical bumrn and you can swallow!" Polly said.

"The party was terrific," Michael said. "I totally expected that I'd go to swank Hollywood dinner parties eventually, but I thought it would be way in the future, when I'm a famous screenwriter. This makes it twice in as many weeks. I hope I used the right spoon for the soup!"

"You did very well, sweetums," Polly said. "I'm delighted that you enjoyed our wee repast. And I guess it really was a Hollywood dinner party, wasn't it? I never think of our little gatherings as such. But I suppose a bajillion people would kill for an invitation to be at my table. Many others—two of whom are in this room as I speak—don't understand my market value."

"You're 'the catch of the day,'" Placenta growled. After a moment during which Tim was weighing whether or not to compare his mother's fame to the price of a barrel of crude oil, Michael said, "Steven Benjamin has a bit of a problem, don't you think?"

All eyes turned to Michael. Polly said, "Um, that's exactly what I was thinking. Just so that I'm clear with my own suspicion, what's your take on the evening?" Michael took another swallow of his drink. "The dude is pathetic. Every time someone suggested that so-and-so was probably Thane's killer, he agreed. He doesn't have a clue. Can't make up his own mind about anything."

Polly considered the comment and recalled that indeed, when the topic of who murdered Thane came up, Steven suggested it had to be one of the contestants. "He was particularly suspicious of Toe Nail. Then, when Brian Smith suggested that it might be Richard Dartmouth, while everyone thought it an absurd idea, Steven was the only one who said that it made sense. And when Placenta pointed out the police probably had the killer in custody, Steven again agreed. It's weird."

Placenta said, "Maybe he's just an idiot who needs his wife to do the talking for him. After all, he used to be a model."

Polly finished her glass of champagne and said, "I've never known anyone who was successful in Hollywood to be stupid. You can't get to where Steven is without a brain. Or at least a talent for strategy. Yes, I'll give in and say that even Rob Schneider must have a few functioning neurons. Nah ... I take that back."

Tim emptied the last of the champagne into Michael's glass and sat down beside him. "You see Steven all the time at work, what do you think of him?"

"Again, weird comes to mind. I mean, the guy is supposed to be Mr. With-it and sophisticated. That's just an act for television, I guess. In person he's like one of those mice in a maze. Ya know, running around scared to death that he isn't going to find his piece of cheese. In Steven's case he's probably afraid of never getting another job."

Polly said, "The other surprise of the evening was Mr. Resentment."

"You mean Brian Smith," Placenta said matter-of-factly. "Yeah, that was astonishing. I didn't know anyone could harbor so much bitterness about no longer being a Pip. Jeez, man, get another life!"

"No doubt it didn't help that Thane treated him like a complete failure," Polly said. "Castigating him in front of the whole television audience for his lenient critiques of the contestants. Snarling that he was irrelevant to the show, and show business in general, would make anyone resentful and want to kill the bully."

"Nice guys are said to be a volcanic mass of neuroses ready to erupt without warning," Placenta added. "After Brian's performance tonight, I'm almost ready to put him at the top of my list of suspects."

Polly nodded. "Their wives seem to be lovely. Although how they put up with their men is another mystery I'd like to solve."

Michael smiled. "Girls go for dudes like Steven with money and power. Unless they have low self-esteem, in which case they go for guys like Brian." After a beat he said, "And I need my beauty sleep. I feel a yawn coming on." He stood and wished everyone a good night's rest.

"We're right behind you," Polly said, and made an air kiss "Mwah" sound. She picked up Michael's champagne flute and poured what remained into her own glass. "Pleasant dreamies."

When the room was once again their own, Placenta said, "Sweet kid. I'm glad we rescued him."

Tim nodded. "He's smart, too. And fun. We're going clubbing next Friday night."

Polly looked around. "He's a breath of fresh air in this musty, old, world-famous mansion. He's also cute and cuddly. But there's something not quite right. Did either of you notice that he didn't indict Miranda at dinner this evening?"

Tim and Placenta looked at Polly with perplexed expressions.

With a shrug, Polly said, "I just thought it was strange that after his altercation with Miranda last week—here in our backyard—he didn't bring her name up as a potentially more appropriate suspect than the others."

Tim knitted his eyebrows. "Hmm. Now that you mention it…"

Placenta added, "Perhaps I've been too quick to presume that champagne bubbles have marinated your brain cells."

Polly stood up and said, "Sleep on it. Let me know what you think in the a.m. Now I'm really going to bed. Big day tomorrow. We're going to interrogate Michael."

The late August early morning sunshine over Bel Air was enough to draw Michael to the Pepper Plantation garden, long before anyone else in the house was ready to face the day. As he wandered over the property, which was still moist with dew, he admired the roses, peonies, vine-covered arbors, and the trickling waterfall flowing into the koi pond. He found the park bench by the garden wall and took a seat to simply absorb the luxurious tranquility. At that moment, in the midst of the warm air scented by flowers, and the only sounds being the buzzing of busy bees, and twittering of birds, and gurgling of the waterfall, he knew what it was like to be Cinderella.

As he thought about having to eventually leave the mansion and return to the rooming house where his small space was defined by blankets hung over a clothesline, Michael was nearly catatonic with grief. He simply sat and stared into his future impoverishment. As he looked around, he became indignant over the fact that he had nothing in his life, not even a car. "Why do some people have everything, and I have nothing!" he spat. "Life is unfair." His reverie was shattered by a shadow that crept over him. He looked up.

"D'ja ever find what you and that Miranda girl lost last week?"

It was Sergeant Sandy, standing with her thumbs hooked over the waist of her beige uniform pants.

"Um, no. I mean, I don't know what you're talking about."

Sandy nodded. "Never mind. Just thought I'd try to help. If I knew what you were missing … I know pretty much every inch of this property now." She touched two fingers to her cap in a salute and turned to leave.

Michael called out, "As a matter of fact I did lose something last week. It was hardly worth remembering. Just an old CD of some favorite songs."

Sergeant Sandy turned around and looked Michael up and down. "Like I said, I know pretty much every inch of this estate. The gardener found your CD, er, it was actually a DVD. It's in my daily report."

"Report?" Michael asked.

"My minute-by-minute observations of what transpires on the estate."

"Miranda and I weren't fighting that night," Michael said for the record.

Sandy shrugged.

Michael tried not to show his agitation. "Great. You found the disc. Whew! Where is it now?"

"Last I heard, Placenta tucked it away. Probably in the great room."

Michael looked at his wristwatch. It was only eight o'clock. "What time does everybody finally get out of bed around here? Placenta's up early, isn't she?"

"It varies from day to day," Sergeant Sandy said. "I've only been here a week. But since it's Sunday, and y'all didn't get to bed until two forty-seven—it's in my partner's report—it may take a while for the star and her entourage to drag themselves away from their gilded dreams."

Michael finger-combed his hair. He looked at his watch again. He feigned a cough. "I guess if Placenta's not getting up for a while, I'll have to make myself a cup of coffee. Can I get one for you?"

Sergeant Sandy shook her head. "Had my tea. I'll finish my rounds."

Once the security guard had wandered past the koi pond, Michael hurried across the lawn toward the house. As he walked around the pool and stepped onto the patio he glanced in every direction. As quiet as the place seemed, he couldn't tell if he was actually alone. He furtively opened the French door leading into the kitchen. The first thing that Michael noticed was that the Mr. Coffee pot had not been turned on; a sure sign that no one in the house had yet awoken. Still, he walked around as silently as possible. He made his way out of the kitchen, passed the great room, and down the hall to the foyer. There, for a moment, he stood like a statue listening to every noise in the house. When Michael was confident that he was alone, he slowly and as quietly as possible opened the top drawer of the mirrored breakfront.

The only light in the foyer came from a stained glass window above the double entry doors. The sun was shining in the right direction and the room was flooded with enough illumination to clearly see into the dark drawer. Michael lifted out a *Harry & David* catalogue, an old copy of *Time* magazine, and a handful of fast food and take-out pizza menus. He realized this was a catchall drawer, and with each layer of junk he was farther away from anything as new as the security report from a week ago. He returned the contents and closed the drawer.

In an instant he realized that a DVD probably would have been returned to where he'd seen thousands of titles on built-in shelves. He cautiously made his way down the long hallway and entered the great room. He crossed the floor and stood before the enormous library of thousands of films and television shows that Polly and her family had amassed. His heart sank as he tried to figure out where to begin. "Jeez, these people are so freakin' anal about putting things away," he whispered to himself.

As Michael went from shelf to shelf he realized that there were multiple categories and subcategories for all the titles. There was a section for movie musicals in general, and within that section were rows devoted to MGM, Paramount, Twentieth Century Fox, and Columbia. Then the titles were further reduced to films starring Judy Garland, Fred Astaire and Ginger Rogers, Kathryn Grayson, Betty Hutton, and Ann Miller. The dramas and comedies were similarly categorized with Humphrey Bogart, Roz Russell, Tallulah Bankhead, Marilyn Monroe, and Jack Lemmon. All that Michael could remember about the disc he was looking for was that the title was hand-printed in blue Sharpie. He searched beyond the professionally pressed DVDs and homemade ones.

Michael looked at his watch. It was nearly eight thirty. Surely, he thought, by this time Placenta would likely be getting up. There was no time to waste. He pulled the library ladder over and climbed to the second step in order to reach the upper shelves of discs. He dragged his fingers across the spines of hundreds of jewel cases. Finally he came to a section that seemed to be for miscellaneous discs. He withdrew the first one from its slot. Through the clear plastic case he read the handwriting on the disc. *Abbott and Costello Show, 1966.* He slipped it back into place and took out the next one. *Actors Studio: Kim Hunter, 1948. Alfred Hitchcock Presents: Judy Canova, Robert Redford, Gena Rowlands."*

Michael looked at the shelf and knew it would take at least an hour to go through every title. He slipped the next jewel case out of its slot and read, *"Anything Goes. Part One of Six.*

"Yes!" he nearly shouted.

"You like old movies?"

At the unexpected voice of Placenta behind him, Michael was startled and lost his balance on the ladder. As he fumbled to regain his footing he knocked a dozen discs off the shelf and they crashed to the floor with the sound of plastic bouncing off the sandstone floor.

"Oh my God," Placenta cried, holding the ladder steady. "I didn't mean to scare you!"

His heart racing, Michael stepped off the ladder, avoiding the discs scattered at Placenta's feet. He forced a laugh and said, "You must be part cat."

Placenta and Michael simultaneously bent down to pick up the DVDs and their cases. "You looked bored walking around the estate and I saw you come in here. I figured you were probably watching television," Placenta said. "I just came to see if you were ready for breakfast. I'll put those back," she said, taking all the discs from Michael.

"Sorry about the mess," Michael said. "I can put them away."

"Nonsense," Placenta said. "Polly likes them a certain way. She's fussy about some things." She set the stack of discs on the custom-built cabinet and shelves. "The Sunday *Times* is on the patio table. I'll bring you a cup of coffee. Pancakes? Eggs? What would you like?"

Michael looked longingly at the stack of discs. "Pancakes would be awesome. Bacon, too, if it's no trouble."

"Your wish is my command." Placenta smiled, happy that she could show off her breakfast-making skills for someone who would appreciate her efforts. "Take a look at the headlines and let me know if we missed that dummy in the White House blowing up the planet while we slept."

By the time Michael was served his first cup of coffee, Tim straggled down from his room and took a seat opposite him. When Placenta handed him a mug she looked at Michael and said, "Don't take any offense, but Mr. Tim is a ceased engine when he sleeps. He can't get his jaw to move along with his thoughts until after his caffeine rush. He'll be a real, live, talking doll in a few minutes."

Tim looked up at Placenta and made a sound like something weak and dying.

"That's my boy," Placenta said. She retreated into the house and opened a carton of pancake batter.

After a few long swallows from his mug, Tim made the effort to say, "Hey."

"Hey, back," Michael responded. "Did you sleep well?"

"Mmm."

"Me too. Except for a dream about Thane," Michael said. "Obviously triggered by all that talk about who killed the son of a bitch."

Polly's voice was suddenly behind Michael's ear. "Such language on the Lord's Day. Oh hell, did I startle you, dear?" she asked as Michael spilled half his mug of coffee. "Join me for a BM. That'll settle you down." She took an empty juice glass and poured in a quarter of the Bloody Mary that Placenta had set at her place, and handed it to Michael. Picking up her little tea bell, Polly rang it aggressively.

"In a bloody minute!" she heard Placenta call from the kitchen.

"Must be pancake morning," Polly said. "She always makes a fuss when she's trying to get the edges just brown enough." She looked at Tim. "Did my boys sleep well? Oh, right, something about a Thane nightmare. Did he tell you where to find the buried treasure, or whatever it is?"

Michael looked at Polly with a blank stare. "Yo, ho, ho?"

Polly shrugged. "You once mentioned that Thane said there was a treasure. I was just hoping he came to you in your sleep and told you where X marks the spot."

Michael chuckled. "Right. Um, no. No nocturnal messages. No secrets from the dead."

Placenta appeared with a tray bearing a plate of blueberry pancakes, a stack of bacon, and two Bloody Marys. She set the meal before Michael and both glasses in front of Polly.

"Michael wants one too," Polly said, pointing to her drinks. Before she could object, Placenta removed one of the glasses and placed it before Michael.

"Are you up to eating solids this morning?" Placenta asked Polly.

Polly rolled her eyes and withdrew a stalk of celery from her glass. She playfully flicked it at Placenta, then defiantly took a large bite from the celery.

Placenta laughed as she retreated into the house to fetch another breakfast plate. When she returned with Polly's and Tim's meals she said, "By the by, I think we have an old-movie buff in our midst. Michael was having a swell time looking at all the DVDs in the library. Maybe you've finally found someone who'll watch *The Dolly Sisters* with you. God help the unfledged."

"Don't fall for the trap," Tim managed to say to Michael. "If you see one Betty Grable film you'll end up stuck with June Haver, Penny Singleton, and Dorothy Lamour. Save yourself, man!"

Polly took a long swallow from her glass and glared at Tim. "If you insult the memory of Betty Grable, you insult the industry that provided all that we have here. She was my idol. You've got your Bouncy—"

"Beyoncé ..."

"—I had Betty, and Doris Day, and Lena Home. Give me an MGM Technicolor musical over a Batman movie any day," Polly snapped.

Michael said, "My mother liked Doris Day. I'd love to watch one of her films with you."

"Brownnose," Tim mocked.

"Romance on the High Seas at one o'clock!" Polly smiled with satisfaction and finished her drink.

Tim stretched and moved his chair away from the table. "Thanks, Placenta," he called into the kitchen. Looking at his mother and Michael, he said, "I'd better call Royal Flush and get Trevor out here to fix the toilet. While you two are visiting with Miss Day, I'll be learning about what to do with a ballcock valve."

As Tim walked away from the table he called back, "Let's meet up at Lush Hour. Here. By the pool. Ta!"

Polly placed a hand on Michael's arm. "At last. It's just you and me. A full day of chitchat. We might sneak in an Esther Williams musical!"

CHAPTER 20

—◡—

"You've got mail!" Polly always felt a slight tingle of anticipation when the voice inside her computer announced that she'd received a message. Although the majority of the missives guaranteed improbable ways to lose a hundred pounds in a week, or nonsurgical methods to enhance the size of her penis, Polly still enjoyed thinking that people were taking a personal interest in her. She rubbed her hands together, touched her mouse, and rolled her cursor to the postage stamp icon. A dozen messages popped up, most of which were lascivious ads that she had triggered when she made the mistake six months earlier of visiting one of Tim's favorite adult entertainment sites.

One subject line instantly grabbed her attention. We adore you! Polly beamed and clicked her mouse. She read:

29 August

Dear Polly,

A proper handwritten message will follow, post-haste, but we wanted to express our sincere appre-

ciation straight away for a brilliant evening at your dinner table last night

If we appeared gobsmacked at first it was the result of meeting you in person and admiring your famous house. I trust that we eventually behaved ourselves, and that last night won't be a one-off.

We will reciprocate within a fortnight I promise.

With all good wishes,
Tiara and Steven

P.S. I'm so very sorry for all the spilt blood!

Polly smiled, and printed out the letter for Tim and Placenta to read. She looked at the clock on the upper left-hand corner of her screen. "Damn," she uttered, realizing that it was well past the time she had promised to meet Michael for a movie in the great room. Polly signed off from her e-mail account and shut down her computer. She raced out of her bedroom suite and flew down the Scarlett O'Hara Memorial Staircase. At the bottom step she saw Placenta and as she hurried by she called back, "Don't miss the first song!"

The double doors to the great room were closed. In her haste Polly pushed the panels and dashed into the room. "I'm hee-er!" she exclaimed. "A million apologies for keeping you—"

She stopped midsentence and looked in astonishment at Michael. He was standing by the DVD shelves and appeared to be stashing a DVD under his shirt. "Sweetums, you can have whatever movie you want. Just ask," Polly said.

"I. Um. There were six of the same," Michael explained. "I, er, was going to watch it in my room later and just didn't want to forget."

Polly didn't know what to do. She hadn't been around much of the time while Tim was growing up, so she didn't know how to handle a boy who was obviously lying ... and stealing.

Placenta arrived with a tray of glasses and a pitcher of lemonade. She instantly sensed that something wasn't right. "Did Doris Day's romance on the high seas drown?" she said.

Michael handed Polly the disc and left the room. "What's the preoccupation with this stupid old movie?" Polly said, looking closely at the disc. "I walked in here to watch a movie with Michael and I find our guest stuffing *Anything Goes*—the same disc that Sergeant Sandy found—under his shirt."

Placenta examined the disc. "Michael was in here this morning going through all the titles. He must have been looking for this one. I wouldn't have guessed that he was a Bing Crosby fan."

Polly looked defeated. "Damn! I was in the mood to play mentor and show another generation the magic of movie musicals."

Placenta walked over to the large-screen television and pressed the *On* button for the DVD player. "Hell, we're here. As much as your old musicals bore the cellulite out of me, and God knows this one is a snooze-fest, I'll take the afternoon off and have a look with you." She slipped the disc into the DVD tray and picked up the remote. Placenta walked back to the sofa and filled a glass with lemonade. "This'll tide you over until Lush Hour," she said, handing a tumbler and napkin to Polly. Then she picked up a glass for herself and settled down next to the mistress of the manor. They both took small sips from their glasses as Placenta pushed the *Play* button on the remote control.

The television screen instantly came to life. "Jeez, what a lousy copy!" Polly complained. "Must be a gazillion generations away from the original. It's not even in color, for crying out loud. I should have let Michael have the damn thing."

"I'll get another copy," Placenta said, and stood up to retrieve *Anything Goes—2 of 6* from the disc library. As she looked for the DVD, Polly suddenly cried out, "JesusJosephandMary! "

A startled Placenta turned, expecting to see that Michael had returned and was holding a knife to Polly's throat. Instead she saw Polly with one hand over her smiling mouth, and the other pointing to the screen.

Placenta followed Polly's stare. "Holy moly!" she exclaimed. "What the hell? *Anything Goes,* indeed!"

Placenta sat on the sofa next to Polly without taking her eyes off the screen. The images, in poorly lit black-and-white, revealed a man and a woman methodically removing each other's clothes. The film quality was atrocious, and the camera didn't move with the action. But there was sound. And the noises that Polly and Placenta heard were ones usually reserved for the intimacy of a bedroom.

Polly looked away for a moment and fixed her eyes on Placenta, who looked at Polly and laughed. In a moment, they were both hysterical with amusement, as if they were kids spying on an older sibling's date. "Wait! What was that?" Polly said, and listened more closely. "Turn up the sound."

"Steven! Oh yeah, Steven, baby!" a woman's voice cooed.

"Miranda, you fox," the man's voice responded. "Steven?" Polly cried out.

"Miranda?" Placenta screeched.

Tim came into the room. "Whatcha watchin'?"

Lush Hour finally arrived and Placenta opened the first bottle of Veuve. She poured three flutes and served Polly and Tim before taking a long swallow from her own glass. "This has been the longest day of my life!" she said. "Don't expect me to cook tonight."

Polly rolled her eyes, then raised her glass. "I trust you both know what we have in our hot little DVD player. That's right. The keys to the kingdom!"

"The Golden Chalice," Tim said.

"The Holy Grail," Placenta added.

"It's what Lisa called 'the treasure map,'" Polly continued. "This absolutely boggles my mind. Steven and Tiara seemed like an ideal couple. But we've just watched six films with six different contestants, and one horn dog named Steven having assignations with all of them in their dressing rooms!"

"Whoever edited the tapes knows how to build suspense!" Placenta said. "The cuts of Steven arriving at the studio, then skulking around the hallways, before knocking on Taco Belle's door, then Amy Stout's, then Toe Nail's, and even Danny's, all playing casting couch. They're really well done!"

247

"I know this is Hollywood, and I've seen just about everything there is to see, but for crying out loud, the backstage intrigue at *I'll Do Anything to Become Famous* is more scandalous than *Desperate Housewives* and *Days of Our Lives* combined!"

"We're dead," Tim moaned. "We're all *The Man Who Knew Too Much.* Obviously, there were people who knew that these discs exist. Thane and Danny must have known, too. That's probably why they're dead. Now Michael knows exactly where they are. Someone's going to come after us, and there's nowhere to hide."

"That's why we have security," Polly said. She stood up and walked to the intercom, and summoned Sergeant Sandy into the house.

"We should go to the police," Placenta said.

"And say what, that we found someone's homemade porn?" Polly answered. "Long before Rob Lowe, and Pammy Anderson and Tommy Lee, filmed their boring smut, do-it-yourself triple-X-rated videos have been a ubiquitous part of Hollywood family mementos. The way families used to film little Ashley's piano recital, or little Gregory's Little League game. Everyone does it. Anyway, all the people in *Anything Goes* are of legal age. They looked to me as if they were all very much consenting adults."

"But Steven obviously took advantage of them," Tim said. "They probably promised to do something for him in exchange for him doing something for them. Quid pro quo can still mean sexual harassment."

"It's an arrangement as old as Hollywood, dear," Polly said. "And, as far as we know, no one has filed a complaint."

"One could package and distribute this like a *Girls Gone Wild* DVD and be financially set for the rest of one's life," Tim said.

Polly raised her eyebrows. "How much do you think we could get?"

Tim looked at his mother. "Six or seven big ones."

"Millions?" Polly perked up.

"Bullets to the head!" Tim sassed.

Placenta tsk-tsked. "If you hadn't lifted those damn discs from Lisa's apartment in the first place we would not be in this mess!"

"How did I know that *Anything Goes* was code for how far the contestants had already gone to try to win the game and achieve fame? Sleeping with the host is like sleeping with the boss at the office! So tacky!" Polly scoffed.

Sergeant Sandy knocked on the open door and stepped into the room. She stood with her thumbs hooked over the waist of her uniform pants. "Yes, ma'am?"

Polly offered Sergeant Sandy a glass of champagne, which she declined. Polly said, "Our houseguest is gone for good. He must not be allowed onto the estate again."

"Yes, ma'am," Sergeant Sandy said with a curt nod. "He already told me that he wasn't coming back."

Polly continued. "And we'd better ramp up security." A glow appeared in Sergeant Sandy's eyes. "Yes, ma'am. I need to be briefed. What's the nature of the situation?"

Polly took another long swallow from her glass and passed it to Placenta for a refill. "Let's put it this way, the Terminator—and I don't mean our charming Austrian former governor—may be on his way over to blow us all to smithereens."

An unusually agitated Placenta interrupted. "What Polly means is, we've suddenly found ourselves in a potentially deep ditch of doo-doo."

Polly shot her a stem look. "That's putting it succinctly. It appears that we're in possession of something that other people want, and we think that they've already killed two people to get hold of it."

Sergeant Sandy asked, "Do I have to play twenty questions? Is it the Renoir in the living room? The Emmys over there?" She pointed to the lighted glass shelves. "Your flashy jewelry? You shouldn't wear so much in public."

"It's a DVD of *Anything Goes,*" Placenta said.

Sergeant Sandy made a face. "Not that Bing Crosby piece of dung that my grandmother used to watch? Excuse me. I know that your friend Mitzi Gaynor is in that piece of crap. Er, excuse me again."

Polly made a "pfflft" sound. "No, what we have are DVDs that are labeled '*Anything Goes,*' but the discs don't contain the old movie. At least not *that* movie. They're copies of security camera coverage of some very private encounters in the Sterling Studios dressing rooms. We obtained them accidentally, and now someone is out to get them back. I'd oblige if I knew the rightful owner. But it seems as though there are at least two people— Michael and Miranda—who are after them. I'll bet Dead Danny was too."

Tim looked at Sergeant Sandy and said, "This could be really dangerous. If the wrong person gets hold of the DVDs … there are six discs … they could ruin careers, or make zillions of dollars selling them on eBay, or … But to get the discs, they have to come here. They'd have to go through Polly and Placenta and me, and you too. As I said, we're dead."

"This is the one time that having a police detective boyfriend is not going to help," Polly said. "Randy would be furious with me for taking something from a crime scene."

"You stole the discs?" Officer Sandy said.

"No!" Polly protested. "Polly Pepper doesn't have to steal anything! She's rich and famous and fans give her tons of useless garbage for free."

"Didn't stop Winona Ryder," Sandy said.

"I'm not a klepto! I merely borrowed an old movie. Or what I thought was an old movie," Polly said. "And please don't compare me with a talented young actress and friend who made a stupid mistake, and will probably have that sorry business brought up in her obituary."

"Randy would insist that you take the evidence to the police," Placenta said.

"But you can't do that without getting yourself in trouble," Sergeant Sandy said. "And if he knew that you had this material and didn't turn it in, he'd be in trouble for aiding and abetting, or some such thing. I don't know exactly how that works, but I'm sure that he'd never speak to you again."

Sergeant Sandy rubbed her jaw, as if she were stroking a beard, as she thought of a plan of action. Then, transforming herself from pseudo law enforcement officer to a take-charge military field marshal, she ordered, "The first thing you've got to do is get those discs out of the house. Give them to me and I'll stash them safely at my place."

Polly thought for a moment. "I wouldn't want you to get into trouble. Tim will take them to our safe-deposit box."

Tim nodded. "In the morning, when the bank opens. But in the meantime, what if someone tries to break in tonight?"

"No one will get past me and Dak. I'm calling her in for backup," Sergeant Sandy replied. "Next, I want a list of all the people on the surveillance tape and anyone who may know about the discs. Everyone is a potential suspect. Finally, I need to watch the DVDs myself."

Tim said, "I wouldn't mind watching 'em again. Especially three and six. Toe Nail has more talent than I gave him credit for, if you know what I mean." He sniggered. Sergeant Sandy did not. "They're actually more funny than sexy. I mean, especially since we know all the people. There's definitely a reason why Steven was a model. He still has the goods! His partners in the films may have been sleeping with him to score points on the show, but it couldn't have been that difficult, if you know what I mean."

Sergeant Sandy looked sternly at Tim and said, "No. I do not know what you mean! When someone in authority takes advantage of his position, that's never acceptable. I don't care how consenting the subjects are. It's wrong!"

Polly, Placenta, and Tim all looked at Sergeant Sandy with admiration.

Tim nodded. "You're right. Steven should be held accountable."

Polly returned her attention to Sergeant Sandy. "Dear, I'm starting to become a wee bit disillusioned with Hollywood. It's all well and good to come to Tinseltown to make an attempt at becoming a household name like me, but if my intuition is correct, one of the contestants on the *I'll Do Anything to Become Famous* show is either trying to stop these tapes from surfacing because they're potentially embarrassing, or they want them for personal gain."

"They're all caught in the act, so to speak," Tim said. "Whoever wants these discs enough to kill for them is probably someone who sees dollar signs."

"I've always had things that other people wanted," Polly sighed. "Talent. Fame. Fortune. Pepper Plantation."

"Husbands," Placenta said with an insolent tone.

"We could be killed for something as stupid as having closed-circuit TV evidence of hanky-panky," Tim said.

Sergeant Sandy seemed to take offense. "No one will be harmed during my watch," she said with such force and assuredness that made Polly, Tim, and Placenta instantly at ease. Although Sergeant Sandy probably couldn't stop so much as an invasion of carpenter ants, her presence made the family feel more at safe, as though she could somehow protect everyone at Pepper Plantation from whoever might be lurking around.

Polly raised her near-empty glass to Sergeant Sandy. "Cheers! To our knight ... er, our knightress? ... um, our Lady of Divine Intervention?"

"When Dak gets here, I'll need a private room in which to view the evidence. By the way, if you have an edited copy, where's the original?"

Polly, Tim, and Placenta looked at each other. They hadn't considered that they weren't the only ones with the material.

"This stuff is usually stored on a hard disc drive," Sergeant Sandy said. "I suppose whoever maintained the security cameras has the original raw data."

Tim said, "I guess that would be Sterling Studios' security department. But wouldn't it be illegal for them to monitor a dressing room? It's like spying in a public bathroom."

Placenta said, "There could be a crazy person in security who wanted pictures of future stars. In fact, what is there to prevent someone at NBC or Disney or MTV from infiltrating dressing rooms for up-close and personal images to sell on the black market? With the way technology is today, if I were a star, I'd want my dressing room on every show scrutinized for bugs."

Tim shook his head. "If not a Sterling Studios security freak, then how about the show's producer, Richard Dartmouth?"

Polly was intrigued. "Hmm. Good looking but ruthless television reality show executive, climbing the ladder to success, finds that it takes more than charm to build a career, so he secretly videotapes his contestants. Just in case…"

"But why?" Placenta said. "They're not famous. Unless cameras were installed to keep an eye on the possibility that someone would cheat—at the game, that is. But how do you cheat at a talent competition, unless you lip-synch to Cher?"

Tim snapped his fingers. "Maybe, since the show is about proving they'll go to the ends of the universe to win, the cameras were installed to catch anyone who might harm another contestant."

Polly considered Tim's suggestion. "But why then would the judges' rooms also be under surveillance?"

"To protect you from the contestants. One might have held a judge for ransom," Placenta theorized.

Polly huffed. "So many possibilities. But there is one person who I'll bet has all the answers."

Tim and Placenta each simultaneously spewed forth practically everyone in their Crime Contact List:

"Steven!"

"Michael!"

"Miranda!"

"Toe Nail!"

"Thane! No, he's dead," Tim corrected himself. "Amy!"

Polly quietly poured herself another glass of champagne. "For pity's sake!" she groaned. "Listen to yourselves! And after all the years of watching *CSI* and *Cold Case* and *Matlock*! We can't talk to Steven. Heck, even if he knows the discs exist we couldn't go to him for information. Same with Michael, Miranda, and Toe Nail. They're all on the surveillance videos!"

Tim smacked the palm of his hand against his forehead. "Of course! Brian Smith!"

"Duh!" Polly said. "It's Lisa, for crying out loud! The discs were in her apartment!"

Placenta poured herself another glass of Veuve. "Obviously, we're going back to jail tomorrow."

CHAPTER 21

—⁓—

"By now, we should have a reserved parking space," Tim said as he glided the Rolls into the parking lot of the Beverly Hills Police Station. Although it was only ten in the morning, all of the slots were taken. He let Polly and Placenta off at the entrance to the building. "I'll join you as soon as I can."

Placenta held open the door to the station allowing Polly to make a grand entrance. She strode through the lobby with all the confidence of a runway model, and spied policewoman Betty with her feet up on her desk and chatting with Garrett, the rookie who had caught Tim's eye the last time they visited. As Polly drew nearer to the desk, Garrett looked up and beamed a smile. He looked behind Polly, hoping to see Tim. Betty looked up too.

"I see it's the Princess of Pepper Plantation," Betty quietly said as she leaned farther back in her chair and touched her fingers together in a "here is the church, here is the steeple" fashion. "To what do we owe this insincere pleasure? Don't tell me I missed another big fat celebrity murder and you're

here to interrogate the lone and somehow dubiously innocent suspect?"

Polly smiled, reached into the clutch purse she carried,
and withdrew a packet of Tic-Tac mints. She took one for
herself, then rattled the plastic box to motion an offer to
Betty. The policewoman declined. Polly sniffed the air.
"Two hard-boiled eggs and an onion bagel for breakfast?"

Betty's face turned red, she took her feet off the desk, and
sat upright in her chair. She tried to smell her own breath
against the palm of her hand, then slapped Garrett's arm.
"Why didn't you say something?" she complained. Betty
took a sip of Coke from a can and then accepted the prof-
fered mint. Betty sighed and said, "I may as well petition
the mayor of Beverly Hills to give you your very own card
key for twenty-four-seven access to the prisoners who end
up here."

"That would be lovely!" Polly beamed.

"I'm being facetious," Betty deadpanned. "But for all the
time you seem to spend here, it's not a bad idea." She stood
up. "I'm setting the timer for fifteen minutes. I can't give
you any more than that."

"You're a love," Polly purred as she and Placenta followed
the policewoman to the steel security door. Polly called back
over her shoulder, "Garrett, dear. Be a gem and take care of
Timmy when he arrives. You're a doll. Mean it." And then
she disappeared into the wing of the building reserved for
Beverly Hills felons and doyens with nothing better to do
than slap their illegal immigrant maids.

"Company!" Officer Betty called as she rapped on the
door behind which Lisa Marrs sat in deep despair. Betty

unlocked the cell and held the door for Polly and Placenta to enter. "Do your business fast," she said as she left the star and her maid with the prisoner.

Polly didn't waste a moment of her precious time. "No need to offer a seat on your bunk, but thank you anyway, dear. We'll only be staying a tick or two."

Lisa was dazed from sleeping all day long. She looked up at her visitors and shook her head. "Is this like *Groundhog Day*? Because I swear we've done this before."

Polly folded her arms across her chest. "Not to worry your little felonious fanny, I'm as tired of this as you are. I'm here for one last rattle of your brain. You claim innocence, and I was on your side for the longest time. However, I've just been shocked into reconsidering my hasty judgment."

Lisa stared at Polly for a moment, before looking at Placenta. "I am innocent. I didn't kill Thane Cornwall. I haven't harmed anyone."

Polly sighed. "Question. What looks like gold but smells like trash? No, it's not Charlie Sheen. But close. Give up? Good, because I don't have time for riddles. Answer. The set of six DVDs you had in your apartment, all of which you planned to show to Richard Dartmouth before selling them to *Access Hollywood,* thereby ruining the career of your nefarious boss and raking in a good chunk of coin at the same time."

Lisa looked at Polly with an incredulous stare. "DVDs? Show to Richard? Chunk of coin?" She blinked her eyes with incomprehension. "What the hell are you babbling about?"

Polly faltered. "The DVDs labeled '*Anything Goes.*' I found them in your apartment."

Lisa shook her head. "You're funny. I'm in stitches right now."

Polly pursed her lips and arched an eyebrow.

Lisa stood up from her bunk and moved the few inches to her washbasin. She turned on the tap, splashed water on her face, and used the back of her hand to mop her cheeks. "Think this through with me. I am … er, was … a lowly assistant to Wannabe Big Cheese in television. You with me so far? I used to get to the office by seven a.m., spend twelve hours in hell then it was off to Thane's for lousy sex and being told I need to work out, or that I shouldn't have had a second glass of wine. Jeez! Nothing was going right in my life. I wanted a change.

"For a paycheck that maxes out at a net of six hundred fifty-five dollars a week, I played the slave to Richard Dartmouth," Lisa continued. "When he tells me to copy a set of DVD discs and then personally take them to his house and place them in the safe, I figure they must have some market value, so I do what anyone who hates their boss and wants to move up would do. I made a spare copy of each disc. I did the same with the false expense reports he submitted, the love letters he exchanged between television's number-one Little Miss Morning Sunshine weathergirl on KRUQ, and sports commentator Matt Roth … yeah, you heard right."

As Lisa went on about her sneaky activities, Polly wondered if every assistant in Hollywood practiced the same level of unethical behavior, and would everyone on the planet, including the Dalai Lama, qualify to be a contestant on *I'll Do Anything to Become Famous*? "I suppose you were saving all those gems for a time when you thought they'd be of use to you," Polly suggested. "Something to exchange for a promotion and raise, or to negotiate a lucrative exit strategy from a job you hated. With all the sex on those discs, why not just blackmail Steven Benjamin?"

Now it was Lisa's turn to look incredulous. "Sex? Blackmail? Steven? What am I missing here?"

Placenta placed her hands on her hips and made a scornful sound. "If you didn't know what was on the discs, why did you bother to have 'em copied?"

Lisa shrugged. "Richard wanted them in his vault. Only his most valuable materials go in there, so I knew they were important. If I'd had some *free* time…" She looked around her cell. " … I would have reviewed the discs to decide just how to use them."

"Why did Richard trust you to take the discs in the first place?" Polly asked.

"'Cause Richard thinks I walk on water," Lisa preened. "He trusts me with the combination to his house security system, and to his vault. I have a strong reputation for reliability. He'd never question my integrity. Fool."

"You would betray that trust?" Polly asked.

"Let's get back to what's on the discs," Lisa said. Polly waved away the momentousness of the discs and what they contained. "If you were so important to Richard, why hasn't he come to visit you in jail? I know your bail's been denied, but he could offer moral support? Instead, he placed his precious buns on Thane's throne as a judge on the program and has already hired a new assistant. He doesn't seem to have any time for someone who was supposed to be indispensable to him."

Lisa looked crestfallen. "That's showbiz. People love you when you're on the rise, but they disappear when it looks like you're on the way down."

Polly leaned her back against the cinder block wall and looked through Lisa. She had slipped into a zone of contemplation and, as if in a trance, was unaware of her surroundings. She thought about the serendipity of finding the DVDs in Lisa's apartment in the first place, and having the potentially career-exploding discs in her possession for several days before happenstance again intervened, and made her aware that what she thought was an innocuous old movie turned out be the hottest ticket in town. "Where did those DVDs come from?"

Lisa was quiet for a moment. "I suppose confidentiality agreements go out the window when you're sitting in a jail cell accused of murder. Okay, here's the deal. Nobody knows this except Richard and me. Promise you won't tell? At least not until *I'll Do Anything to Become Famous* is over?"

Polly looked at Placenta, who grimaced and nodded. "Very well." Polly pretended to pull a zipper across her lips. "Spill it."

Lisa sat for a long moment contemplating her loyalty to Richard Dartmouth and how he had not reciprocated her fidelity. With a sigh of resignation she spat, "Screw it. The son of a bitch hasn't had the decency to think twice about me. I'm just the girl to forget all about my promise to keep secrets. This is it. When Richard got the green light from Sterling Studios to produce *I'll Do Anything,* he had all of the dressing rooms bugged with surveillance devices.

His plan was simple. From day one, he wanted to tape the behind-the-scenes activities of the cast and collect every outrageous thing they might do or say that could give the viewing audience a reason to put one contestant over the top in terms of votes. I figured the discs I had were just copies of dumb stuff that Miranda or Toe Nail or Taco Belle had said after a bitter exchange with Thane. I was backstage during rehearsals as well as the first show, so I heard how much they hated Thane Cornwall, and everybody said they wanted him dead."

"If you suspected that those discs contained threats to Thane's life, why haven't you said anything to the police? Any one of the contestants might be the real killer," Polly said.

"I figured that Richard would hand over whatever might contain even a hint of evidence," Lisa said.

Polly shook her head.

Lisa looked defeated. "I guess the fact that I'm still here answers my questions. That lousy bastard! I'll kill him! He could very well be personally responsible for me rotting away in here!"

Polly clicked her tongue. "Life is strange. Everything can change in an instant. You hated your job and were determined to get out of it. And it happened, but you ended up here. The contestants on *I'll Do Anything* have been working hard to beat the others, but no matter what they do, the surveillance videos may change the course of the game, as well as the direction of their lives. If these images get out, Steven Benjamin's career path will definitely be heading south, straight on down to hell."

Polly looked at Placenta. "Our time's up," she said. Then Polly looked at Lisa. "Sweetums, is it possible that Thane knew about the surveillance cameras?"

Lisa thought for a moment. "As I said before, it was a secret between Richard and me. But they were friends, so…"

"The people who installed and maintained the surveillance equipment would have known what had been filmed," Polly suggested.

Lisa pursed her lips and cocked her head. "Never thought about that. I wonder if Richard ever considered that."

"What about the other contestants?" Placenta said. "How do you think they found out about the discs? Perhaps a techie was working on the equipment and Toe Nail or Miranda or Danny or someone saw them. One of them found out, then told another, who told someone else, et cetera. Maybe?"

Polly grabbed Placenta's arm. "That's all very interesting, dear, but it's time to leave. I'm sure this poor girl needs her beauty rest." She turned to Lisa and blew a kiss. "We'll have a party for you at the plantation when this is over."

The women turned to the door but found that it didn't have a knob. Polly knocked on the thick window. "Police-woman Betty! We're ready to make our exit!" Nobody responded. She began to visibly panic.

Lisa looked up and smiled. "It's rather cramped in here. And it's getting so warm! I was never claustrophobic before coming to this rat trap, but…

Polly banged on the door and pleaded for help.

CHAPTER 22

—✍—

"Trapped, I tell you! Caged! Like the cast in an Alec Baldwin play!" Polly berated Tim for monopolizing Garrett and Officer Betty and not coming to her rescue sooner. "Placenta and I could be locked in a room with Michael Bay and you wouldn't have cared!"

"Hey, it's not as though I left you two alone with Shia LeBeouf!" Tim said as he drove along Santa Monica Boulevard toward Rodeo Drive. "The fact that you wanted out of Lisa's cell early only means that you got all the info you wanted from the jailbird and you're champing at the bit to investigate a new source or allegation. What did you pummel out of her? The demento psycho killer must have revealed something of value."

Polly suddenly forgot that she was peeved with her son. "I'm very excited. Drive over to Steven Benjamin's house. And step on it!"

During Tiara's career as a top runway model in Europe, she amassed a fortune flaunting the designs of Versace,

Dior, and Cavalli. When she began appearing in print and television ads for Noxema and Maybelline, she tripled her wealth. Steven, too, had made a killing as a model. First recognized for his appearances in sophisticated ads for Brooks Brothers clothing, he made a bigger fortune when his agent negotiated a deal for him to be the spokesperson for the upstart online dating service E-Chromosome.

Although the company was new, and had almost zero dollars to invest in advertising, Steven's sexiness made them the number-one online dating service in the world. His television ads were cutting-edge erotica and could only be shown after ten p.m. Women signed up for the dating service because they dreamed of finding a man who looked like Steven. Guys joined because they wanted to sleep with the kind of women seen in bed with Steven. And, thanks to his astute agent, Steven accepted a relatively small paycheck in exchange for company profits.

As Tim drove through the streets of Beverly Hills, he turned left onto La Dolce Vida Drive and maneuvered the car up a steep incline.

"I haven't been in this area for ages," Polly marveled, looking out the window at older Beverly Hills homes.

Making another left at Picasso Place, the car came to a stop in front of an immense iron gate, behind which one could see a home that nearly rivaled Pepper Plantation in size.

Polly whistled. "Let's see what Beverly Hills Barbie, and her perfect-10 Ken, are up to on this lovely summer afternoon."

Tim rolled down the car's window and reached out to press the intercom keypad. Soon, a muffled voice asked, "Jes?"

"*Hola*—" Tim began to say but was interrupted by his mother.

"*Hola*, sweetums, it's Polly Pepper. From the television? The show that Mr. Benjamin is hosting? I'm expected, I'm sure. I've brought a wee prezy for Mr. and Mrs."

"Si. Come," the voice answered.

As the twin gates parted, Placenta nudged Polly. "Prezy? You mean a bottle from the trunk?"

"As long as it's not our last."

As the trio stepped from the Rolls and walked to the frosted-glass front entrance doors, Tim rang the bell. In a moment, a maid in uniform opened the door and made a slight bow to welcome them. "*Bienvenido*," she said with a gesture for them to follow her.

Polly looked at Placenta, raised an eyebrow, and cocked her head toward the maid.

Placenta snapped, "Don't say it! Don't you even think it!"

"I was just wondering—"

"Keep on wondering—to yourself. If one word about putting me back in a uniform escapes your lips, someone will be investigating *your* disappearance!"

After a few moments of waiting in the living room, Tiara Benjamin came in looking frantic. "Polly!" she called out with exhaustion in her voice. She greeted the television legend with a quick peck to her cheeks. She smiled at Tim and Placenta and hugged them, too. "If I'd known that

Maria had let you in, er, I mean, that you were dropping by, I'd have made myself a tad more presentable. Things are a bit … loony today. Steven's unwell. A dreadful toothache."

Polly stepped forward and handed Tiara the bottle of Veuve. "It's not chilled, but I guarantee it'll make you and Steven feel like a million. It works especially well dimming all sorts of pain."

"Thank you for thinking of us," Tiara said. "Your timing is impeccable," she said with a slight edge to her voice.

Then, from the distance, Steven called out for Tiara. The summons sounded more like an old man's death rattle.

Tiara looked panicked. "Please, have a seat. I'll be back in a tick."

As Tiara rushed to her husband, Polly took the opportunity to look around the room. "It's changed so much," she sighed. "When dear, lovable, and vibrant Rita Hayworth lived here, it had an abundance of old-world elegance. She learned a lot from being married to Orson, however briefly." Polly looked back through the years and pictured every detail of the room as it had been in the 1970s. "Rita had a grand piano over there." Polly pointed to what was now a seating area with expensive modern Le Corbusier furniture. She looked at the modern stone fireplace. "There used to be a very ornate mantel there, above which was a huge portrait of Rita posing as Gilda. The place was so well decorated then. Now it's as sterile as an operating room," she scoffed.

"This place is so antiseptic that I defy any germ to survive long enough to ever make Steven or Tiara ill!" Placenta said.

Polly spied a crumpled piece of beige-colored notepaper on the floor of the otherwise spotless room. "Oh, Maid Sweetheart," she called out, forgetting the name of the domestic. She bent down to retrieve the paper, then looked around for a trash receptacle. "They don't even have a goddamn ashtray," Polly whined as she walked from one end of the room to the other, searching for a place to deposit the paper. Just as she was about to place it on a glass end table, her curiosity coaxed her to open the paper and take a peek.

Polly unfolded the wrinkled ball and read to herself, *There are no secrets in Hollywood. However, l am willing to protect yours—in return for U.S.$ ...*

Polly's eyes grew wide, but before she could finish reading the sentence Steven suddenly stumbled into the room, leaning on Tiara for support. Polly instantly squeezed the paper into a ball again and surreptitiously dropped it to the floor.

"Polly," Steven said, in a weak voice, "I'm sorry you have to see me like this. Can we arrange a visit in a day or two? I don't want you coming down with whatever I've picked up." He forced a cough.

Polly ignored the dramatic change in diagnosis. "I'll chance it," she said in a motherly coo, and touched the back of her hand to Steven's forehead. "Polly Pepper hasn't had a cavity or a cold in years, probably because I have a teensy bit of OCD when it comes to washing my hands a bajillion times a day and always flossing after every meal. Please don't let us bother you anymore. Off to bed! Let Tiara tuck you in. We'll catch up when you're one hundred percent! Go! We'll let ourselves out."

Placenta and Tim both offered their wishes for Steven's speedy recovery and then the trio turned to leave. "*Gracias,*" Polly said when they met Maria in the foyer. "*Adios.*"

When they were safely back in the car and heading down the driveway toward the estate's gates, Polly slapped her knee and said, "Steven's sick all right, but it's not a virus or a cold or food poisoning or a silly toothache. He's ill because he's about to lose a ton of money *and* his career, and probably his wife, too. He's being blackmailed!"

Tim looked at his mother in the rearview mirror. "You picked that up just from touching his forehead?" He grinned.

"Shush!" Polly interrupted. "He's in trouble with someone who's shaking him down for a big payday advance. That crumpled piece of paper that I found on the floor? It was a note that instructed him to transfer money or his career would be over."

"How much?" Tim asked.

"D'know."

"I don't suppose it was signed," Placenta said.

"Didn't get that far," Polly fumed. "Steven and Tiara came in and I had to ditch the damn note. However, it was on Crane stationery, and printed from a computer. The font was Helvetica. The type size, twelve point."

Placenta rolled her eyes and in a voice meant to sound like a psychic on *Larry King Live,* said, "The perp is five feet seven inches, works as a dental hygienist during the day, writes screenplays at night. He wears a toupee, walks with a limp, and collects *Captain America* comic books."

"Don't be rude," Polly said.

"D'ya think the letter is from one of the contestants?" Tim said.

Polly shrugged. "Run-of-the-mill blackmailers wouldn't use expensive stationery. Who among them has any taste?

Hell, I wouldn't be surprised if everyone involved with this show has discovered that Steven is on the surveillance tapes and now's the time to score big money by ratting him out! If we find the blackmailer, we'll probably get to the killer too."

"Richard Dartmouth?" Placenta said. "If Richard knows, then Brian Smith may also. And whoever transfers the videos, too."

"We're back to everyone being a suspect!" Tim ranted. "It's been nearly two weeks since Thane bought the farm and we're not any closer to finding his killer. I think we should just give up, and let Lisa fend for herself."

Polly said, "You're wrong about our not being any closer. We know that it can't be Lisa writing blackmail notes. Jail is a pretty good alibi. Same for Danny. Dear, dead Danny. Two down. As for Richard Dartmouth, it's improbable that he'd be tied up in a blackmail scheme. He's got loads of moolah. Plus as Thane's replacement judge he's becoming a celebrity."

Tim honked the car horn out of frustration. "That doesn't mean that he didn't kill for the job."

"Doubt it," Polly said, and folded her arms across her chest. "Oh, what am I talking about? This is Hollywood. Anything that one can imagine happens here in real life. On this one show alone we've got a killer, a blackmailer, an adulterer, a cast of six whores, a pervert who goes around secretly videotaping people in private acts. And everyone— except the dead bodies—is a suspect! It's *The Twilight Zone* and *General Hospital* and everything dear Jackie Collins ever wrote, all on one lousy reality show!"

As Tim drove the car through the East Gate of Bel Air, and followed Stone Canyon Road along its serpentine length toward the plantation, the passengers all remained silent. As they reached the PP-monogrammed iron gates of Pepper Plantation and waved to Sergeant Sandy, who sat under an umbrella in the late afternoon sun on a folding wooden stool, Polly broke the ice. "While I'm having my hair done tomorrow, you'll take Placenta back to the Benjamins'."

Tim and Placenta both made faces. "And do what, take Steven's temperature?" Tim asked.

Polly looked at Placenta and reached out to take her hand. "Sweetums. Dear heart. Friend. You know I'm not in the least bit prejudiced about any minority group, with the possible exception of young casting directors who are too stupid to know that *The Polly Pepper Playhouse* remains a seminal show in the history of television, and have never seen my films or heard my number-one hit record. So I say this with all due respect." Polly cleared her throat. "You have to go back to the Benjamins' as a..." She waited a beat, then said, " ... domestic engineer."

"A maid?" Placenta snatched her hand out of Polly's.

"Just *pretend,*" Polly begged. "Anyway, that's what it says on your W2 Form!"

"I knew you'd find a way to get me back into that stinking uniform!" Placenta snapped as the car pulled up to the front portico. "Why can't *you* befriend the senora? I could tell that she recognized you when we walked in."

"But you speak her language!" Polly complained.

"Me, no hablo español." Placenta retorted.

"I mean, you two work for rich and famous stars. You have things in common. I need you to go there and make nice with the help and get that letter for me," Polly begged.

"I need to find out who sent it to Steven. Please help me out? Just this once?"

"Once?" Placenta huffed, and leaned as far away from Polly as she could. "I'm on your side twenty-four- seven! Aren't I, Tim?"

"She's right, Mother," Tim said as he turned off the ignition and opened his door. He walked around the car to the passenger side and pulled on the handle to his mother's door and reached out to help her.

Polly walked to the front steps, punched in the security code, then turned and looked at Placenta. "I'll give you a thousand bucks."

"Si, Senora! Es un placer servir a usted durante el tiempo que me necesite!" Placenta beamed.

"No hablas español, my Bob Mackie-clad butt!" Polly snapped.

As the trio entered the mansion, Placenta and Polly both had satisfied smiles plastered on their faces. They headed for the great room, and Placenta said, "Cash, up front, Mrs. Scrooge." While she was uncorking a chilled bottle of Veuve, Polly went to the floor safe in the kitchen panty. When she returned, she exchanged a flute of champagne for five one-hundred dollar bills. "The balance upon delivery of that blackmail note," she said with an edge to her voice. She seated herself on the sofa and took a long swallow of her drink.

Placenta gave Polly the evil eye, then looked at Tim. "You're my witness. Your mama owes me five hundred! And I won't take it in trade for cocktails at the Polo Lounge!"

CHAPTER 23

—⌖—

W hen Placenta breathlessly rushed into the great room at Pepper Plantation waving a photocopy of the note that she retrieved from the Benjamins' maid, she panted, "Steven *is* being blackmailed!"

"What did I tell you?" Polly said as she grabbed the paper out of Placenta's hand.

> *There are no secrets in Hollywood. However, I am willing to protect your secret—in return for U.S. $500,000. Place the banknotes in a black suitcase tied with a red string on the handle. Take a room at the Beverly Hills Hotel on Friday, 10 August.*
>
> *Park the suitcase in the closet. Leave the hotel and drive to the Barnes & Noble at the Grove. Place the hotel room card key in a volume of* Wuthering Heights *(classics section of the store).*
>
> *Don't be a wanker. There will be bloody hell to pay with your career and marriage if you don't perform precisely as instructed.*

Polly looked up again and her eyes met with Tim's and Placenta's. She looked back at the note. "August tenth. That's the day after tomorrow!"

Polly looked at her watch, then held out her wrist to Placenta. She tapped the crystal.

Placenta rolled her eyes and started for the wine cooler but stopped as she reached for a bottle of Veuve. "First things first," she said. "Cough up my dough. I wore this stinking costume and made nice with the Benjamins' maid. By the way, the whole meek and subservient routine is an act. She's tough-as-nails Cybill Shepherd masquerading as vacuous Melanie Griffith playing the role of an obsequious Mexican maid. As for her '*Bueno. No speaky ing-gee, por favor*' routine' it's a great big snow job. Not only does she speak English better than me ... er, better than I ... she's got ears like a Doberman's and picks up everything she overhears from her employers. She has an enormous talent for spying on Steven and Tiara. The CIA or the KGB could learn a trick or two. Maria, actually her real name is June Smith, has a hidden trove of documents that, if she wanted to use, could embarrass the Benjamins and maybe even get them a cell next to Lisa Marrs's. So, where's my loot? Oh, and throw in an additional three hundred. That's how much Maria, er, June, charged me for a photocopy of that note."

"Three hundred dollars?" Polly whined.

"That was cheap. For a photo of the Mr. and Mrs. swimming with Hugh Jackman and his wife ... photoshopped so they appeared naked ... she wanted twelve hundred!" Placenta said.

Tim perked up. "My birthday's coming up. Remember that picture when you're thinking of the perfect gift for a perfect son."

As Polly went to open the safe, Tim said to Placenta, "Now is the time we should get Randy involved. But Polly won't hear of it. She's afraid that he'll be angry. He'll be angrier when he finally finds out—and he will— that Polly has been hiding her investigation from him."

"On the one hand, it's none of our business," Placenta said as she uncorked the bubbly. "On the other hand, we want what's best for your mama. If we tell Randy what's been going on, he'll never be able to trust Polly again. We have to play this very carefully. He's got to find out, but I don't think that we should be the ones to tell him. Drop a few hints and let him come to his own conclusions. Yes?"

Tim nodded as Placenta poured him a glass of champagne. "I suppose I could have drinks with him and offer a bit of bait."

"Nah. Let your mother's loose lips do their inevitable damage," Placenta suggested. "Once the bubbles begin to kill off her inhibitions, she gets friendly and cuddly. She's bound to say something about the blackmail note. Especially if we surreptitiously guide her."

Polly soon returned. "For three hundred dollars, you should have been able to buy O.J.'s confession," she said, handing an envelope to Placenta.

"Who's to say I didn't?" Placenta smiled and withdrew the original note from her uniform pocket. "That deceitful, double-dealing servant made a photocopy for her own files, and when Tiara called her to explain the reason for a missing cupcake, I grabbed the copy and skedaddled."

"Were you ever planning to give this to me, or were you going to keep it for your own future felonies?" Polly said as she picked up the flute of champagne that Placenta had poured for her.

Placenta feigned hurt pride. "I was planning to make you a present of it."

"I'm not used to paying for my own presents," Polly snorted. Just then, the house telephone rang. "If it's the Benjamins' maid, tell her that Placenta's been dismissed," she said as Tim reached for the phone.

In a moment, Tim brought the phone to his mother. "Randy," he said as he held out the handset. "I think he should know what you're up to."

Polly made a face and covered the microphone with her hand.

Polly plastered a wide smile on her face as she spoke into the phone. "Sweetums, you're avoiding me! It's been two whole days since you were here!"

Polly paused, then swallowed hard. "Who suggested such a ludicrous idea to you?" With a heavy sigh she said, "All right. It's true. But I'm getting very close to solving the mystery of who killed Thane. Oh, and Danny, too. As a matter of fact, I was going to tell you over dinner tonight." After a beat she said, "Forgot? It's right here in my calendar. 'PP. Din-din. Seven. Wear BM, um, Bob Mackie.' Goody! See you then." Polly pushed the *Off* button on the telephone and handed it back to Tim. "Drats! He's coming for dinner," she said. "Of course I want to see Randy, but when he hears how deeply involved I am in this case, he's bound to throw one of his less-than-macho hissy fits. The lovely and talented Officer Betty spilled the beans." She reached for the bottle of Veuve. "We'd better do our homework before he arrives."

She picked up the original letter and read it aloud again. "This is way too queer. Look at the way the blackmailer refers to the money. 'U.S. $.' What about the word *banknotes*? This was written by someone trying to disguise themselves as a foreigner."

Tim took the letter from Polly's hand and reread it himself. "'Don't be a wanker.' I still think that's funny, and definitely not an American expression."

The room became silent for a long moment. "Thane Cornwall may have written this," Polly said. "Steven and Tiara both admitted that Thane was no longer a friend when he died."

"It arrived after his death," Tim said. "Steven wouldn't have been such an emotional wreck yesterday if the note came from a dead man. In fact, he'd be bouncing off the walls with glee."

Polly looked at the letter once again. "The instructions to place the hotel room card key in a volume of *Wuthering Heights* seemed odd at first. But I think whoever wrote this is rather clever. Nobody buys a classic unless they're forced to read it for school, or Oprah beams her mind control techniques at the masses and sends 'em out to a book store. So the chances of somebody coming by and picking up a copy with the card key in it are remote.

"Second, the fact that the writer had to spell out where in the store the book is located tells me that either Steven is a dolt when it comes to literature, and/or the person who wrote didn't want to risk having Steven ask for assistance finding the book and the possibility of a salesperson taking the wrong book or thinking the card key was rubbish and thus throwing it away."

Tim said, "Any decent blackmailer would do their best to conceal their identity. The person who wrote could be pretending to be European. Maybe they're just trying to mislead us."

Polly and Placenta both nodded. "Michael worked for Thane," Polly said. "He would have picked up his phrases and the novelties between our two English-speaking countries. For example, the way we write out dates? We'd say August 10, and they say 10 August. And specifying United States currency … one would never spell that out, unless one wanted foreign money. As a matter of fact, whoever wrote this is a fool for not asking for Euros!"

"Wait!" Tim said. "Maybe we should add another name to the list of suspects. What about the Benjamins' maid?" He looked at Placenta. "She's obviously duplicitous. You said she was one of the most astute women you'd ever met. She's around Tiara all the time and would easily pick up her idioms and way of speaking and writing."

Polly whined. "No. Please. Not another suspect! We have too many as it is. Let's just hang the guilty charges on someone and be done with it."

Placenta was taken aback. "The whole reason you got involved in this case is to clear the name of an innocent!"

"But it's getting so confusing," Polly complained. "Okay. I started this. I guess I have to follow through. But please, someone, get me on the first flight to the Mars the next time a body lands at my feet."

Placenta said, "What about *Wuthering Heights*? Might that be a clue? Does Emily Brontë have any significance here?"

"I saw the movie," Polly said. "As I recall, Larry Olivier was a hottie. I don't know what the hell he saw in Danny Kaye as a lover. Unless it's true what they say about redheads." She looked at Tim. "Is it true?"

Tim was irritated. "I. Don't. Know! You're the redhead."

"Formula 271!" Placenta called out.

"And what is it that 'they' say anyway?" Tim asked.

"Never mind Tim," Polly said to Placenta. "His taste is so vanilla. He's still hung up on the adult Doogie Howser and Niles Crane, for crying out loud.

"Oh, and I recall there was a lot of retribution going on in *Wuthering Heights*. Which sort of takes us back to considering everybody who hated Thane."

Tim shook his head in bewilderment. "With so much animosity going on behind the scenes of a show that's based on foul play, the blackmailer could be anyone."

"Nope!" Polly said, and drained her flute. "I can't agree. It had to be someone with either too much to lose, or someone who'd already lost everything and wanted vengeance. This leaves a very intimate group."

Placenta poured more champagne all around.

"No. The group isn't so small. The killer, at least Thane's killer, could still be one of the contestants on the surveillance tapes, or Lisa or Richard or Brian. They all have more to lose if those tapes get out and circulated on the Net," Polly continued.

"Let's wait and see what Randy has to say," Tim suggested. "In the meantime, let's catch Steven again in *Anything Goes—Disc 4 of 6.*"

At eight o'clock, Sergeant Sandy announced that the driver from Spago had arrived with dinner. She opened the gate and allowed the Mercedes-Benz delivery car to enter the estate and park near the front entrance. Tim tipped the man twenty dollars and took the warm bags into the kitchen. As Polly and Randy rubbed noses in the great room, Placenta and Tim set the table, and ladled the spring-green asparagus soup into four bowls, and placed the Cantonese roasted duck in the warming oven. Rather than ringing a bell to call Polly and Randy to dinner, all Placenta had to do was pop the cork from another bottle of champagne, and the infatuated couple stopped what they were doing and came to the dining room.

Always a gentleman, Randy held out the chair at the head of the table for Polly, and did the same for Placenta, whom he seated to Polly's left. Randy took his seat opposite Placenta while Tim faced his mother from the other end of the table. After a few sincere comments from Randy about how great the soup looked, and oh, boy, was he hungry, everyone simultaneously picked up their spoons and began to eat. Amid sounds that could be mistaken for amorous pleasures, Polly took another long swallow from her champagne flute and said, "Did you notice the lovely new addition to our estate security?"

Randy nodded. "I was going to ask about her. I should be on a permanent list of approved guests. She's not very adept at frisking men."

Polly nodded. "Absolutely!" She turned to Placenta. "Be sure that Sergeant Sandy places Randy's name on the 'A' list. Remind her that Tim and I are the only ones allowed to do a strip search."

"Do you really need the Secret Service?" Randy asked as he scooped up the dregs of his soup.

"Tim has the bizarre notion that just because we may have major evidence to exonerate Lisa Marrs in the Thane Cornwall murder case, we're all going to be dead soon." Polly suddenly checked herself and looked up at Randy. "Oh, drats!"

Tim and Placenta shared an infinitesimal smirk.

"Dead?" Randy said, taking a sip from his water glass.

"Timmy overreacts." Polly smiled. "The fact that the boy we almost adopted, Michael, a kid who was living in the most degrading circumstances, which I'll tell you about some other time, discovered that we unwittingly possessed the secret surveillance sex tapes of Steven Benjamin and the cast … and I mean the entire cast of *I'll Do Anything* … and tried to steal them from us, which is what dear dead Danny was probably trying to do when he got yanked out of the physical world, and the fact that everybody else on the show seems to know that we have these amazing and undoubtedly extremely valuable DVDs of *I'll Do Anything for an Orgy* … Tim got paranoid and said we were as good as dead. That was before we discovered that Steven was being blackmailed, but now that we're certain of that, I think it's a good idea to have the extra security."

Polly came up for air and took a long swallow from her glass. "If nothing else, it's good for potential Polly Pepper killers to see that it isn't so easy to barge in on the estate of the queen of television!"

Tim put down his spoon. "Mother, we all agreed that it was wise to have the extra help since the dumb security alarm service can't keep our unit working. Sergeant Sandy is a very good investment in our safety."

Randy sat back and folded his arms across his chest. When Polly noticed his eyes boring into her own, she smiled. "Yes?"

"Adoption? Sex tapes? Blackmail?" Randy smiled. "If I act all innocent and full of wide-eyed wonder, would you indulge my naiveté and elaborate?"

Polly touched Randy's arm. "I'm so happy that you're not angry with me! I just couldn't involve you until I had all the evidence I need to clear Lisa Marrs of the crime of murdering Thane Cornwall. Actually, I don't have any evidence, but I'm close. And you can help."

Randy shook his head. "Unbelievable."

Polly smiled with pride. "I'm getting pretty good at this sleuthing business, aren't I?"

Randy sighed. "I mean, it's unbelievable that you would suggest that I help you continue this crime spree you're on."

"I'm not the one committing crimes," Polly said. "I didn't know that I had important evidence until I watched the DVDs of *Anything Goes,* which really wasn't *Anything Goes,* which we inadvertently stumbled across in Lisa's apartment. Oh, I know what you're going to say. You'll want to know what we were doing there in the first place. Then you'll ask how we came into possession of the evidence. It's all a long story and I'm too hungry to discuss it right now."

"I'll wager it's rather a very short story," Detective Archer said. "Here's how I see it. You either broke into Lisa's apartment or conned your way in. Then you burgled the place. The end."

"Polly Pepper is not a burglar," she insisted. "I simply borrowed an old movie that turned out to be new, and not even what I thought it was. Bing Crosby was nowhere on those DVDs! Look, I probably did the wrong thing taking anything out of Lisa's apartment. And I should have asked you for help a long time ago. But I didn't think you'd let me get involved. You know how dreary my days have become. This is the most excitement I've had since—"

Randy could not stay mad at Polly. He touched her arm and smiled. "What can I do to help?"

"That's more like it!" Polly squealed. "What you can do is get a few of your police pals to attend tomorrow's taping of *I'll Do Anything to Become Famous.* It's the final night of the competition, and I'm going to insist that J.J. get my old job back as a judge. By the time he gets through with Richard Dartmouth, I'll probably get a raise, too. Anyway, I have a hunch I may say something that will cause a bit of a stir."

CHAPTER 24

—⌇—

"Tell me again how you made him cry," Polly laughed into the phone as Tim and Placenta eavesdropped on her conversation with her nefarious agent, J.J.

Polly smiled when she had completed her call. "J.J.'s a gem. Chipped and most definitely cracked, but he got me back on the show, starting tonight!"

"What about that Saddleback creature who replaced you?" Tim asked.

"Booted back to the coffee klatch, *The Shrews*."

"Consorting with J.J. is playing with the devil." Placenta tsk-tsked. "What sort of evil did J.J. perpetrate against Richard?"

"That's the best part." Polly smiled. "Apparently, Richard and J.J. frequent the same, shall we say, massage therapist. J.J. threatened to let America's mommies know how Richard spends his weekends—special uniforms, and all. The country's little kiddies would be yanked away from watching *Lafayette and Boom Boom*, and those darling teen heartthrobs on *Youth and Eyes* on the Sterling Channel as quickly as one could say the Jonas Brothers have zits. Sterling's stock would plummet, and soon handsome but kinky Richard would be out on his butt alongside that former Sterling senior VP, Shari Draper."

Tim looked at his watch. "It's nearly noon. What's the call time? You'd better get ready. And start thinking up crazy questions for the interview segment of the show. It's your last chance to find out who will proudly say, 'I'll Do Anything to Become Famous.' I'm going outside to check on the gardeners."

Polly and Placenta hurried out of the great room and hustled up the Scarlett O'Hara Memorial Staircase. At the second-floor landing, they both rushed toward Polly's bedroom suite. "I'll draw the bath!" Placenta called back as she passed Polly in the corridor. "You decide what you want to wear."

"What I want is a medicinal glass of bubbly!" Polly said as she entered her boudoir and opened the door on her bedside wine cooler. "I'll take care of the bath. You, open the bottle and lay out my new Dolce, please!"

The two were happy to be engaged in an activity that kept them working together and focused on a mutually agreed upon outcome: turning the lady of the manor into a reasonable facsimile of the Polly Pepper that a generation remembered from her glory days on television. "This is my last time at bat, and I need to be stunning!" Polly said. "Oh, and I want to smell good too. I'll be on set all day and J.J. said to expect the media to be out in full force covering the meteoric launch of another fifteen seconds of blame, er, *fame*."

As a euphoric Polly immersed herself in the bubbles of her Jacuzzi tub, she set her champagne glass among her herbal body oils and lotions on her tub caddy, and felt herself melt into the fragrant suds. "I pity the poor people," Polly cooed.

"I don't see you volunteering to alleviate the suffering on this sick planet," Placenta grunted.

"I mean, the poor people who aren't judges on a popular TV reality game show," Polly said. "If I do well tonight, perhaps replace someone in their *Dancing with the Stars* chair. I mean, everybody in town must know that I survived Thane Cornwall, so I can certainly hold my own with any ol' meanie!"

"Considering that Thane died after one show, I'd say that you survived him only in the same sense that you survived Danny ... by him preceding you in death," Placenta said. She added more champagne to Polly's glass, and busied herself with straightening the colorful bottles of perfume on the granite-top sideboard that served as a vanity in the vast bathroom. "We'll see how well you take on Richard Dartmouth tonight."

Polly splashed in the tub. "After the way ol' J.J. slaughtered him, Richard'll probably go for my jugular," she said, taking another sip from her glass. "However, America loves me, and I'll come out smelling like the rose that I am."

"You're a thorn!"

Polly and Placenta both looked up when they heard Sergeant Sandy's voice. Sandy stood in the bathroom doorway, pointing a gun at Polly.

"JesusJosephandMary!" Placenta said.

"Forget about roses, you'll soon smell like fried flesh." Sergeant Sandy pointed her revolver at Placenta. "Sit!" she barked.

Placenta did as instructed and took a seat on the white leather chaise. "What the hell are you doing? You're supposed to be protecting us, not robbing us!"

"Robbery?" Sergeant Sandy said, her eyes darting between Polly and Placenta. "I'm not stealing anything. Except a few DVDs—and your lives."

Polly gasped. "Why? What for? What did we ever do to you?"

"It's what you *didn't* do," Sergeant Sandy said. "You didn't mind your own business. You had to take those DVDs from Lisa Marrs's apartment. You beat Toe Nail and Michael there by mere minutes and ruined all our plans by pinching what you thought were copies of that stupid old movie musical. We—Lisa, Toe, Michael, and me—had everything worked out … until you got in the way."

Polly clicked her tongue. "I see. You were aware that Steven Benjamin's sexual proclivities were captured by surveillance cameras, and you were blackmailing him." Sergeant Sandy looked at Polly as though she were an idiot. "We weren't blackmailing Steven Benjamin."

"But the note?" Polly said.

"Note?" Office Sandy sneered.

Placenta whispered, "Skip it, Polly. There isn't any note. You're fantasizing again."

"Never mind," Polly said. "It may seem fun to be a megastar like me, but the bright studio lights have a way of melting one's marbles."

"Just shut up!" Sergeant Sandy spat. "Where's the hair dryer?" she asked Placenta.

"We don't have one," Placenta said.

"What do you call that thing?" Sergeant Sandy said, and pointed to a handheld hair dryer attached to the wall above the vanity. "Get it! And don't try anything heroic, or I swear I'll blast you first. You're not spoiling *this* plan."

"What plan?" Placenta asked.

"According to the statement I'll give to the police, I caught you after you murdered your boss by electrocution and I had to shoot you in self-defense."

"No one'll buy that," Polly said as she wondered why her knight in shining armor was never around when she needed him. "Placenta and I are best friends. The *National Peeper* even hinted that we're lovers, which is ridiculous since Jodie Foster is far more my type. That is, if I had a type. I mean, if I liked ladies instead of men, which I actually thought about after my second husband, the asshole, left me. But then I realized that I'd miss a certain accoutrement that nature gave to only one of the sexes. But everybody knows that Placenta and I are devoted to one another. She would never do anything to harm me, nor I her!"

"Shut up!" Sergeant Sandy growled through gritted teeth. "One more word and you're dead!"

"Isn't that where all of this is leading anyway?" Polly said. "Before you kill me I want to know what I'm dying for. How does my having those discs of surveillance coverage have anything to do with you?"

Sergeant Sandy looked at Placenta. "Get the hair dryer. Now!"

Placenta moved to the vanity as slowly as possible and unplugged the Conair dryer. She stood with her back to the intruder, but could see her reflection in the mirror.

"What are you waiting for?" Sergeant Sandy huffed. "Let's get this over with!"

"Placenta, don't move," Polly commanded. "Not until we're told why we have to die."

Sergeant Sandy shook her head. "For an actress, you don't take direction very well." She gave in. "Your time as a living legend is up because I need those discs, and because you know too much. My baby is going to win *I'll Do Anything to Become Famous* when she proves that she indeed would—and did—more outrageous things than the others."

"Your baby?" Polly said. "You're Taco Belle's mother?"

"Socorro!" Sergeant Sandy snapped. "Her name is Socorro Sanchez. That bigot, Thane Cornwall, insulted her by nicknaming her after a fast food restaurant."

"She killed Thane?" Polly said.

"No! She seduced the show's host!"

"She intentionally slept with Steven Benjamin. In my book that makes her fast food," Placenta said. "If the burrito fits…"

Polly sniggered and Sergeant Sandy pointed her gun at the star.

"I'm sorry," Polly said as she pulled a meringue of frothy suds toward her breasts. "You do know that Steven slept with all the contestants?"

"I only pretend to be stupid," Sergeant Sandy said. "Playing the 'dumb as cement' game helps when I'm working for brain-dead rich people, like the ones at Pepper Plantation. I've watched all the discs. Remember? Tonight, when the DVD with Socorro is broadcast—which will demonstrate the lengths she has gone to become famous—she'll be the winner. To make her victory even more assured, Socorro will explain that after seducing Steven Benjamin, she convinced all the other contestants that if someone had sex with the host they'd have a better chance of winning."

"And each thought they were the only ones to go through with it," Polly said.

Placenta forced a weak smile. "Very Hollywood. Everybody screws everybody else to win."

Polly looked perplexed. "You said that you didn't know anything about a blackmail letter," she said to Sandy.

The security guard shrugged. "I'd never put anything in writing. Anyway, we didn't want anything from Steven, except the tapes filled with him and Socorro and Toe Nail and Amy and Miranda and Danny."

"Talk about 'reality,'" Placenta said.

"You used Danny to collect the discs from Pepper Plantation and then you killed him," Polly said. "As an employee of SOS, you were able to interrupt the alarm system, get Danny into the house to look for the DVDs, and then snuff out his life to keep him quiet."

"I had nothing to do with Danny's death," Sandy insisted. "Yeah, Michael and Danny came here to find the discs, but when they heard someone else in the house, Michael freaked and left Danny alone. Someone else killed him."

"Did you know that the discs were here before you came to work for us?" Polly asked.

"It was logical," Sandy said. "Lisa befriended Michael after a particularly nasty day for him with Thane. They got together for drinks to commiserate about their loathsome bosses, and in no time she was yakking about Richard secretly filming the contestants … and judges … in their dressing rooms. Yeah, I know it was part of the reality contest, some sort of bonus for contestants to score extra points if they plotted and schemed and made a big enough noise while backstage. Lisa said that she didn't have time to put the discs in her bank security deposit box because she was arrested for the murder of Thane Cornwall on a weekend. She told him where to find them. But then you got into her place and took them home with you. Thief."

"Did you plan to have Michael stay with us?" Polly asked.

"You did that all by your own stupid self," Sandy said. "We could never have planned a better scenario for getting Michael into your house. If he'd succeeded in absconding with those discs, we wouldn't be here today. However, the idiot failed at your dinner party when he lost one in the grass on the estate, then screwed up again when he had full reign of the house."

"So why isn't Michael dead like Danny?" Polly asked.

Sergeant Sandy took a deep breath and said, "Let's just say that he's no longer living in that hellhole of a rooming house."

"Poor boy," Placenta said. "I think he sorta liked Tim—in a big brother way."

Polly suddenly looked horrified. "Tim! What have you done with Tim?"

"Relax. It's Friday. Hector the gardener day. Last Friday I noticed that between twelve thirty and two Hector and Tim disappeared into the cottage over by the south end of the estate. They're having a tea party again—if you get my drift. Too bad he and Placenta plotted against you for their inheritance. Again with the self-defense theme."

Polly shook her head wildly. "What the hell are you talking about? He would never … You won't get away with this! Not a single person on the planet, especially our friends, will ever believe you!"

"You should have taken the time to read my daily reports. If you had, you'd have discovered that I kept meticulous notes and quoted long conversations between your son and so-called maid. They planned elaborate ways to get rid of you." Sandy sighed again. "For crying out loud, I take the time to use my creative writing talents in my daily reports and nobody reads in this house! A shame."

Sandy pointed to an electrical socket near the Jacuzzi tub. "Time's up. Plug in the dryer over here. Then turn it on and play catch with your mistress."

As Sergeant Sandy backed away from the tub for a wider view of the women, Placenta moved forward. Then she stopped in the middle of the room and turned toward Sandy. "Look, I don't have to die. I can help you. I've wasted the best years of my life working for this drama queen, so I don't care what you do with her. But I'm not ready to go. I have a full life ahead."

The expression on Polly's face turned from fear to injured surprise. "Placenta! We're best friends."

"Not if I can escape from this mess that *you* got us into," Placenta said. Then she turned to Sergeant Sandy again. "You're not going to get away with this crime unless you either hire a very expensive lawyer, or escape to a country without extradition treaties with the United States, both of which will cost a fortune. I have access to all of Polly's money. Plus, we have plenty of very wealthy friends abroad."

For a moment, it seemed that Sergeant Sandy was considering Placenta's offer. "How much money?" Sandy asked.

"Lots!"

"Nah, Socorro's win tonight will land us not only that 'get out of jail free' card, but a movie deal and endorsements, too."

"Not when the police begin thinking about how far the lovely and talented Socorro went to win the big prize, and how many real-life bodies you and she scattered around Hollywood," Polly said. "It won't take any time at all before they come to the conclusion that a certain mother/daughter team is responsible for all the killings. And I don't mean the Kardashians. They'll discover that you were the mastermind behind my death, and Placenta's. Then the police will accuse you of killing Thane and Danny," Polly said.

Sandy looked as though she hadn't considered that scenario. "Don't forget the grand prize, the 'get out of jail free' card!" Sandy stuttered.

"One card. One crime. No felonies," Placenta said. "And it's Socorro's card, not yours."

The color drained from Sandy's face. She stood frozen for a long moment, then pointed her gun directly at Placenta's chest. "Stop it! I'm tired of you and the so-called legendary

Polly Pepper getting in the way of things! Plug in the god-damned hair dryer. Now!"

Shaken, Placenta plugged it in and stood motionless.

In a softer voice, Sandy said, "Turn the power on."

Placenta looked helplessly at Polly. "I wasn't serious a moment ago when I said that I'd wasted the best years of my life with you. I was born into a horrible life, just like you, and I actually got to escape my destiny all because you liked me. I'll thank you again when I see you in heaven. I know that St. Peter will let you in."

"And you, too, Placenta," Polly said with tears in her eyes. "You were a sassy ol' thing, but we were a terrific team. At least we won't be seeing the likes of this bitch inside the Pearly Gates. I'll be sure to tell St. Peter all about how she treated us. Hey, I'll have that immortality that every celebrity who dies young receives. I'll probably surpass Elvis for the most Polly Pepper sightings! But damn, I always wanted a Kennedy Center honor!"

Sergeant Sandy raised her Beretta subcompact to Placenta's temple. "Do it. Now!"

Still, although Placenta's entire body was shaking, she did not move.

Placenta pushed the On button and the machine began to whir and blow warm air. As she pointed the gun-shaped dryer at Polly, the force of air caused the foam in the water to part, revealing one of Polly's lovely knees. As Placenta stood helplessly on the precipice of actually killing her best friend, Sergeant Sandy let out a stream of curses and swacked the dryer out of Placenta's hand. Placenta lunged forward and tried to catch the blow dryer, but she fumbled and the unit plunged into the water.

Polly and Placenta screamed simultaneously. Polly screamed again. And again, this time softer. And then they all realized that nothing had happened.

In the split second between the hair dryer sinking into the water, and Sergeant Sandy looking incredulously at the lack of any electrical charge, Placenta grabbed the neck of the bottle of champagne and bashed it with full force onto Sandy's skull. The security guard dropped to the floor and her handgun discharged, sending a bullet into the travertine of the shower at the opposite end of the room.

Polly laughed with satisfaction as she stepped out of the tub. With suds dripping from her body, she accepted a plush bath towel from Placenta.

"We showed her!" Placenta said, pulling the hair dryer cord out of the wall socket, and reeling in the device from the water. "Contrary to Sergeant Sandy's high opinion of her intellect, she's as dumb as they come. She picked the wrong bathroom grooming tool to use for execution."

"She should read *Consumer Reports,*" Polly agreed.

"Since 1991, hair dryers have ground circuit interrupters, which prevent electrocution whether on or off," Placenta recited.

As Polly stood looking at the body of Sergeant Sandy, and listening to Placenta quote an article they'd both read about the special features on the top ten hair dryers, Tim bounded into the room without his shirt on.

He looked at his mother, wrapped in a white towel, and Placenta using long strands of dental floss to bind Sergeant

Sandy's hands behind her inert body. "I heard a gunshot! What happened?" he said, his eyes wide with fear.

Polly looked at her handsome son's well-developed upper body. "I'm shocked that you could hear anything above the noise you were making out in the cottage," she said with a loving smirk.

CHAPTER 25

—✍—

The EMT unit sopped up the blood on the floor from the crack in Sergeant Sandy's skull. The crime scene investigators photographed every vein of travertine and marble in the master suite bathroom. They tweezed and bagged the last strands of hair in every drain. Detective Archer made his official preliminary report and chastised Polly for not checking the references of the people she hired. And field news reporters from channels 4, 5, 7, and 11, and Access *Hollywood,* finally left the estate to embellish out of all proportion the story of Polly Pepper's too-close-for-comfort brush with a psychotic security patrol assassin. Now it was time for the star to zip her hiney into her new D & G dress and play *Beat the Clock* to get to the live broadcast of *I'll Do Anything to Become Famous.*

Dressed to impress a platoon of paparazzi along a celebrity-clogged red carpet, Polly followed Tim and Placenta and hustled to the Rolls-Royce. "Step on it, sweetie," she called from the backseat. The car cruised off the estate and sped down Stone Canyon Road and onto Sunset Boulevard.

Finally gliding up to Sterling Studios' legendary (if not infamous) lightning-bolt-logo wrought-iron gates, Tim stopped at the guard kiosk and pushed the control to roll down his and Polly's windows. Polly's favorite security guard, Jack, was on duty and waiting for her with his clipboard in hand. "One for Miss P.," he said, handing a computer generated self-adhesive drive-on pass with her name printed in large bold type. "One for Tim. One for Placenta. Better make it snappy, Miss Pepper," Jack said as he raised the arm of the black-and-white-striped barrier. "Your show starts in thirty minutes. I'll call ahead so they'll know that you're here!"

Polly called out, "You're in my will, sweetums!"

Tim drove down narrow streets between the soundstages, searching for a parking space close to Studio B's stage door.

"There!" Polly shouted, pointing toward a block-long empty space that ran the length of Stage 37. "Fire zone," Tim said as he continued on.

"Don't be a sissy," Polly protested. "Studios don't burn down. If you don't count Universal. Still, if anyone makes a noise, you can move the car then. In the meantime, I have my own emergency. I've got to get into makeup!"

Tim was used to following his mother's instructions, regardless of the potentially dire consequences. He parked parallel to the enormous soundstage and rushed Polly and Placenta into the studio. Just inside, a production assistant was waiting to usher Polly to the makeup room. Another PA escorted Tim and Placenta to their seats in the VIP section of the audience.

As Polly followed the PA, she joked, "I would have arrived earlier, but a deranged killer attacked me!" The production assistant, who like all the other unpaid production assistants on the show was a freshly minted actor from the Holly-wood Academy of Stage and Screen. *The pians* (the *s* had been missing from the sign on the dilapidated building that housed the so-called academy for as long as anyone could remember), politely, if disinterestedly listened to the old star.

Polly summed up the blond ingénue and said, "You'll practically pee when I tell you that my intruder turned out to be that darling *Mama Mia* boy—in drag! You know the one. Hot bod, yet pretty enough to model Vera Wang."

The young escort said, "No way!"

"Not a word of truth, dear," Polly reassured the young girl. "But he's pretty enough to get away with wearing Val-entino. Don'tcha think?"

Finally settled in the makeup chair, Polly was given a quick touch-up of powder and lip-gloss and a dark pencil to her eyebrows. "Am I soup yet?" she said, smiling at Katie, the makeup girl. "Ah yes! A lovely tomato bisque. You'd do wonders for any old puss. Just tell me that the Saddleback creature was a makeup artist's worst nightmare."

"Absolutely," Katie lied. "And you don't look quite as constipated as Miss Thinks-She's-the-Voice-of-American-Political-Reason."

"One rounded tablespoon of Colon Cleanse mixed with champagne twice a day. That's my regime! It would work wonders for her," Polly declared. "By the by, gossip? Gossip? Gossip?"

Katie leaned in close to Polly's ear. "You know I never dish my clients."

"Just an initial or two?" Polly smiled. "Please, please?"

Katie grinned. "Okay. But this is more informational than simply the fun of ruining someone's reputation with slander and defamation. I have it on reasonably good authority—the studio massage therapist told one of the interns, who told Kelly, the wardrobe lady, who whispered it to me—that Lisa Marrs is not Thane Cornwall's killer!"

Polly yawned. "Oh, hon, everybody who's paid the slightest attention knows that! But can you name names?"

"Let's just say that Kelly says she heard that Thane's ex-gofer, Michael What's-his-name, plans to drop a major WMD tonight. Might breathe some excitement into this dead cow of a show. She said he'll massacre a couple of powerful reputations."

Polly suppressed a laugh. "Anyone we love to despise?"

Before Katie could say more, the PA received a text message on her iPhone. *Showtime, Miss Pepper! Gotta get you to the judges table right away.*

The color drained from Polly's face. "This is my favorite feeling. The horror of when I'm about to face a live television audience is like an orgasm, only it lasts a hell of a lot longer!" She turned to the PA. "Let's go, Peaches."

As Polly moved through the backstage area of the studio, she absorbed the vibrations from the drone of the audience in the distance. She inhaled the scents of perspiration from the hardworking grips and gaffers. With each blink of her eyes Polly captured mental pictures of the backstage tumult. When she arrived at the judges' table, she involuntarily smiled with a combination of excitement and fear. Just as her PA was leaving, another arrived with Brian Smith. "Sweetums!" Polly smiled and accepted a peck to her cheeks. "I'm thrilled to be home. What have I missed?"

"Nothing as exciting as your *real* life! I just saw the news on television. And someone told me it was Zac Efron disguised as Ashley Tisdale or Vanessa Hudgens. Are you all right?"

"I should be so lucky to have those cuties in my home. No, the intruder was just a crazed fan who broke into the wrong twenty-seven-room Bel Air mansion. Apparently she was aiming for Barbara Eden. For years I've been telling Barbara to answer fan mail more promptly! Loonies are just waiting for us to disappoint them. All of the Polly Pepper fan blogs commend me on authentic autographs. The particular crazy who wandered into my boudoir wanted to bottle Barbara up as Genie again and send her back to Babylon." Polly shrugged. "Remind me who's left among the contestants on this dangerous show!"

"Where've you been, girl?" Brian said. "It's down to Toe Nail and Taco Belle."

Polly shivered. "Don't let her mother hear you call her that."

As Polly scanned the audience, the crowd suddenly erupted with boos; Richard Dartmouth was walking toward the judges' seating area. "Oh Lord," Polly said, nudging Brian. "I sense that I'm in for a rough night."

"Success and power have gone to his head," Brian said. "Richard is as bad as Thane Cornwall. The contestants are sullen, but I can tell they're petrified of how he'll slam their performances, and the way he'll mock their answers to the interview questions. I'm surprised that he hasn't joined Thane down in Hades."

When Richard arrived he coolly ignored Polly.

"He's ticked off because my lovely agent coaxed him into bringing me back to the program," Polly whispered to Brian.

Richard took his seat, and the lights dimmed and the orchestra began to play. With a drumroll from the percussion section, the announcer called out, "Live! From Sterling Studios! Deep in the heart of the San Fernando Valley. Just over the hill from the real Hollywood. This is *I'll Do Anything to Become* Fay-*mous!*"

The orchestra played the show's theme song, an eerie Metallica-flavored arrangement of "Live and Let Die," and the studio audience applauded wildly and stomped their feet. They divided their attention between the live action onstage and large television screens showing what the home viewing audiences were seeing. The announcer continued. "Ladies and gentlemen. Please welcome. Your host. Steven. *Ben*-ja-min!" The crowd cheered even more loudly as Steven bounced into the spotlight. His smile advertised the whitest, most perfectly arranged teeth. His eyes sparkled like glitter. His dimples dimpled. And the cleft in his chin was deep enough to require flossing after meals. He held up his hands to quiet his adoring fans.

"Here we are!" Steven said as the applause died down. "The final night of our competition! To celebrate, let's welcome back that very special legend from the last century, the still lovely ... and ambulatory Polly Pepper!"

Blowing kisses, Polly stood up to accept the ovation. "I'm not quite ready for the Neptune Society." Then she added, "I have the lovely and talented Richard Dartmouth to thank for inviting me to return for this auspicious final installment of the program." Polly applauded Richard and was accompanied by a half-hearted response from the crowd. They weren't as eager to salute the man they loved to hate. Instead, they wanted to hear Toe Nail and Taco Belle sing, and to find out who would be voted the most likely to make an easy meal out of their family and friends in order to reach the top rung on the ladder of success.

Richard Dartmouth studiously inspected his cuticles.

Before Polly could take her seat, the camera returned to Steven Benjamin. "Let's set history in motion!" he said, rubbing his hands. "Please welcome our two remaining contestants. Toe Nail! And … Socorro Sanchez!"

The two walked across the stage. Their lack of camaraderie was evident. Neither did they hold hands, nor did they smile at each other, or at Steven. In fact, they stood on opposite sides of the host looking as bored as prostitutes working Main Street, Disneyland.

However, gracious master of ceremonies that he was, Steven pretended not to notice the lack of congeniality between the contestants. "As you remember from last week, darling Miranda and sweet Amy said goodbye to our shrinking family here at *I'll Do Anything to Become Famous.* Shall we take a look at some of their more memorable parting shots?"

Projected on the large screens throughout the studio soundstage was a montage of film clips showing Amy's three weeks on the show. Her singing was flat, and what appeared to be mean-spirited jibes from Thane and Richard were mostly spot-on. Then came the moment from last week when Steven Benjamin had to open a sealed envelope and read, "You'll *never* be famous," which were the dreaded words telling the contestants that they were being ditched from the show.

The screen revealed Amy in shocked skepticism. Then the smug faces of the remaining members of the contest were shown. A handheld camera followed Amy as she stomped off the stage to return to her dressing room. In the cinder block corridor, she looked into the camera and said, "I was promised! I swear, when I write my book, I'll let the freakin' cat outta the bag!"

The camera returned to Steven. "Such a good sport. *Not!* And of course, Miranda departed last week, too. I'm biting my nails all over again. Let's take a look at that inauspicious occasion." The large screens showed the tense moments as Steven opened the envelope and spoke Miranda's name. The eliminated contestant put her hands on her hips, curling her lips. Then she slapped Socorro. "You know what that's for!" And she slapped Steven while sputtering, "Liar! Cheater!"

Backstage, she said, "Some so-called big people are gonna become very small, very soon." Then she slapped the camera out of the videographer's hands, breaking the thirty-five-thousand-dollar piece of equipment.

When camera number one again focused on Steven, he smiled and said, "Owww! That still hurts!" He good-naturedly rubbed the side of his face where he'd been slapped the week before. "Let's get on with this final show. But first, take a minute to watch these great commercials from our amazing sponsors!"

When the stage lights dimmed, and the lights in the audience were turned up, Polly nudged Brian. "Where's your beautiful Lyndie on this special night?"

Brian pointed into the audience. "She and Tiara are together. Isn't that your son with them?"

Polly looked in the direction that Brian was pointing. "That's my Timmy. And Placenta, too."

Brian suddenly looked startled. "Oh, damn! I forgot to give this to you." He reached into the breast pocket of his suit jacket and retrieved an envelope. "It's from Tiara."

Polly smiled and slipped a finger under the sealed flap of the envelope. She withdrew a sheet of expensive notepaper and began to read silently. When she finished, she smiled and looked up at Brian. "She's a darling. I'm invited to their anniversary party celebration. Ten September."

Brian nodded. "Guess we'll see you there."

"Anniversary," Polly said in a cynical tone.

"Something wrong?" Brian asked.

Polly shook her head. "I'm such a ninny. I couldn't keep two husbands, so I suppose I'm a bit suspect of others pretending domestic bliss."

"Are you suggesting that Steven and Tiara aren't as happy as they appear to be?"

Polly smiled sheepishly. "No relationship is perfect."

Brian looked across the audience to Lyndie. "Steven and Tiara are both nice people, but…"

"But?" Polly said.

Brian looked at Polly, trusting that she was a clam. "I don't like to spread rumors, but…"

"Spread 'em!" Polly pleaded. Just then, the lights in the studio dimmed and the stage shone brighter. Polly whispered to Brian, "What rumors?"

"I'll tell you during the next commercial break," Brian said, and turned his attention toward the stage.

Polly huffed, but plastered on a wide smile for the camera.

"And we're back!" Steven said with his boyish enthusiasm. "Toe Nail and Taco Belle, oops, Socorro, flipped a coin backstage, to determine who would be the first to perform this evening. Oh, and to make the competition just a little bit more exciting, Toe Nail and Socorro each chose the other's song. So, please welcome to the stage, Toe Nail, singing 'Muskrat Love'!"

Wild applause ensued as Toe Nail ambled onto the stage, showing obvious disdain for the song he was about to rap.

"Muskrat Suzie! Muskrat Sam!
Do the jitterbug out in Muskrat Land!
And they shimmy! Sam is so skinny!"

When his performance was over, he didn't bother to bow. He simply walked forward and, with his arms defiantly folded across his chest, placed himself in line for a direct hit from the judges.

Steven put his arm around Toe Nail's shoulders. "To celebrate the return of our very own living legend, let's allow Miss Polly Pepper to be the first to assess your performance.

"Oh, jeez…" Toe Nail said.

As cameras focused on Polly she smiled and waved to the audience. "Darling, Toe Nail! I love that song! I loved it a hundred years ago when The Captain and Tennille made it a hit. You weren't even a guppy in your father's glands, but trust me, they were the cutest couple. Not the glands. The singers. You'd have to have been there to appreciate 'em. We had corny acts then. Husbands and wives. Brothers and sisters. Entire families. Black ones and white ones and Christian ones and Mormon ones. La, what a lovely musical period. Of course, they all appeared on my show at one time or another. Purchase the new collector's edition boxed DVD set from the first five seasons of *The Polly Pepper Playhouse*. You'll see what I mean."

"And the clock keeps ticking," Steven Benjamin said.

"Anyway," Polly continued, "you did a marvelous job. You *nailed* it, Mr. Toe Nail. I could tell that you really felt those lyrics. *".. and now he's ticklin' her fancy, rubbin' her nose ...'* So deep and yet you brought a genuine sense of what those two sexy muskrats were up to. I say, bravo!"

"What the hell's a muskrat, anyway?" Toe Nail said. "And does 'ticklin' her fancy' mean what I think it does?"

Steven interrupted again and said, "I think this is a family show. So let's hear from our very own best brownie baker in the country, Brian Smith!"

Brian smiled and accepted the applause from the audience. "I'm with Toe Nail—and Polly Pepper. The lyrics are stupid, but Toni Tennille made it seem sweet—more than a quarter century ago," he said. "Considering the material, which I suspect was selected by Socorro specifically because the song is so dreadful, you did a decent job. At least you spared us from clearly hearing all the lyrics. For that we're grateful. Good job, man."

Before Steven had an opportunity to introduce Richard Dartmouth, Richard spoke up. "Christ allmighty! Man, you're a drag! You have a lousy song to begin with, one that I thought couldn't be any worse than the record, and you succeed in proving me wrong. You've just wasted three and a half minutes of my life! Did it ever occur to you to save what little dignity you may have and refuse to perform that tripe in public? Jeez!"

The cameras refocused on Steven, whose dimples seemed to grow deeper by the minute. "A novel thought from Mr. Positive! I think we're off to our usual interesting start! Now let's see how Socorro handles the song that Toe Nail selected specifically for her. Please welcome back to the stage Socorro Sanchez, to sing 'Torn Between Two Lovers.'"

As the key light followed Socorro to her place on the stage, the audience's applause was tepid but she maintained her straight posture and held her head high. Polly was convinced that Socorro's confidence was a result of believing that she held the trump card: the DVDs of the sex-capades between Steven and her, and Steven and the other contestants. Although her mother obviously wouldn't be delivering the discs as they had planned, her friend Michael wouldn't let her down. She was certain that he'd ride in at the last moment and prove that she was the most nefarious of them all, and would thus win the grand prize.

As Socorro began to sing, Polly leaned forward on the table and looked intently at the performer. *With her mother in the jail ward at Cedars Sinai, why is Socorro even onstage?*

Sure, the show must go on, but your mother's been accused of attempted murder, and she's suffered a concussion at the hands of her almost victims.

When the spotlight was again focused on a beaming Steven Benjamin, Polly nudged Brian Smith and whispered, "Remember that kid Michael who was at our dinner party? Have you seen him today?"

Brian shrugged and stuck out his lower lip. "I don't think so."

Richard Dartmouth was the first to send his verbal daggers toward the stage. "I'm torn too," he said to Socorro, "between suicide and murder. Honey," he continued, "you didn't display an ounce of genuine feeling. It's a song about a tramp who's wracked with guilt because she's cheating on two guys, both of whom she desperately wants to bang her. You acted as though you were torn between the Big Mac and the chicken nuggets!"

As the audience booed, Socorro gave him the finger. The audience broke into wild applause with hoots and whistles thrown in for good measure.

When the camera again found Richard, he was smirking and shaking his head.

From the stage, Steven called on Brian Smith to offer his evaluation of Socorro and her rendition of "Torn Between Two Lovers."

"Heya, Socorro," he said, "I've been there. I think we all have. It's tough when you can't decide, but here's a bit of advice, forget the heart, go for the gold!"

Again the audience erupted with applause, as though Brian had said the only sensible thing. Brian continued and said, "I'm only suggesting that if you love two guys, and one has money, catch the one with the dollar signs sparkling in his eyes!"

Steven looked out toward the audience. "Brian got lucky. His wife is stunning *and* rich. Stand up, Lyndie! I saw you sitting in the audience." The camera found Mrs. Brian Smith. She halfheartedly waved and smiled uncomfortably.

"Good advice, my man," Steven said to Brian as the camera now captured a smiling Polly Pepper.

Polly looked at Socorro and said, "Lovely, dear. And nowadays, having two people who love you is rare. The song is very hopeful. And I sincerely hope that your mother is feeling better."

Steven Benjamin acknowledged that Socorro's mother had been hospitalized for "a trauma to her head." He then shot Polly a stern look.

"I'm sure that if they allow television in the lock-down ward at Cedars, your performance tonight is helping your mother to recuperate," Polly said. "Plus, there's a rumor spreading like intestinal bacteria in Mexico that we're in for a very special surprise!"

When the lights in the audience again went up, Polly found Tiara Benjamin standing by her side.

"Lovely to see you again, Polly," Tiara said. "I wanted to say hello before the cocktail crush after the show. You know how those things are, with a sea of studio execs and all the wankers who've worked on the show mingling and drinking, I might not be able to find you."

Polly stood up to embrace Tiara. "Love your outfit. Valentino?" she said, holding Tiara's hands and stepping back to view her clothes. "I know you never come to the show, but I'm happy that you decided to make an exception for me tonight."

"I'm here as much for Steven," Tiara said.

"And thank you for your kind invitation. Love the stationery. And the type font is precious! I always think it's a grand idea to celebrate milestones in our lives. An anniversary. Nothing could be more exciting!" She looked into Tiara's eyes. "My goodness! Ten glorious years of love, comfort, honor, fidelity, et cetera. All that crap that one has to promise to one's partner. I don't know that I could ever do that again. Sounds good on paper, but there are so many temptations, especially in this town where everybody is beyond gorgeous!"

Tiara sighed. "Yeah, I suppose marriage has never been a breeze for anyone. Still, I like being attached to one bloke. Especially a chap who is as attractive and seductive as my Steven. Even if he wanted to leave me, I'd never let him go."

"Toothache all gone?" Polly inquired.

"Toothache? Oh, absolutely! Steven cracked a tooth on something silly like cotton candy." She looked up at the stage searching for a glimpse of her husband; then she looked at her watch. "I'd better scatter back to my seat. The show's about to continue. See you in a tick or two. Yes?"

As Tiara left the judges' area and wended her way back to her seat in the VIP section of the audience, Polly took out her invitation to Steven and Tiara's upcoming anniversary party. She caressed the fine linen paper and stared at the words for such a long time that Brian Smith leaned over and said, "Are you memorizing the invitation?"

Polly smiled. "I was just thinking what an amazing woman Tiara is. And I adore how Brits use the English language better than we do. Steven should be in heaven." Polly placed the notepaper back in its envelope and slipped it into her clutch purse. She looked down to the end of the table and saw Richard speaking into his cell phone. "Can you believe that man?" she said to Brian. "He hasn't said one word to me. I dug out an expensive bottle of Veuve to bring as a gift. I'm glad I decided to drink it myself. "So, Brian, you were about to tell me rumors…."

The announcer counted down, "Five. Four. Three. Two..

CHAPTER 26

—⁓—

"And, we're back!" Steven said from the stage.
"Since this is our last time together, and before
our popular interview section of the program, let's walk
down memory lane, and take a look at a few of the more
exciting moments from the past five weeks."

Instantly, the lights in the studio dimmed, the curtains
behind Steven parted, and a large movie screen was revealed.
A montage of images of the contestants and judges filled
the screen, as a documentary about the making of *I'll Do
Anything to Become Famous* began to play.

Polly and the studio and television viewing audience
watched as potential contestants first auditioned for the
program. Some were mortifyingly awful, while others,
especially Toe Nail, seemed at home in front of the camera
and found an easy rapport with the audience. Images of
the first night and the cruel treatment that each contestant
on the stage had received from Thane Cornwall made the
audience boo. But then there were the backstage rantings
of the contestants, each of whom had scathing words for

Thane, and threats of being accountable for his quick demise. These made the audiences roar with approval, despite the fact that each of the contestants' promises for retribution had come to pass. Thane was as dead as they'd all pledged.

As the montage continued, Polly watched clips from the shows that she had missed. She found herself rooting with the audience when the screen filled with Richard Dartmouth proclaiming, "Miranda's diaphragm must be filled with nuclear waste because there was no other way to account for her freakishly deformed and mutilated singing."

"Boo!" Polly joined the audience.

And then the orchestra began to play the somber Dvorak classic *Goin' Home* as the screen momentarily went to black and the words *in memoriam* appeared. A moment later, a photograph of a smiling Thane Cornwall appeared, accompanied by his name and the years of his birth and death. The audience was respectfully silent. Then, an image of Danny Castillo filled the screen. Again, the audience was reverent. Finally, the screen faded to black. As the lights in the studio illuminated the audience, Steven Benjamin returned to the stage and led the applause.

"Thane Cornwall. Danny Castillo," Steven said. "Both men provided their unique talents to this show and we will always be grateful for their contributions." After a short moment of dignified silence, Steven continued his job as host. "Toe Nail and Socorro have come a long way, but tonight only one will receive the coveted *Get out of Jail Free* card for proving that they'll do anything to become famous. Up until now, our television viewing audience has voted each week, but tonight, the studio audience will determine the winner. And there's still one more hurdle to cross for our two remaining contestants."

On cue, both contestants ambled center stage into the spotlight. Looking like juvenile delinquents being summoned before a criminal court judge, they stared down at Richard, Brian, and Polly, with looks that dared anyone to ask a question more difficult than to remember what they'd had for lunch.

Steven asked if Brian would be the first to pose a question to Toe Nail.

Brian smiled and said, "Man, I shouldn't say this, but I think you've already nailed it. You said you'd do a lot of stuff that I'd be too much of a sissy to try. But when you said you'd even work with Vince Vaughn in order to succeed, I figured for that misery you deserved to win. But for tonight, I'll just ask, 'What have you done over the past few weeks that you never in a million years thought you'd do in order to win this game and be on your way to becoming famous?'"

Toe Nail thought for a long moment. Finally, he said, "I'm not a 'what goes around comes around' kinda guy. Morals and ethics are for tree huggers and dudes who believe in karma and divine retribution, and stuff. I don't care about saving the planet or the spotted white owl. I'm into saving me! So I'm not afraid of going to hell for doing what I had to do to stay in the running to win this contest. I took out an obstacle that would have given Taco Belle the edge."

The audience started to chant, "Toe Nail! Toe Nail! Toe Nail!"

"I mean, the dude was going to reveal something pretty shocking. We're just keeping him quiet until I win the game," Toe Nail said.

Brian continued his questioning. "So what did you do to this person? Is he or she still breathing?"

"I'm not a killer, like some people around here," he said, looking into Brian's eyes.

Brian evil-stared back at Toe Nail. "What did this person have that threatened you and your own dishonesty and illegal activities?"

Toe Nail shrugged. "I could have won this idiotic contest without kidnapping, but I didn't want to take the chance. Plus, holding someone against their will is a pretty good way to keep racking up the points, too," he said. "The dude is cool about it."

The audience chanted his name.

Steven Benjamin lifted his microphone to his lips and said, "Way to go! I'm sure the audience will give you a ton of credits for abduction! Wow! Who would have thought?" And then he looked at Richard Dartmouth. "Mr. D.! It's your turn to make 'em squirm. Go for the gold, man!"

Toe Nail adjusted his stance as if to withstand a blast from Hurricane Richard.

Richard leaned back in his chair and folded his arms across his chest. "You're a wily one, aren't you? Every week you come before this tribunal and tell us tales of the things you'd do to win fame. I don't believe half of the things you say. Now you've added kidnapping to your improbable resume of felonies. I'd like to take a wild guess as to who that someone is with the ability to reduce your chance to win."

Toe Nail shrugged.

"We've been missing an assistant for the past few days. Michael. That kid who used to work for Thane. He hasn't shown up for work since Wednesday. I'll wager that he's the victim of your crime."

Again, Toe Nail shrugged.

"What were you were afraid he was going to reveal? Could it have been…" Richard Dartmouth stopped for a moment and let Toe Nail sweat about what he feared Michael had planned to say, and the possibility that Richard already knew and was going to do the job himself.

"Michael and Socorro were plotting against me," Toe Nail said with a defiant sneer.

Socorro shouted, "No! Michael has to be here!"

"Your mama's not coming to your rescue either," Toe Nail said. "Just be glad that I have a heart. He's safely watching the show." He looked to the camera. "Yo! Dude! You'll be free after tonight. We'll grab a beer, okay? No hard feelings."

Richard leaned forward and put his elbows on the table. "You're not going to tell us why you kidnapped the kid?"

"Specifically?"

"What else."

"Nope." Toe Nail stared at Richard, knowing that the producer-turned-judge had to be fully aware of the drama that would have unfolded had Toe Nail not taken measures to remove Michael from the equation, and daring him to make any accusations.

"I know why he kidnapped Michael," Socorro yelled. "Because Michael has a ton of evidence showing how far *I've* personally gone to eliminate the losers on this show, and prove what I've done to become the winner!"

Richard shook his head. "Curiously, when I developed this show, I wanted to prove that some people would literally do anything, and I mean anything, to get a few minutes of face time on the tube. You're both exactly what I'd hoped for. You're deceitful, crafty, scheming, untrustworthy, dishonest, and unscrupulous. You're my poster kids for Machiavellian behavior in Hollywood."

"A man after your own heart?" Toe Nail said. "Hollywood corrupts. Maybe it's true that you can't get to where you're going in this town without killing off a few rivals along the way. I have my own means to the end."

Richard Dartmouth gave a self-confident smile. "As I always say, one does what one has to do."

"Right on, bro," Toe Nail said.

"Me, too!" Socorro cried out.

In the studio's sound booth, the director spoke into the cameramen's headphones. "Camera number one to Steven Benjamin. Camera number two, wide angle on the judges' table. Number three, stay with Toe."

When Steven received the director's signal, he smiled and ad-libbed for a minute about the fate of Michael and how a kidnapping charge was pretty much proof that indeed Toe Nail was the challenger most likely to win the competition. Then he cut to the next bank of commercials.

Brian Smith leaned over to Polly and asked, "What the hell's Toe Nail talking about? What's his 'means to the end'?"

Polly smiled and shook her head. "You'll see. It's coming up after the break." She then reached into her purse and speed-dialed Tim's cell phone number.

Tim's phone vibrated in his pants pocket. He surreptitiously removed it and, seeing Polly's name on the readout, accepted the call. "Yeah?" He listened for a moment, then ended the call. Tim turned to Placenta and winked. "I need to leave for a moment."

Placenta gave him a knowing look. "She's sure?" Placenta asked.

Tim nodded his head and excused himself as he squeezed past Lyndie and Tiara and the others in his aisle.

In a moment, the show was back live. Steven Benjamin looked at Polly. "Miss Pepper, would you pose a question to Toe Nail, or graciously pass? We're running out of time, so if you'll allow us to move on, you'll definitely interview Socorro first."

"I'm fine," she said into her microphone. "I just want to wish Toe Nail good luck!"

Steven was visibly delighted. He called Socorro back to the stage. "You look a little rattled."

Socorro grimaced. She looked at Polly and said, "Hit me with your best shot, star lady."

Polly took her microphone out of the table stand, stood up, and faced the stage. "And I wish you all the luck in the world, too, Socorro. I know you've worked hard at being dastardly throughout the course of the competition. In fact, I've seen the evidence in so many unexpected ways. You may be happy to know that even without your mama or Michael to help you out tonight, I'm the next best thing."

Socorro forced a smile. "I figured you might be smarter than people give you credit for being. Hell, kidnapping is small potatoes compared to what I had up my sleeve."

Steven Benjamin said, "Tick, tick, tick."

"Very sorry," Polly said. "It's just that since this is the last night of the competition, there's so much I want to say. I know that I don't have all the time in the world, so let me just pose one teensy question.

"Excuse me for one moment, dear," she said to Socorro. "I do have a question, but I must direct it to ... Steven Benjamin."

Steven gave Polly a warm smile. "Reruns of *Mary Tyler Moore* start in twenty minutes," he said in his charming voice. "Can't let the nation's fans be deprived of Mary and Ted and Valerie and Ed and the Happy Homemaker."

"This'll just take a sec, dear." She was quiet for a moment, then said, "Steven, hon, why did you kill Thane Cornwall and Danny Castillo?"

The audience roared with laughter. But when Polly didn't laugh with them, they started to murmur among themselves. Steven's smile, however, grew wider. "No wonder you're famous, you're a very funny lady."

Polly grinned. "I try. Sometimes I make people wet their pants." Then she looked up to the control booth. "Mr. Director, dearest, would you please run the DVD that my darling son, Tim, brought to you a few minutes ago? You're a doll. You're in my Will!"

Then the lights above the stage were dimmed, as were the lights in the audience. A large screen rolled down automatically from the ceiling and hung in front of the stage. The DVD marked *Anything Goes—2 of 6* began to play.

The audience began to laugh; then they sniggered and began a series of noisy wolf calls. As they oohed and aahed, the orchestra conductor picked up his baton and led his musicians in an unrehearsed rendition of Ravel's "Bolero." Soon there were whoops and whistles from the audience.

And when the DVD played itself out and the lights on the stage were once again illuminated, Steven stood looking shell-shocked.

Again Polly asked, "Why did you, Steven Benjamin, kill Thane Cornwall?"

Steve shot back, "I had nothing to do with Thane's death! And what has some doctored DVD showing people engaged in lewd activities got to do with Thane or me? It was his assistant, Lisa Marrs, who killed him. She's in jail for it!"

Polly shook her head. "Oh, pooh. She certainly wanted to kill the son of a bitch. But she was just one of many on a long wait list. You forced your way to the head of that line. Why? You used to be friends."

Steven gave his signature smile to the camera and said, "We'll be back after these messages." He continued smiling, waiting for the director to announce that they were no longer in the live feed.

"Nobody wants to cut away when the story is getting so juicy, sweetums," Polly said. "So let's give 'em a really good drama, shall we? Think of the ratings!" Steven stopped smiling. He walked over to the tall staircase on the set and sat down on the second step. With his microphone in one hand he resembled a denim-clad version of *The Thinker.* "I'm all ears."

Polly came out from behind the judges' table and walked up to the stage. She stood in the spotlight and for an instant she was back on the set of *The Polly Pepper Playhouse.* She could feel herself drifting back in time and almost unable to keep herself from asking if the audience wanted to see her popular sketch comedy character Bedpan Bertha, the klutzy nurse. Or Madam Zody, the fake psychic. Suddenly, Polly began singing "Send in the Clowns." When she completed the song, the audience gave her a standing ovation.

"Comfortable up here?" Steven's patronizing tone reeled her back to the moment.

As the audience buzzed about what they were seeing, Polly asked, "Steven. Do you remember the night that Thane was killed? Of course you do. What I should ask is, do you remember your little sparring ritual? Thane asked you why you seldom wear your wedding ring."

Steven shot her a deadly look. "And I told him that I sometimes forget to put on my wedding band."

"Remember his response?" Polly asked. "He said, 'My Willy is more discerning than yours.'"

Oohs and boos erupted from the audience. Polly said, "It was a reference to you having sex backstage with each of the contestants—just as we showed a few moments ago in that priceless film clip. And that's why he stopped being your friend. He may have been a troublemaker, but he hated your marital infidelity. You realized in that moment that his assistant, Michael, and Richard's assistant, Lisa, had become chums and that she must have told Michael about the surveillance video. In fact, Lisa told me that Richard had brought you into his office to warn you about your conduct. He's the first one who told you about the surveillance cameras. Lisa confided in me that her boss told you he promised to destroy the tapes."

Polly looked toward the judges' table. "Isn't this true, Richard?"

Dartmouth nodded, as captivated by Polly's analysis as the rest of the audience.

"You realized in that moment that Thane Cornwall was your blackmailer!" Polly said.

"My what?" Steven stood up. "A blackmailer? That's nonsense. No one is blackmailing me!"

"Yes, and no," Polly said. "After the show that night, you waited for Lisa to leave Thane's estate. Then you entered the house. You'd been a guest there so many times, you knew your way around. I suspect that you were wearing latex gloves when you picked up a knife in the kitchen. You found Thane sleeping soundly in his bedroom."

Steven folded his arms across his chest, daring Polly to continue.

"Very clean work, Steven," Polly said. "Best of all, Thane probably didn't feel a thing. Second best of all is that Lisa Marrs's fingerprints were on the handle of the knife. She tells me that when they argued she'd picked up the knife with the intention of killing Thane herself. But she couldn't go through with it. However, and this is where it gets more icky, a few days after Thane's death another blackmail note arrived, and you realized that you'd killed the wrong person."

"*Another* note?" Steven roared. "Am I supposed to have a drawer full of blackmail letters? Is that what you're suggesting?"

Polly nodded.

"You're as crazy as Norma Desmond," Steven snapped. "You'd better prove something soon or Sterling Studios' security will take you away to a place you belong, and I don't mean Pepper Plantation."

Polly took a deep breath. "Remember the day that I dropped by with a gift of a bottle of champagne? You were in so much pain. Tiara said it was a toothache. You said it was a virus. A double whammy. I felt awful for you. You were sweet not wanting me to catch anything so you booted me out quickly. But you weren't sick with a cold or flu. You'd received another blackmail letter. I know, because I read it. You'd crumpled it up in anger and thrown it onto the floor. While you were in the bathroom heaving up your guts from fear and regret, I got a glimpse of what your blackmailer was after. Five hundred thousand U.S. dollars. The letter stipulated U.S. dollars. Odd, isn't it?"

Steven sat down again, helplessly sinking.

"But who was really behind the blackmail letters?" Polly asked. "I've given this a ton of thought. It didn't seem logical that Thane Cornwall, who was wealthy, would shake anyone down for money. No, I thought it had to be one of the contestants, or even Lisa Marrs, after all. But the contestants on film were all over eighteen, and from watching that interesting DVD a few times, it seems your encounters were consensual. They probably figured that by having relations with you, it would help their chances of winning. That ploy is as old as Hollywood. By the way, my Tim and Placenta were impressed with your endowment. Me, not so much. Killers are unattractive—regardless of how cute they are."

The audience roared with laughter.

"I thought and thought about this case. It was driving me nuts!" Polly said. "Then I received the sweetest thank-you note from your lovely and darling wife, Tiara, expressing her appreciation for that fun dinner party we had at the

Plantation. The Brits are so polite and well raised, don't you agree? Then something jumped out at me. I reviewed the blackmail letters—you really should get more loyal household help—there were several common denominators among them and Tiara's thank-you note. For one, the stationery was exquisite. Regular bond paper would have sufficed for a common blackmailer. Also, the way the missives were dated. The British always put the day before the month, unlike Americans. And the punctuation. In the States, we place our commas inside quotation marks. In England they're placed outside."

The director ordered a split screen of the unfolding events, and the studio audience and television viewers were treated to simultaneous reactions from Polly and Steven. On the left, Polly looked glamorous in her Dolce. On the right, Steven looked tired and his shirt wrinkled with perspiration. "What is this, Remedial English 101?" Steven raised his voice. "What you're telling us is completely stupid and insane and has nothing to do with Thane Cornwall's death!"

"I thought so too," Polly said. "Then my darling maid and bff Placenta got to be buddy-buddy with your maid, Maria. The two shared their tiffs about their employers. Although I'm a perfectly wonderful mistress of my manor, it seems that your beautiful Tiara had confided in Maria that she suspected that you were having affairs behind her back. Tonight, Tiara told me that she loved you so much, and would never let you go, even if you wanted to leave. She also used a couple of words that appeared in several of the blackmail letters. Do the terms 'wankers' and 'bloke' mean anything to you?"

Polly turned to Tiara Benjamin. "I'm so sorry, honey. I'm sick to death about having to rat about your broken marriage on national television. You weren't really blackmailing your husband, were you? No, just trying to scare him into fidelity. You couldn't have known how far he'd go."

The television screen suddenly split into quarters, showing Polly, Steven, Tiara, and the audience. Tiara was weeping into a handkerchief.

Polly continued. "Steven, your rags-to-riches story is indeed an inspiring one. From a trailer in Newhall, to a career as a model, to acting on daytime dramas, and now as the host of *I'll Do Anything to Become Famous*. You've got that great mansion, the expensive cars, and commercial endorsements. But you were about to lose everything because you couldn't keep your fly zipped. So you killed Thane because you presumed that he was about to take it all away from you. But why did Danny have to go too?"

Polly was quiet for a long moment. Then she answered her own question. "I couldn't understand why anyone would murder such a darling boy, and in *my* personal mansion! Then I realized that Michael obviously couldn't keep his trap shut and talked about the surveillance videos. I remembered that Lisa said she'd become friendly with him as they commiserated about how much they despised their respective bosses. So, armed with knowledge of the DVDs, each of the remaining contestants set out to steal the discs to use against the others. Miranda tried at my dinner party. Danny must have come to my home at the same time that you and Michael did. The funny thing is, I didn't know what was on those discs until Michael tried to steal them from my house."

Steven screamed, "You can't prove one thing that you're saying! So you have a motive. A lot of people did. Where's your evidence? You haven't any!"

Polly opened up her clutch purse, withdrew a clear plastic sandwich bag, and held it up. "It's not much, but it belongs to you."

As the television camera moved in for a close-up, Steven peered intently into the bag. "What?" he asked, shifting his eyes to Polly.

"A little something the police found in my home, a few inches from Danny's body."

Steven looked puzzled.

"You must spend a fortune to keep your perfect teeth looking movie star bright. I'll bet you have a strict regimen for brushing and flossing and rinsing. Oh, it must have hurt to chip one of your pearly whites. In fact, I know it did. I stopped by when you were experiencing that horrid toothache! Remember?"

Steven shook his head. "So what if I had a toothache? I had a cavity."

"It's no use. The police have already matched your DNA to that tooth," Polly said. "As for placing you at the scene of Thane's murder, well, that was a little harder."

"Because I wasn't there!" Steven insisted.

"Surveillance videos tell a different story." Polly smiled.

"Thane's security system was out of service," Steven said triumphantly. "He had SOS, the same as you. That wretched company can't keep their equipment working. Even the police said the cameras were inoperable that night!"

Polly snapped her fingers. "Dam! You're right. Thane and I have that same crummy service. I suppose that's how unwanted guests keep finding their way into my house."

There was a collective sigh of disappointment from the audience.

"You were wise to go with Mayday. I'll be calling their installation service first thing in the morning. They really are a better grade for celebrities such as us. In fact, your cameras are always working just fine."

Steven looked uneasy.

"They take such good pictures, in fact, that even in the middle of the night, with very little light, you're as clear in the image as you are sitting in front of this live television audience."

Steven blanched.

Polly tsk-tsked. "It was fairly easy for me to put you at the scene of Danny Castillo's death," she said. "The bit of tooth was all the evidence I and the police required. But I didn't know how the hell to connect you with Thane's death. The blackmail notes weren't enough. Sure, the finger was pointed, but I had no hard evidence. And when the security system at Thane's failed, I thought, well, I guess Lisa Marrs is going to fry like bacon.

"But as I kept thinking about security cameras, it occurred to me that yours might have been working just fine. Guess what? Those darling technicians and customer service agents at Mayday Security were able to access the hard drive on which your cameras' footage was uploaded. At first I couldn't understand what you were doing up so late! Then I figured it out." Steven put his face in the palms of his hands.

Polly looked out at Tiara. "Honey, it's two a.m. Do you know where our Steven is going in the middle of the night?"

Steven stood up and pointed at Toe Nail. "It's his fault! Yeah, Richard Dartmouth told me about the surveillance footage, but all the contestants wanted me. They thought it would help them win."

"Na-ah!" Socorro spat. "We all agreed you were at the top of the boring lover list."

Steven continued. "I trusted Richard to destroy the evidence. He promised. I didn't count on his evil little assistant making copies. I promised Toe Nail that he'd win the competition if he and Michael got hold of the discs. They broke into Lisa Marrs's apartment, but you beat them to it, stupid woman."

"Polly Pepper is not stupid, nor is she a thief," she said with indignity in her voice. "How often do I have to say that I borrowed the DVDs? I thought they were old movies with my girl chum, Mitzi.

"Back to your own thievery," Polly continued. "When your two little assistants returned empty-handed and told you that I took the evidence, you decided to pay a visit to me at Pepper Plantation. Fortunately, I wasn't home and the alarm system was on the fritz. However, Danny must have heard your plans because he was already there when you and Toe Nail and Michael arrived."

"If only that were the case." Steven sneered. "Yeah, Danny insisted that he hadn't found the DVDs at Pepper Plantation. But all these kids are liars. I suspected that when he heard us enter the house, he'd ditched the discs. While Toe Nail and Michael were scouring the house, Danny was out of control. He threatened to go to the *National Peeper* and tell them what we'd done, and the surveillance tapes would have been proof. I told him that I'd arrange for him to be the winner of the contest, but he said he wanted more than that for his silence. He wanted money and a house and a car. I knew he'd always hold the strings in my life, so I..."

"Killed Danny," Polly said. "And in the struggle you hit your mouth on the floor, and there went that precious tooth."

Polly looked into the camera. "I think we have a winner! Who in our studio, despite not being *in* the competition, has proved that he'll do anything to *stay* famous?"

The audience erupted: *"Stee-ven! Stee-ven! Stee- ven!"*

Polly applauded the audience, then turned and applauded Steven. "We can save the interview questions for the prosecuting attorney." Polly looked into the audience, shielding her eyes against the bright lights. "Where's my adorable BHPD bf Randy Archer? C'mon up with a batallion of your finest and let Steven have Lisa Marrs's room at the Bastille."

CHAPTER 27

—✑—

As Steven Benjamin was escorted out of the studio by a platoon of police officers, a PA approached Polly. "Mr. Dartmouth wants you in his office, pronto," she said.

Polly looked at the assistant. "I'm pooped. Tell the big D that we'll celebrate our success over something bubbly when I wake up—in a week or two."

"If you aren't there in five minutes, the studio security team will drag you by your gray roots."

Polly blanched and tottered on her heels.

"I'm merely the messenger."

Polly waved to Tim and Placenta, who were wending their way to the stage through the sea of tweens leaving the studio. When they were at Polly's side and offering hugs and congratulations, Polly grimaced. "I've been summond to Dartmouth Dungeon."

"A commendation for sure." Tim smiled.

"A spanking, I presume." Polly sniffed. "Damn J.J. He goes way too far when he threatens to make pretty men not so pretty."

Polly and her troupe followed the PA out of the studio and across the lot to the executive building, otherwise known as Sterling Stalag. Regardless of the reason for one's business in this stark steel and glass structure, which housed Sterling's global headquarters, entering the building generated more discomfort than preparing for a colonoscopy.

The young PA escorted her charges into the elevator and ascended to the penthouse of the twelve-story building. When the doors parted, the only illumination in the foyer was dim amber light emanating from modem decorative sconces on the walls. "This way," the leader said. At the end of the long hallway was a set of tall, frosted-glass double doors, as ominous as the portal to the throne room of the Wizard of Oz. "Just knock," the young woman said as she quickly peeled away and disappeared down the hall.

The trio exchanged uneasy glances before Tim rapped his knuckles on the door.

"Yo!"

Tim pulled the handle on one of the massive doors and held it open for his mother and Placenta.

The room was impressively large. Richard's desk, designed to complement the rest of the building, was chrome and glass. The only objects resting there were a telephone and a banker's box with an Emmy Award resting on top of papers, books, and picture frames. Richard was seated on a white leather Barcelona chair in the middle of the room.

Polly offered her most effulgent movie star smile. "Don't pout, precious. I know that J.J. has you rattled, but trust me, FOX News is the last one on the planet to care about your silly 'Mummy and Me' Egyptian-themed sacrificial altar weekend play dates. They'll never broadcast such a trifle."

Richard shook his head. "Sit." He motioned toward a twin sofa and two matching La Corbusier chairs.

Polly looked around. "I'm parched. Where do you keep the champers?"

"Damn. I totally forgot about your habit. Er, your preference," Richard mocked. "I won't keep you but a tick. Then you can run along to your Pepper Plantation and guzzle to your ulcerating kidneys' delight." He looked away from Polly. Then in a small voice he said, "I've been fired."

"But ... the show is a hit," Polly exclaimed.

Richard snorted. "Good ratings are generally a sufficient reason to keep even the most malevolent producer or studio exec at the helm of a show. However, Sterling prides itself on keeping its vault of secrets tamperproof. Tonight, you let a few of the most feral cats out—so to speak. As the producer, I'm the fall guy."

"I didn't say anything to the millions and millions of television viewers around the world that wasn't true."

"Millions," Richard sighed. "Sterling's stockholders are a money-grabbing and not-so-liberal slice of old-fashioned Americana," Richard said. "They can tolerate one of Sterling's employees murdering Thane Cornwall. It made for huge ratings. But hanky-panky in the dressing rooms? Caught by Big Brother's surveillance eyes? That's a little too weird for people who actually think we're a Pollyanna family empire. The big cheese CEO is livid with me for not saying bupkis about Steven fooling around backstage."

"You gave that Cock of the Walk a warning," Polly said.

"I should have fired the killer. That might have saved Danny, too." Richard took a deep breath. "I've been a jerk. I was trying to fill Thane Cornwall's Frankenstein shoes 'cause the show needed conflict to keep audiences tuned in."

Polly tried to feel sorry for Richard. However, she looked him in the eye and said, "Sweetums, you got exactly what you wanted: contestants caught sabotaging each other, ruining established showbiz careers, and destroying any hint of the myth that Hollywood is only for the talented few. You decided that if you showed how cruel and crass people can be when their egos want to slurp from the well of celebrity, then your own career would skyrocket. And it did. At least until a little ol' inconvenient truth popped up. The only real talent on this show was a talent for murder."

Polly stood up. She looked at a forlorn Richard Dartmouth. "Honey, you know as well as I do that in Hollywood, when an executive is fired from one position, he gets an even better job at another studio. It's called 'failing up.' It worked for Shari Draper. She used to occupy this very office. Not to worry your impossibly handsome kisser. Call J.J. if you need a reference. You'll have to kiss his butt. However, you made it this far in H-wood, so I suspect you've perfected that skill."

Suddenly, the office door opened. Polly, Tim, and Placenta looked up as a young man wearing tortoiseshell eyeglasses, and un-tucked white satin twill shirt, faded blue jeans, and a Bluetooth cell phone headset embedded in his ear confidently walked into the room. "Time's up, Dartmouth," he said.

Polly studied the man for a moment. "Combat pay?" she asked.

A smile played across the young man's face. "Not anymore. J.J. fired me. But Seymour Tallowschmid hired me. I'm now his director of development here at Sterling. This is my new office. Oh, and my name's Shawn."

Tim looked at J.J.'s former temp receptionist. "We knew you'd quickly move up the ladder, but this is ridiculous," he joked.

"Only in Hollywood, eh? One day you're a Nobody receptionist earning ten bucks an hour. The next, you're producing TV and films, with a six-figure salary, a BMW, and an expense account," Shawn said.

Suddenly the kid from J.J. Norton's office became serious. "Polly. Er, Miss P. Your performance tonight killed us. That song. Mwah! Your stage presence. Wow! Awesome! Stellar! Seymour and I wanna make you a star. D'ya follow me?"

"I'm already an icon, dear." Polly looked down her nose.

"Sure. Of course. We all know that. Right. But you're from my parents' generation," Shawn said. "However, there's still a place for you in Hollywood. Seymour thinks so. I know so. Seymour thinks you should do a special. I say a big event in Central Park. No. A talk show, like *Ellen*. Hmm. No. A sitcom about a famous star who solves murder mysteries?" Shawn put his fingertips to his temples. "I'm getting a vibration about this one."

"It's the radiation from the cell phone embedded in your head," Polly said.

"I'm calling J.J. to set up a lunch. Tomorrow. The Ivy. Two o'clock," Shawn said. As he turned to leave the room he looked at Richard Dartmouth and his box of personal effects. "Don't think about using that Emmy to get rid of me. It's no longer an original idea," he said. Then, at the door, he faced Polly again. "You were nice to me at that sucky job."

—⌒—

In the great room at Pepper Plantation, Polly, Tim, Placenta, and Detective Archer clinked their champagne flutes together. "Cheers! To Polly Pepper, the egalitarian!" Tim proclaimed. As you always say, 'Be nice to the little people in Hollywood, because eventually they'll be running this town.'"

Polly "hear-heared." She turned to Tim. "Party time!"

"Ugh," Tim sighed. "I figured this was coming."

Next Saturday," Polly continued. "Something utterly amazing to celebrate Lisa being released from that smelly Beverly Hills Gulag, and Steven taking her place. Oh, and Shawn, and Seymour Tallowschmid—whoever he is—getting my career back on track."

"I've actually been playing with party theme ideas for a couple of weeks," Tim confirmed. "Catherine the Great Caterer is on board. I've already met with the mayor. He's assigned the DWP to flush out your hole so our guests can go down there and play 'What's My Phobia?' I'm thinking … maybe secret closed-circuit TV coverage down there. We can sequester our chums, like John Travolta and Zac Efron. Large-screen monitors will show everyone else how well they dance in the dark. Oh, and maybe my silver-fox idol Anderson Cooper and Placenta's fave, Daniel Craig.

They've all got a ton of talent that's hidden from all but the *National Peeper.* It would be a scream for the other guests to watch!" Polly smiled and raised her glass to her son. "A hole is only as good as the people who fill it."

"That's what I always say." Placenta clinked her glass against Tim's.

Polly said, "We have tons to celebrate! I solved a couple more murder cases. That cute kid from J.J.'s office—by the way, I think he's son-in-law material— wants me to do another TV show. Lisa Marrs is free from jail. Steven Benjamin is facing a lethal injection. Officer Sandy is strapped to a bed in the lockdown ward at Cedars. Hollywood dreams do come true!"

Placenta cleared her throat. "I have to know one thing. When did you send that chip of Steven's tooth to a DNA lab?"

Polly smiled. "You're a maid. Can't you tell the difference between a grain of Uncle Ben's converted rice and a chip of someone's bicuspid?"

Placenta shook her head and smiled.

"What about Steven Benjamin starring in his own home surveillance footage?" Tim asked. "You're in our sights twenty-four-seven. When did you have a chance to get to Mayday and check out their coverage of Steve's property from the night of Thane's murder?"

Polly shrugged and took another sip of champagne. "No one ever gives me credit for being a great actress!"

"A great con artist," Placenta said.

"Another bluff?" Tim guessed.

"Whatever. I deserve an Oscar for playing the role of the grand inquisitor tonight," Polly said. She turned to Detective Archer and purred, "What prize do I win for being so amazing and talented and glowing with star shine?" She smiled.

He smiled.

Tim and Placenta faked yawns.

"I guess I'll be setting another place at the table for breakfast," Placenta said as she took one last swallow from her glass. She leaned over to hug Polly good night.

Polly reached out and affectionately caressed Placenta's cheek. "Celebrities, like Anne Hathaway, are manmade," she said. "Stars, like me, are *God* made. You, my dear, are a saint."

"In other words, better than … but not as good as." Tim mocked his mother's attempt at tribute and helped Placenta to her feet.

"There's nothing wrong with limbo!" Polly hissed.

Placenta shook her head and bade good night with a pat to Detective Archer's head and a peck to Tim's cheek. "Purgatory is more like it. But at least I'm in an exclusive zip code," she said, and walked out of the room.

About the author

—◆—

R.T. Jordan served for 30 years as a Senior Publicist with the Walt Disney Studios motion picture marketing division, where he worked on over 500 feature films. In addition to his many published books, including the *Polly Pepper mystery series*, and untold numbers of feature articles, he also wrote the seminal nonfiction Hollywood/Broadway book, *"But Darling, I'm Your Auntie Mame!"* a history of the immortal fictional character created by author Patrick Dennis. He enjoys living half the year in the Lake Arrowhead area in Southern California mountains, and the other half in a cottage (a converted 18th-century stable) in the English countryside.

FUN FACTS ABOUT R.T. JORDAN

- Enjoys cooking
- Loves music from the 40s and 50s
- Attended Doris Day's 90th Birthday
- Can't change a tire

- Loves traveling, especially to Europe
- Had the worst holiday of his life in Amsterdam (ask him why)
- Loves old movies, especially "Cover Girl" starring Gene Kelly and Rita Hayworth, and "Auntie Mame" starring Rosalind Russell
- Wants to be among the first "space tourists"
- Cries when he sees suffering anywhere on the planet
- Has never met Michelle Obama, but attended her book tour in Los Angeles
- Discovered author/poet Maya Angelo
- Is happy to spend time with himself

LOVE POLLY PEPPER?

Enjoy all of Polly's adventures!

Final Curtain is the one where Polly lands the title role in the off-off-off-off Broadway musical production of Mame only to have her big comeback thwarted by some thoughtless Emmy-wielding hit-man who murders the director.

A Talent for Murder is the one where Polly becomes a judge on a cheesy reality TV show and somebody kills the nasty Brit that everyone in the music world loves to hate.

Set Sail for Murder is the one where Polly's scene-stealing nemesis is killed with a deadly DVD box set on a celebrity cruise for fans of Polly's old television cast and its once-famous guest stars.

But wait … there's more! Amalfi Books is proud to announce that more Polly Pepper mysteries are being written now. Don't miss out. Join our email list and we'll notify you when new books are available.

Plus, you can get a special R.T. Jordan novella for free right now. Sign up and we'll send you the e-book edition of Naughty or Nice by R.T. Jordan. This holiday comedy romance gives readers a peek at what happens to your love life when your Mom is America's sweetheart.

Keep up with your favorite author.
Visit Polly Pepper Central:

WWW.AMALFIBOOKS.COM/POLLYPEPPERCENTRAL

Made in the USA
Middletown, DE
14 April 2022

64272346R00208